TIER 1

BOOK 1 IN THE TIER TRILOGY

CINDY GUNDERSON

Button Press

To my Eric. Who is actually named Scott.

"How will it work?" the woman in the room asks, gently tucking an errant strand of hair behind her ear.

"We need to move sensitively. Grace, you'll need to do your research on this one," the man responds, scanning through information on his display. Just outside the door to the room, a man slowly shifts his weight to the other foot, trying to catch a glimpse of the face in the chair. The room is clean and sterile, the light blue shirt on the man standing out like a spring flower against the dismal hues on the walls.

"Is this completely necessary?" the woman asks hesitantly.

"We believe it is. All of the data we have analyzed— "

"It's a lot to ask of them," she whispers, cutting him off. He smiles knowingly, folding his arms and leaning back against his chair.

"Not when you think about the effect this could have on individual lives over the next two hundred years. We are at the cutting edge. Humans are like any other mammals, after all. Cerebral mammals, but stimuli-driven nonetheless. With the technology we have available, nobody will suffer." He pauses, tapping his fingers lightly on the metal table in front of him. "Is that your concern?"

She doesn't answer and the silence is deafening.

"Grace, if there is a problem here," he says, a warning in his tone.

From his limited vantage point, the man in the hallway sees the woman's shoulders stiffen.

"No. No problem," she replies.

The scraping of a chair against the floor sends a shot of adrenaline through the watcher's arms, leaving his hands tingling. He knows he should go, but his curiosity pushes him to stay put.

"Your compassion will serve you well in this position, Grace. This transition will be infinitely easier under your sensitive care. There aren't many I trust to have the perspective needed to do the hard things."

"Thank you, sir." Her voice is audibly shaken, and she clears her throat. "Compensation? Shall we discuss—"

"All taken care of," he interrupts. "Exactly what you would expect."

Hearing footsteps approach the door, the man in the hallway propels himself around the corner as noiselessly as possible. He wipes the sweat from his forehead and sits down on the bench in the hallway. Breathing deeply, he tries to calm his frantic heart rate.

"Something to do. I need something to do," he thinks, forcing himself to breathe normally. He reaches down and unties his shoe, then begins to re-tie it.

"Nick? I didn't realize you were coming so early." At the sound of his name, the watcher looks up to see the Director walking toward him. "You and Grace have already been introduced," the Director says cheerily, motioning to the woman next to him. "Come with us. Let's get started."

CHAPTER 1

I GASP AWAKE TO see a pair of eyes an inch from my face. A lock of blond hair is swept across the still sweaty forehead of my seven year old, but the eyelashes are what get me. They are impossibly long and thick. Life isn't fair.

"Good morning, Mom" Bentley says with an impish grin. "Did I scare you?"

"Yes," I groan, reaching out to pull him in next to me. "Why do you have to be so creepy? It's disturbing to wake up to someone that close to your face."

He giggles and cuddles in under the blankets, his pointy toes like daggers against my thighs.

"It's not my fault, I have your genes," he retorts.

"I was never that strange," I sigh, squeezing him tight. "I'm not ready to get up yet, so I guess you're just stuck here awhile."

"But I'm really hungry! That's why I came in," he complains in a muffled voice, squirming to escape my arms.

"Tell your dad. He's the best at making breakfast." I kick my leg over to the opposite side of the bed and catch Eric in the calves.

"Mom's making that up. She's just trying to make me feel good about myself," he groans, rubbing his eyes. "She is far superior at making a good breakfast. Right Bent?" he continues groggily, rolling over and ruffling his hair.

"Dad! I just brushed that!"

I suppress a laugh. Bentley has suddenly taken an interest in hygiene the last few months. It's adorable and frustrating, but mostly adorable. I can't complain. At least he is bathing now.

"You brushed your hair before breakfast?" I ask in mock horror.

"Doesn't everyone? And I'm really hungry! Can you please get up?" he whines, slipping out from under the covers and pulling on my arm.

"Dad wanted to make breakfast, remember? He told me he wanted to make pancakes today." I barely get the last word out because Eric is tickling me.

"Bent, think of those pancakes Mom made the other day. The best. You want those right?"

"Yes! Can we have chips in them?" he asks eagerly.

"Ok, I give up!" I say, throwing my hands up in surrender and gasping for breath. "I will make pancakes! But no chips, sorry bud. We hit our weekly max for refined sugar yesterday and it doesn't reset until the weekend. But, we still need to get in some fruit for the week, so how about blueberries?" I ask, hoping to avoid any resistance.

"Yes! Ok, I'll go get the flipper. Can I be the flipper this time? Tal did it last time."

"If Tal did it last time, then yes. Your turn."

His little legs kick out of the room before I even finish my sentence.

"We have got to get him some pants that don't fall off. All I see every day is little boy bum," I mutter.

"Good luck with that. He got my non-hips. I still can't find pants that fit," Eric laughs.

"I'm okay if your pants fall off."

"Yeah, but kind of inconvenient in the lab."

"True." He kisses me softly and then flips the comforter off of me, exposing my bare legs to the morning chill.

"You better get on those cakes."

"I hate you a little bit."

"I can't wait to eat them."

I smack him lightly as I get out of bed and pull on my robe.

"You won this one, but I'll get it back," I say, flashing him a sinister grin.

"Mmmm. The sweet smell of victory. And pancakes." He pulls the covers back over his head. I might be annoyed if I didn't know his sensor was going off in two minutes.

I walk downstairs to find Bentley ready by the stove, on the step stool, flipper in hand. The sun is streaming in through the window over the sink, making the colors in the kitchen warm and inviting. When we were assigned this house, I felt like the luckiest girl in our territory. In an effort to save resources, the Committee refurbished different sections of the city as soon as possible after the Crisis. They used materials collected from some of the more dilapidated areas, but obviously had to put everything through a cleansing process. It took years to open up permanent housing. I shudder, imagining trying to raise a family—or even taking care of your own needs—crammed into a safe zone holding center.

"Mom, here's the measuring cup," Bentley says, pulling it out of the drawer and handing it to me as I put the rye berries into the grinder.

I don't take for granted that it could have been us in that situation. Pioneers in the initial Tier system. In terms of societal progress, we aren't that far removed. After the Crisis, we weren't picking up at society's peak. We were in recovery from almost eighty years of decline and societal rot. Any industrial or scientific progress that had been made up to that point was in a state of exponential loss. We had to recover that knowledge, re-invent those processes, rebuild the prototypes. Stop the bleeding. It didn't take long for the Tier system to eliminate the initial chaos, but the gaping fissure in our collective advancement wasn't so easily filled. We are still battling to regain what was lost.

I let Bentley mix the dry ingredients while I heat up the griddle. It should only take a minute or two to get to temperature, which is just enough time to add the goat's milk and eggs without wasting energy. I swoop around the kitchen, gathering the last few ingredients, and allow Bentley to add them.

The simple act of cooking with my son causes my heart to swell, overwhelmed with gratitude for those who came before. They prepared a foundation for me to live a comfortable and meaningful life. The fact that Eric and I could pair and immediately have a permanent home is incredible. The fact that it fits us so perfectly is my little secret.

I pause and watch Bentley carefully pour the batter. An unintended drip falls to the counter, and I quickly sweep it up with my finger. Then I pull up his pants.

CHAPTER 2

THE DISHES CLATTER pleasantly as I stack them on the drying rack. The boys have gone for conditioning, and I revel in the momentary stillness. Hanging my apron on the hooks near the stove, I load my tablets into a canvas messenger bag, securing the straps. Through the window, I notice that the car is already waiting for me. I fight the urge to rush unnecessarily, knowing I still have a few minutes before I absolutely need to leave. Eventually, having double checked my supplies for the day, I slide into the seat, setting the navigation.

I'm assigned to Washington Park and for that, I'm glad. Technically, every neighborhood in Tier 2 is supposed to have an equal demographic, but I'm not convinced. I encounter much more apathy in some of the neighborhoods east of City Park. Today should be standard if not downright pleasant. Though the thought of diving into preparation is tempting, I look ahead, knowing that reading on the sideways will inevitably cause nausea. Finally, as the car hits the straightway, I lie back and begin familiarizing myself with today's files. Motion sickness is one variation I could do without.

I stop on file thirty-one. Cassidy. By the looks of it, she has qualified for Tier 1 initial testing. I hope she shows up to hear the good news. The car slows and, glancing out the window, I see the lily pond ahead of me. I prefer to have the car drop me at the corner of Virginia and Franklin before parking. It would be faster to go directly to the lake, but walking in the cool morning air— watching the dappled sunlight dance along the path—always provides much-needed perspective before seeing patients. Gathering my things, I exit the vehicle and a smile involuntarily crosses my lips as I begin to move through the trees.

"Hey Kate!" a voice calls from behind, pulling me into the present. I turn around and see Shane running my direction. His sleeveless shirt accentuates his lean musculature and, even from this vantage point, I can see that he has worked up quite a sweat.

"Are you working Washington Park today?" he asks as he catches up and slows to a stop.

"I am. I was just walking to the boathouse. Are you headed there, as well?"

"Nope," he says, still breathing heavily. "It's my rec time. They switched me to Highlands so that I could jog in the mornings. It seems like my body does better with exercise before noon."

"Oh, that's great! How are you liking it so far? Different patient base up there, I hear."

"Yes, definitely a change, but honestly, I think it suits me. We don't have as many transfer options, but people are compliant. They are willing to work with the program despite not having much hope of progressing. It's nice to see people just...living."

"That's good to know," I say, smiling, searching for something to keep the conversation moving along. Whenever Shane and I have chatted, Lily is usually there to fill in the gaps. "Is Lily still working over here on Fridays?"

"Occasionally, but they try to keep us together as much as possible. I could see it phasing out in a year or so. You better catch her while you can," he admonishes, tilting his head for added effect.

"Will do," I promise, hearing a warning beep from his sensor.

"That's my exit, sorry. I have to keep my heart rate up for another twenty minutes," he says, already beginning to jog up the path. "Have a great day! Hopefully I will see you and Eric at the next training?"

"We will be there. Bye Shane," I say, waving, trying to keep the relief I feel from entering my tone.

My shoes pad along the familiar wooden floor of the boathouse. When I reach my station, I gingerly unload the tablets from my bag. Patients are already waiting along the dock. After securing the connection to my display, I announce the first name on the schedule.

Berg's protocol change, reverting back to health meetings in person, was instituted early this year. In my opinion, it was absolutely the right call. The digital scans were more efficient, yes, but getting positive feedback from someone in person really can't be appropriately replicated digitally. The increased physical connection has the added benefit of breaking up isolationist patterns, and we are already seeing health improvements.

A small woman sits down at the table. Her clear skin and symmetrical bone structure belie her true age and I find myself questioning my memory of her chart. While I double check, I slide a tablet across the stainless steel surface, allowing her to scan her sensor and officially check in for her appointment. Her most recent brain scan shows major markers for diabetes, glioblastoma, and dementia. Again, extremely surprising that she looks to be in such good health.

"Hi Tia," I say, smiling and holding her eyes, intentionally working to create a physical connection. "My name is Kate and I will be collaborating on your health today. How have you been feeling since the last time you met with a health specialist?" I ask genuinely.

"I am doing well, but," she scoots her chair forward and leans in, as if about to let me in on a secret, "I haven't seen much difference after trying my new hydration plan. I feel the same and my scan came back similar to last time."

"Have you been keeping notes on mental acuity? I know you were noticing a negative change in your memory and clarity of mind in November. Is that still progressing?"

Her shoulders relax, but her mouth remains in its downturned position. "Well, I guess that hasn't changed much," she ponders.

"That's actually good news," I say, smiling reassuringly. "As you know, you have a marker for dementia and that is known to start kicking in anytime after the age of 35. Now here you are, 52, and still one hundred percent lucid. Tia, that's remarkable. Only twenty years ago we would be expecting your body and mind to be breaking down at an incredible rate."

Her eyes are riveted on me, hanging on every word. I reign in my cadence, giving her time to process.

"We are in uncharted territory for our generation. I am sure you know that people used to live to almost a hundred years old, which I can't even begin to fathom, but seeing your results makes me think it's going to be possible again. And you are Tier 2," I add excitedly. "You have been able to accomplish this level of health with your genetics stacked against you. Really impressive work."

A smile flickers across her face, but her eyes are still creased with worry. I reach across the sterile surface and squeeze her hand in mine.

"Tia, the most important thing you can do is resume your relaxation techniques, stick to your health and nutrition regimen, and allow your body to function. If it's true that you haven't experienced any more decline, I would also recommend that you stick to your added hydration. I can imagine that aging causes anxiety, but stress will only contribute to decreased brain functioning. Have you been attending your meditation sessions with Dr. Siene?"

"Yes, mostly." She looks chagrined. "Sometimes I am tired and it is easier to stay in bed awhile longer."

"I understand. I can help you set some achievable goals if it would be helpful. We want to see you hit your 60th birthday, ok?"

"Me too. I want to experience being a grandmother. Did you see in my notes that my daughter has been cleared to have a baby next year?" she asks hopefully, her eyes brimming with tears.

"Oh wow, that is incredible. You are one of the lucky few. If I have the pleasure of meeting with you again, I hope you'll tell me all about your grandbaby."

She stands up and scoots her chair back as I release her hand. "Thanks, Kate. I will keep working."

"Thank *you* for keeping your appointment today."

As she walks away, I find myself wishing I could see the end of that story. I don't have the luxury of seeing people consistently enough to keep track of them. I like to think that they all end up in best-case scenarios, but every once-in-awhile it would be nice to see concrete evidence.

Not immediately seeing my next patient, I assuage my complaining bladder and walk to the back of the shelter to use the washroom. Turning the corner briskly, my shoulder is impacted and I spin, hitting the rough planks of the wall with enough force that my breath is expelled from my lungs momentarily. A hand grasp onto my arm, steadying me. I regain my balance and am attempting to catch my breath, when I look up to notice a young man I don't recognize. His broad shoulders are inches from my nose and deep, blue eyes are frantically searching my own. I take in his soft, blond waves and for a moment, I am speechless.

"I am so sorry," I belatedly eek out, regaining my bearings. "I was on a mission to get to the washroom and I didn't even look." He releases my arm, allowing me to stand up straight.

"Don't worry at all, I wasn't paying attention. Are you ok?" he asks, concern evident in his tone, as he continues to survey my head and neck.

"I think so, thanks," I say with a shaky smile, rushing through the washroom door. Even if he hadn't been unusually attractive, that was just embarrassing. I wonder if he is Tier 2? Not likely. Tier 1? Possible, but what would he be doing down here? He is too young to be a specialist. I realize that I am thinking far too much about this, so I focus on washing my hands. Thoroughly.

Back at my table, I notice the handsome stranger sitting on a park bench across the grass to the side of my station. I didn't get his name, I muse. He glances my direction and I sharply look away, pulling up my next file. That was a little unnecessary. And obvious. I have always been such a dolt when it comes to men. Especially attractive men, I think, remembering the first time Eric and I met.

I was seventeen, sitting at the cafe near our house, working on training assignments. Since I wasn't paired yet, I lived in group housing, and it was sometimes difficult to find a quiet space. Not sometimes—always. My roommate Alyssa was constantly chatting with someone on her display, a habit I both loved and found incredibly perturbing at times.

When Eric walked into the cafe with his friends that day, his eyes met mine and I...looked down immediately and began furiously scrolling. Apparently this was—and still is—my signature move.

You would think that after being paired for 11 years I could be somewhat normal, but apparently not.

My hands are slightly shaky, whether from the impact or the shock that I am still capable of feeling attraction, I can't decide. Thinking of Eric, I wonder if this ever happens for him and immediately regret it. Yes, of course it does, but Eric wasn't ever as awkward as I was. And that realization isn't comforting in the least.

My next patient approaches the table before I even call his name, snapping me back to reality. My movements are frazzled and disjointed as I attempt to begin the check in process. When I think to glance back at the bench a few minutes later, my handsome friend has been replaced by a middle-aged woman sitting peacefully, a book propped in her lap.

Five more patients arrive and leave before I am able to break for lunch. Recognizing the tension that has accumulated in my shoulders, I take purposeful, cleansing breaths as I walk to the mobile distribution center located at the opposite end of the boathouse. Scanning my sensor, I receive my portions of chicken breast, chard salad, fonio, and raspberries. The man ahead of me has a much larger salad and no grain. Obviously, he hasn't been keeping to his vegetable requirements on his own.

I prop myself up against a tree and enjoy the varying textures and flavors of my meal. Though it's difficult, I remind myself daily to focus on these simple pleasures. I truly believe in the work that I am doing—both at home with my children and here with my patients—

but that doesn't prevent my life from feeling tedious at times. I yearn to make an impact. To contribute in a massive way. Yet I often feel stilted. Always pressing against some invisible boundary. Self-created? Perhaps. Or maybe it's just not my season. Rationally, I know that I am doing the most important work with my family, but I also know I have a lot more to give. Coming to no obvious solution, I distract myself by self-indulgently resuming my memories of Eric.

That day at the cafe, after picking up his sandwich and ignoring my ridiculous response to his attention, he sauntered directly over to me and introduced himself. We ended up talking for a good half hour. He didn't care that I had seeds in my teeth and a crumb stuck to my cheek. I didn't care in that moment either, but only because I was blissfully unaware until I got into the car a few minutes after he left. My first, real experience with delayed mortification.

Even after his friends were gone, he stayed put, not giving any sign that he intended to follow. I remember watching the corners of his eyes crinkle as he smiled while telling me about his training and desire to work full-time in the lab. I don't think I heard a single detail, I was so distracted by noticing everything about him. The strong angle of his jaw, his dark hair, the humor in his smile, the lean muscles visible through his cotton shirt...

"Pull it together, Kate!" I mentally scold myself, pressing my hands into the soft grass, tethering myself to the here and now. I must be ovulating.

After my lunch break, I am seated back under the awning and

Cassidy is approaching. She has obviously taken the time to dress for the occasion with clean pressed slacks, a collared shirt, and her long, auburn hair pulled into an attractive knot.

"Is it one o'clock yet?" she questions excitedly, her cheeks flushing. "I don't think I can stand waiting any longer to hear my results!"

Checking my tablet, I see that her appointment is still twenty minutes away and there is one person yet to be seen in that time. I don't, however, see anyone physically waiting at the moment, so I quickly shift her position in the queue.

"It's not, but I am excited, too. Let's go for it," I smile.

She rushes to sit down and nearly knocks over the chair. "Kate, thank you. I feel like my heart is about to burst!"

"Cassidy," I laugh, "Take a slow breath and hold it for a few seconds. I promise it's good news." She covers her mouth with her hands and squeals.

"I can't handle it! Tell me!"

"Ok, ok!" I say, my pitch mirroring her own. I open her file and start reading. "Cassidy Turner, you have been cleared to begin Tier 1 initial testing and conditioning, effective immediately. As you know, this will require significant life changes both for you and your family—" I stop there because she has now entered full-blown hysterics. I put down the tablet, walk around the table, and wrap my arms around her. She sobs and laughs, but eventually I feel her breathing return to normal.

"Would you like me to read the rest of the letter?"

She smiles shakily at me. "You know I have it memorized. Just sit down so I can ask you all of the questions I have been obsessively mulling over for years! I didn't feel like I could ask before I was cleared. It seemed pretentious."

I move back over to my seat, still grinning. "Ask away."

"Okay, first. Is there any chance that my gene mapping could sink below Tier 1 levels again? Like, if I continue living this way forever, will I be safe?" she asks, her hands gesticulating nervously.

"That's complicated, but I can tell you current policy states that once you have been cleared for Tier 1, you remain Tier 1 forever. Even if your DNA becomes damaged at some point, you will still have all of the opportunities and responsibilities as such."

"Do you think it's likely...that I will be able to pair?" she asks hesitantly, then rushes to explain. "I know that I can most likely pair in Tier 2, but it wouldn't be guaranteed that I could have a child. I am hoping that will be an option for me." Her hands land in her lap, awaiting my reply.

"Cassidy, I have been meeting with you for years. I know how excited you are for these new possibilities. Your feelings are completely normal and should verify to you that you are right for Tier 1. Your coding is driving you to find a partner and procreate and that is evidence that you are clean. Embrace it."

A tear rolls down her splotchy cheek. "I guess I hadn't ever thought about it that way. I have always felt selfish. Like I would just never be happy with the options I had."

"You know I can't promise you that you will be approved, even though I would love to. So much depends on who you are attracted to and how your genes match up. But, I can tell you that you need to find someone to partner with who matches you at eighty percent or higher on the thirty disease markers—you specifically will need someone to match at one hundred percent on all five markers for your TSG's, the tumor suppressing genes. Since you only hit four of those markers yourself, you will need someone who has them *all* to be considered for reproducing. Those TSG's are going to be critical for your clearance to have children. If you find the right partner, I think your chances are high."

She looks at me, obviously trying to process, and I realize that I may have thrown out too much information at once.

"For example," I say, backtracking, "before Eric and I paired, we used our sensors to run our genetic numbers. Do you understand that process?"

"Theoretically..." she answers.

"It's simple and quite fun, really." I pull up the app and point to a couple of key markers. "You've looked at your numbers before, right?"

"Of course, I am always checking for improvements."

"Right, so when you find someone you would like to pair with, you both pull up your numbers and then this button here will allow you to combine them and analyze the results. So this marker here," I scroll down my chart, "is where you will find the markers for TSG's. Like I mentioned, you have to match at over eighty percent on all of the other disease markers, but you can pay specific atten- tion to those. Make sure they are in the green." Pulling my sensor back, I smile. "You will get plenty of training on this, so don't feel like you need to memorize it all now. I just wanted to make sure you understood what I was referring to."

"Thanks, that helps," she says, fanning herself with her hands to keep tears from overflowing. "Sorry, I'm really emotionally drained right now. What if I meet someone and we aren't perfectly pairable?"

I sigh. "That's always tough, but if having children is your priority, you will have to keep looking," I say gently. A rush of emotion floods me as I remember the anticipation of reading my results with Eric. I was terrified that we wouldn't be in the green.

"Maybe I will ask to see a guys' TSG markers before agreeing to go out with him," she suggests, waggling her eyebrows.

I laugh. "That would be efficient, definitely."

"Do you have time for a few more questions?"

I glance behind her, seeing my overdue patient leaning on the railing, and lean in. "You can ask one more, but then I have to move on with my schedule. You can always feel free to message me later, as well."

"I totally understand. Ok, most important and practical. I know I will be moving to the Tier 1 side of the city. How does that all work?"

"Yes, I— " distracted by flashing light, I look down at my display and see an alert on the screen. My sensor buzzes and I tap on it.

<Due to a security breach, all consultants are asked to immediately vacate Washington Park. Tap if transportation is needed >

"I am so sorry," I mumble, giving an apologetic frown.

She looks at me, confused.

"I have to go. Send me a message later?" I say hurriedly, jamming the tablets into my bag and racing toward the car. I look back in my haste and see Cassidy still under the awning, my next patient approaching her, looking confused. For a moment, I wonder if I should return and explain more thoroughly. I abandon this thought and, again, tap my sensor, requesting that the car meet me at a closer intersection. I need to follow protocol.

CHAPTER 3

THOUGH SAFELY IN THE CAR, my fingers shake with excess adrenaline and my mind runs wild with possible explanations for the alert. The short search I enter upon getting in the car doesn't produce any new information, so I send a message to Eric. When he doesn't respond immediately, I resign myself to sitting in unknowns for the time being. I will have to ask Shari about it later. I rationalize that if it was something extremely worrisome, I would have received more information by now. Resting my head on the cushion, I close my eyes and fall quickly into a state of partial sleep.

My brief respite is interrupted by my sensor. It's Shari calling. Relief washes over me, and I'm smiling before her face even comes into view. Shari has been my mentor since I was eight years old. She was nineteen at the time and, at our first meeting, she brought hot pink nail polish to paint my toes. To this day I have no idea how she got her hands on that. I succeeded in keeping it a secret from my parents for two days, thinking they would make me take it off. Shari and I have seen each other at least once a week now for twenty years and we talk almost daily. Am I really that old? Twenty-eight this month. I answer the call.

"Kate! I tried calling you earlier, but your sensor was listed as unavailable. Were you working this morning?"

"Yep, so sorry. I have to put it offline when I'm in meetings. It's too distracting! I need—"

She cuts me off. "I know you were just avoiding me, but I forgive you."

I laugh awkwardly. Our connection must not be great.

"Have you talked with Eric yet?" she asks.

"No, why? Is everything ok? Considering your good mood, I assume it's not a disaster."

She scoffs. "Nothing like that, but something I know you will want to hear about. Just call him!"

"I'm literally five minutes from home. But now I get to be anxious for those five minutes, so thanks for that."

"Always looking out for you." She grins.

"I haven't heard back from him. I tried to message him after the alert. I'm slightly annoyed that he has talked with you and not me," I complain, pretending to pout. She looks at me, her eyebrows furrowed.

"Oh, I wasn't talking about the alert. This is something else entirely."

"What?" I question, thoroughly confused. "You know about it, right? I had to leave Washington Park with zero warning, right in the middle of patient evals. Something about a security breach. Sorry, I assumed that's what you were referring to—that's all that's been on my mind since I left."

She nods and looks apologetic. "Totally understand, and yes. The security breach is nothing to worry about at this point. There was a group of Tier 3 individuals who left their assignments without approval. They were in the Tier 2 section of the city, but the Committee didn't know their exact location or their motivations for leaving. One of them has a history of mental illness. They wanted to take precautions since they had consultants in the area. It was probably an overreaction, but I always appreciate that they take our safety so seriously," Shari explains.

"Wow. I can't believe they would vacate us all purely because a few people weren't accounted for. Last time it was because of a weather event. I assumed today was something similar."

"Kate, you know that some people in Tier 3 have erratic behavior— "

"But what could they even do?" I interrupt.

"I don't know! Start a fight? Destroy your property? When someone is unstable, the possibilities are endless."

"I thought you said they were working? If they were that unstable, how would they have been approved for a work assignment?" I say, thinking out loud.

Shari gives an exasperated huff. "I don't know, Kate. Maybe I didn't read everything correctly. It's been a really long day," she snaps.

Shari is never short with me and it stings. I am at a loss for words.

"I'm sorry," she sighs, taking in my expression. "Like, a really long day. But we don't need to get into that. The real reason I was calling was to see if you could be available before training on Monday. We wanted to invite you to help with the Tier 1 introduction ceremony on the fifth. Specifically since you've built such a relationship with a couple of the people who are transitioning. Could you be there about an hour before training starts? I assume it will be a fairly quick meeting," she says, flashing a forced smile.

"Of course. I can't believe I forgot about that," I sigh. "Has it already been three years since my last one? Shari, I think I might be getting old," I joke, attempting to lighten the mood.

A smirk plays on her lips. "Not old, just tired. You have kids, remember? All I have on my task list is watering my plants."

"True. Kind of pathetic when you think about it."

Shari laughs out loud. "I'll remember how pathetic it is when I get a full eight hours of sleep tonight. Which I need desperately. Bye friend." She winks and the signal cuts out. Eight hours. Sounds blissful. I don't wish for a second that I was ineligible for children, but eight hours...

Not for the first time, I wonder what it would be like to remain unpaired. I have talked with Shari about it in the past and she did *not* make the decision lightly. She and I are matched on personality, and we also meet the minimum markers for disease, but Shari has a couple of variations that make pairing difficult. She didn't have many options to begin with, and I know she was anxious that she wouldn't qualify for procreation, regardless of her pair's numbers. She concluded that elective sterilization was safer than taking the risk of perpetuating those genes through accidental pregnancy if she wasn't cleared.

Thankfully, there are still plenty of options for companionship, and of course she still gets her physical and emotional needs met. Berg put protocols in place for that, ensuring satisfaction and safety for all in Tier 1, regardless of pairing success.

To me, though, short-term relationships seem like they couldn't be as fulfilling and enjoyable as being with someone long-term. There are so many facets of a relationship that you aren't able to experience without significant time and commitment. Eric and I have nearly laughed ourselves breathless over ridiculous things that we have witnessed over the years. Little moments that only we find funny because we lived it. We have supported each other through the deaths of loved ones, the birth of our children, and the everyday incidences of frustration or self-doubt. Our depth of connection can't be mimicked in a weekend. We are so interconnected at this point that I can't imagine my life without him in it.

From the way Shari talks about it, being with people short-term is more about the spikes of excitement. The newness. Sometimes, I admit, my heart yearns for the flutters of a first kiss, or the intense elation when a call rings through after the agony of waiting. But this, what Eric and I have. This is solid.

. . .

The strangeness of my conversation with Shari is still tickling my subconscious when I walk through the door to find Eric sitting at the table with Tal. Solely from Eric's posture, I can discern that something isn't right. Glancing next to him, Tal exudes sullenness, his shoulders slumped, chin resting in his hands. His blond hair covers his eyes, and I can't tell if he's been crying or not. I hang my bag on the hook by the door and remove my jacket, absently laying it across a chair.

"Hey guys, where's Bent?" I ask, feigning ignorance of the current emotional climate.

"He's playing in his room," Eric answers with a wan smile. "How was Washington Park today?"

<What's wrong?> I mouth.

<Trouble during conditioning today> he mouths back.

"It was great. I had the chance to give Cassidy some much-needed news." I pause, debating whether to continue sharing. "We had an alert and had to vacate."

"Vacate? That's odd. I have some exciting news for you, actually."

"Now?" I ask hopefully.

"Let's talk about it later. Who is Cassidy again?"

"She is a patient I've been seeing on and off for the past two years."

"That's right," he says, nodding.

"She made Tier 1 initial testing this week and is beyond thrilled."

"I bet. That's fantastic. It seems to be happening more and more these days, isn't it?"

"I think I've personally put through twenty-seven people in the last year. And that's saying something since I see fewer patients than most," I agree.

"That's impressive. What was the alert about?"

I shake my head. <Later> I mouth.

"Nothing important. Hey Tal. How was your day?" I ask, trying to seem chipper.

"I don't really want to talk about it," he mumbles.

"I would really love to hear when you're ready." I say, rubbing his shoulder. "What if I make you a snack while you think about it?"

"Only if it's a good snack," he says, raising his eyes to meet mine.

"Deal."

We move to the patio so I can refill the bird feeders while we talk. I swiftly load all of our empty toiletry and food containers into our refill bin. It's pick-up day tomorrow and I know I'll forget if I wait. Eric speaks first, after giving Tal enough time to eat his favorite pieces of dried fruit.

"Tal, we love you. We are here to help you with whatever happened today, so don't worry about us making a judgment," he says, nudging Tal with his elbow. "I mean, don't worry about me making a judgment. Your mom is pretty judgy sometimes, but I'll make up for it."

"Ahem. Standing right here," I say, pretending to be annoyed.

That gets a small smile out of him.

"What's bothering you?" I ask gently.

"Well, we were discussing history with Mr. Dane, and we got to the section on crime and punishment. He talked about how we don't "punish" people who inflict harm on others. They are a product of their genetic and social conditioning. He said 'the actions of others are purely a reflection of our societal integrity' or some equally benign statement. It felt so wrong to me. Not that I want to punish people, but if people make bad decisions, shouldn't they have consequences?"

Eric and I look at each other dumbfounded. I scan our parenting history, wondering what we did to give him the idea that people should be held responsible for actions they have no control over.

"Okay, Tal," I say, "first of all, you are ten years old and it's completely natural for you to be questioning the world you live in."

"Mom, I know it's normal to a point, but everyone else seems to get it," he shoots back.

Bentley dramatically opens the patio door and struts out to join us. "What'd I miss?" he says loudly, hopping up on Eric's lap.

I laugh as I hang the last bird feeder. "We are discussing something with Tal, bud. Do you have something you could play inside until we're done?"

"No," he says matter-of-factly, obviously not intending to go anywhere.

"Bent, this is my time with Mom and Dad," Tal complains, only to be met with a victorious grin on Bentley's face.

"Okay, enough you two. Bent, you can stay if you don't interrupt," Eric says seriously, and I look at him skeptically. Interrupting is Bentley's strong suit.

"Kate, can you grab that book on the Crisis from the bookshelf?"

"Which one?" I ask.

"The initial issue."

As I move to complete my errand, I hear Tal grumbling behind me. "Dad, I already know about all of that. I learned about the Crisis years ago..."

The door closes, and I enjoy a moment of silence, rifling through the various books and documents. Finally, my fingers brush the faded spine of the issue Eric is interested in. Most of our resources are digital at this point, but there's still something comforting about print. About touching something that was treasured generations before you existed. The distinct smell of aged paper, ink, and dust wafts upward as I thumb through the pages before heading back out to the boys.

On the patio, the atmosphere is tense. I hand the book to Eric and shoot him a questioning look. He reaches for the book, flipping through the chapters.

"Here it is," he says, landing on the page he had in mind. "Look right here at this picture. Tell me about it." He opens the pages to Tal and points to a picture of world leaders in a heated discussion at UN headquarters.

"It's a bunch of old people yelling at each other," Tal mutters. I can tell Eric doesn't appreciate his tone.

"True. Why are they yelling," he asks, maintaining his aura of calm.

"Because of the virus," Tal says in a monotone voice. Eric smirks.

"Obviously I am not touching on anything new, so let's skip ahead. The world is in crisis, nations are at war, resources are being wasted by the few at the expense of the many, yada yada yada," he dramatizes. "So, what did they decide to do after the virus was released?"

Tal's posture shifts, and it seems that this question has momentarily caught his interest.

"I know they decided to put Berg Genetics in charge, but," he hesitates, "I actually don't know why."

Eric leans forward, excited to have a potential teaching moment, though he does a good job of masking his level of enthusiasm. When did teaching our kids become such a touchy endeavor? They used to love hearing our opinions on everything.

"To really understand that decision—the decisions that literally shaped the world we now live in—you have to understand what was happening in the 100 years before the Crisis," Eric begins.

"Dad, I—"

"Can you please let me at least try to explain? I'm trying to help you here," Eric insists, his voice tense.

Tal slumps back in his chair and reluctantly nods his head.

"Over the course of about forty years, more than 1 billion people paid to have themselves genetically tested. They did it through myriad private companies—who charged them through the nose—just out of curiosity. They wanted to know what their lineage was, whether they were likely to die of heart disease or cancer, and what dominant and recessive genes they possessed. Berg Genetics was the first group to recognize what an incredible opportunity this was. They were mostly focused on recombinant DNA tech up to that point, so it was somewhat surprising that they took an interest—"

Tal interrupts, "What is recombinant DNA tech?"

"Each human cell contains around 6 feet of DNA, so up until recombinant DNA technology came around, searching for specific genes was a game of chance. This technology allowed scientists to isolate a specific gene, mutate it in very specific ways, and then reinsert it into a living organism and study the results," I interject.

"Got it," Tal nods.

"Your mom is smart, right?" Eric says, eyes mooning in my direction. Tal rolls his eyes in disgust.

"Yes," Eric continues, "so Berg Genetics recognized that this was the first time in history that they didn't have to pay for genetic material. If they could get their hands on these commercial test results, they would have the world's largest bank of genetic data at their fingertips."

"They started stealing peoples' confidential test results?" Tal looks genuinely horrified.

"Well, steal is a strong word. More like 'politically negotiated' for peoples' confidential test results. They were able to get the results with only basic information like sex, race, and age, but not names or locations of participants." He looks at Tal dramatically. "At first."

"What do you mean 'at first'? Are you saying they then got people's private info?" Tal asks incredulously. He has been effectively sucked in at this point. I cross my arms and watch them interact, my eyes flitting between their faces as they speak.

"A few years later, they were able to lobby for very specific information about these people and actually watch their health over time," Eric continues.

"Seems wrong."

"In some ways, yes, but when we get to the results, you may be willing to justify their methods," he postulates.

"Maybe." I stifle a grin. This kid is black and white.

"Anyway," Eric continues, "Berg has this massive data bank of genetic information. So what do you think they do with it?"

"I am guessing they study it," Tal says, feigning boredom.

"Bingo. They started analyzing the data. Then, when they were able to match the genetic testing with specific individuals, they were able to conduct the largest longitudinal study ever. And nobody even knew they were a part of it." Tal doesn't respond, so Eric moves on. "The results of this study were completely stunning. Their information, along with better technology and understanding of the brain, revealed over 185 new genetic markers for disease, social success, resiliency, and even small variations like loyalty and honesty."

"So, our genes predict everything about us?" Tal questions.

"Yes, along with our social experience, of course. The idea wasn't new, they just finally had the research to back it up. There were other studies, completed ages ago, proving that action precedes the conscious mind, but we can talk about that another day, if you're interested. The takeaway is that each of us, if given the same genetic code and social inputs, will make exactly the same decisions as someone else with the same set of coding and conditioning. Every time."

Frowning, Tal says, "I guess I don't understand how that could be true. I feel like I am making a choice when I stand up, or choose to eat a plum instead of something I don't like. How is it that I am *not* choosing? And how could you ever really prove that?" he asks, his voice gaining energy as he continues. "Why does it matter? If people are misbehaving, does it *really* matter why? They still need to be removed from society."

Eric runs his hands through his hair, his cheeks flushed. "It matters, Tal! If you make a poor choice and I believe you have free agency, I have zero control. I have no way to ensure that you don't make that choice again in the future. So yes, in that situation, under those pretenses, I have no other rational option but to remove you. However, if I believe that you are a product of your genetics and social input, I at least have a starting point."

"So it's about control?" Tal asks, irritating Eric further. To his credit, Eric takes a deep breath before responding. It diffuses things a little.

Bentley is sitting very still, wide-eyed. His quiet voice breaks the silence. "It's about helping people, Tal. That's why we're here, right Mom?" Bentley asks, and Tal groans in disgust, stomping back into the house.

"Is he mad at me?" Bentley asks innocently, his lip trembling slightly.

"No," I sigh. "He is just working through some things."

"It's true, though, right?" he asks.

"What's true?"

"That we're only here to help people," he repeats.

I smile and give his hand a squeeze. "It's completely true. That is our purpose in Tier 1. And the ironic thing is, helping other people is actually what brings us the most happiness, too."

"Win-win," he concludes, hopping off of Eric's lap and giving me a brief hug before running inside to find his brother.

CHAPTER 4

ERIC and I finally have a moment to talk privately while cleaning up after dinner. Tal and Bentley have already run across the street to play at the park with their friends from around the corner. Not having many children in our neighborhood, the boys are always thrilled to look out the window and see little hands waving at them from the playground.

"Tell me about this alert," Eric says, placing a bowl of green beans back in the fridge.

"It was weird. We just got a message saying there had been a security breach and we needed to vacate. Shari told me it was because of some Tier 3 individuals who left their work assignments without approval," I hesitate, "but I still don't understand why it was necessary to evacuate."

"Hmm. Not sure. But I am glad they took precautions to keep you safe. I didn't realize anything had been out of the ordinary today."

"It doesn't make sense that we should be so concerned about

people approved to have service assignments," I say, clearing the last of the dishes from the table.

"I am sure Berg had their reasons. I can ask about it at the lab tomorrow if you want," he offers.

"It's not a big deal," I sigh. "If you hear anything, I would definitely be interested, though." We move around each other seamlessly, like a choreographed dance, putting the kitchen back in proper order.

"Do you think I handled that okay today?" Eric asks.

"With Tal? I think you did a great job. It's so important for him to start reframing his experiences. Kids, at this age, seem to only see things from a selfish perspective." I put a stack of plates in the cupboard.

"I just hope it wasn't too heavy or confrontational, you know? I don't want to place too much on him before he's ready," he says, washing off the table with a checkered rag.

"I think the fact that he is questioning shows he is ready."

"True."

"I have been thinking about the catalyst for this whole thing, actually," I say, pausing and resting my hands on the countertop. "A 'crime and punishment' discussion is what spurred this from Tal. I meant to ask him what he thought about how we handle people who are breaking societal rules. I don't know if he said what he did purely because he doesn't feel comfortable with a lack of free will, or if there's more to it."

"What do you mean?" Eric says, matching my pose across the island.

I return to my task, pondering. The warm water runs smoothly over the frying pan, rinsing the suds and food particles down the sink. When it shines, I run a cloth over the surface before placing it in the rack. Finished, I meet his eyes, finding him still awaiting my response.

"Well, do you think he has questions about what happens to those people? I don't remember how in depth our conditioning went at that age. I wonder if we should take him to a holding and rehabilitation center so that he could see it first hand."

Eric takes the pan from the rack and returns it to its proper place in the drawer beneath the oven. It's mostly dry, so I don't stop him.

"Not a bad idea. Maybe we could do that Saturday," he suggests. "I could probably get clearance by then," he contributes.

"Let's talk with him about it first and make sure *that* wouldn't be too heavy. But, maybe get the clearance just in case?"

"Sure. I'll put in the request tonight." He pauses, a faraway look in his eyes. "Do you remember having worries or questions like that when you were his age?" he asks. I scan my memories and can't initially come up with anything

"I think I must have been a really boring kid," I laugh.

"Why do you say that?" Eric asks, giving a quizzical smile.

"Because, when I try to remember what it was like to be ten years old, I can't focus on anything specific! I remember my favorite foods and that I liked conditioning. I obviously absorbed everything I was supposed to, but I don't have any concrete moments that I can draw from. Is that normal? Do we just let those things go as our brains are filled with other, more pertinent information?"

Eric looks at me, a disbelieving expression on his face. "You seriously can't remember any one moment? Like, when you are going around day-to-day and you see, I don't know, a tree in bloom? Or someone with a certain haircut, or you hear music? It doesn't ever take you back? For me, it is often watching the boys move a certain way or say a specific phrase. Doesn't something like that trigger you to remember a similar time when you were young?"

"Yes," I say purposefully, not enjoying his patronizing tone. "That happens all the time, but it seems like they are always memories from when I was older. Maybe age nine and up?"

Eric tilts his head. "Really?"

My grin evaporates. "Really! You are making me feel like there's something wrong with me, Eric. Shari says that most people discard memories from certain times in their lives. Don't you have a series of years that you don't remember perfectly?" I say, not as calmly as I would have liked.

"I'm sure I do," he says quickly, capitulating. "I'm sorry, I didn't mean to make you feel that way. I guess I haven't spent much time thinking about it. It's one of those funny moments where you assume that everyone experiences life the same way that you do and then..." He meets my eyes and holds up his hands, seeing the look on my face. "For the record, I love these moments! I love having to second guess my assumptions," he laughs. "I don't think there's anything wrong with you. Can we move on?" he pleads.

I close the cupboards, take a deep breath, and sit down on a stool. "Wait!" I suddenly remember. "What is your exciting news? I got so distracted I completely forgot." All of my frustration melts away as I watch his face light up.

"Ha!" Eric throws down the towel and leans on the counter. "Yes. I did too. Ok, are you sitting down?"

"I'm obviously sitting down."

"I mean mentally. Are you mentally sitting down?"

"Let's pretend the answer is yes."

"I feel like you don't understand the intensity of— "

"ERIC! Say it all ready!"

He laughs, tickled at my exasperation. "Ok. You know we have been working tirelessly to find genetic pairing for maximum strength in TSG's?"

"Yes," I say slowly, pulling at threads of old information filed away in my mind. "Your team has come really close multiple times, but in cell trials, it has never fully stopped tumor growth."

"Exactly. Well, today. We did it."

"You did it?"

"We did it."

"Like, you found a variation match that slowed the growth even further?"

"No, like we did it, Kate. We stopped the tumor growth completely. In fact, the tumor was nearly eradicated. We literally solved the problem." The excitement on his face is contagious.

"That's incredible! I am—I mean, I don't even know how to wrap my brain around this! Were the TSG's able to stop sarcoma and glioblastoma cells?"

"Both. They completely shut down sarcoma cells. The glioblastoma took a bit longer, but they also began to die eventually. It's amazing to watch."

"I had no idea you were so close," I say, a mixture of elation and regret playing on my face.

"Neither did we," he assures me. "Every trial looks the same, and usually we check results and see that the tumors are still growing in some way, shape, or form. I thought I was dreaming when I checked the results last week. We replicated this on fifteen different types of cells, all with the same result."

"Why didn't you say something then? I had no idea," I exclaim, standing up and rushing to him. His arms wrap around my waist and I bury my face in his neck, feeling his warm skin against my cheeks.

"I didn't want to get your hopes up. I—didn't want to get my hopes up," he breathes. We stay pressed together until I eventually push back to see his face, my arms remaining looped around him.

"So what now?" I ask, searching his eyes.

"I say we take this to the bedroom," he suggests without missing a beat.

"Later," I laugh, slapping his hands away. "What now with the research? I know when they found the match for heart disease they immediately started pairing people, but that was almost 180 years ago. It's been so long since we found a new disease match, does Berg even know how to handle that anymore?" I step away and start placing utensils in the drawer.

Eric sighs and runs his hands through his hair. "I don't know. You're totally right—it's been a long time and society has changed exponentially. But, the results from the last pairing are phenomenal. I was just at a briefing a couple of weeks ago where they gave the most recent statistics. We are now at a total multi-territory heart disease rate of six percent. Diabetes is *two percent*."

"Those are actual incidence rates or markers?"

"Incidence rates. The percentage for markers is higher, but at least we are preventing the onset."

I nod. "I was going to say, I see plenty of patients with markers. But you make a good point. I don't see many Tier 2 individuals who actually have symptoms."

"Right. One more generation and we will be even closer to making those illnesses complete memories from a past world. We honestly shouldn't even be seeing markers *in* this next generation." He pauses, noticing the look of frustration on my face. "What's wrong?" he asks.

"It seems so—" my hands gesticulate as I search for the right word, "—ridiculous, I guess? We are witnessing the disappearance of some of the most lethal chronic illnesses plaguing our society for centuries, and yet we still aren't projected to live as long as humans did hundreds of years ago. What more do we need to do?" I say, exasperation evident in my tone.

"Kate," Eric says, smiling gently, "you know the answer to that."

I look at him, jaw set, and raise my eyebrows. "Do I?"

"Yes," he says as he walks toward me, wrapping me in his arms. An amused smile plays on his lips. "You know that we have never been purely focused on lifespan. Berg has always considered quality of life to be paramount. I know that you like to pretend this doesn't exist, but we aren't in a position to waste resources on those that are suffering."

He's right. I do like to pretend that we don't cut off resources for people of all Tiers when they become too dependent on outside care. I like to pretend that we don't give people the option of continuing to suffer, or ending their lives peacefully. I do also understand that we can't pretend that we have enough resources to artificially sustain life for no real purpose. I don't expect that we repeat past mistakes through misappropriation of resources. I get it. I only wish that our efforts were having more of an affect sustaining people into old age.

Eric continues, "If we want to increase lifespan, we have to increase quality of life during the aging process. We have to find ways for the body to self heal and require less from society. That's why this research is so important." He sighs. "I honestly think that with heart disease and diabetes finally so low in our generation, we will be seeing lifespan increase significantly. Here and now. I predict we will witness it, Kate. I don't anticipate that we will experience the same decline seen in past generations." He walks back over to the counter. "But, with cancer rates continuing to increase, we have to get our soil toxicity under control before we will truly see how far reaching this will be. If we start now with this TSG match..." he trails off and turns on his display, using his stylus to scrawl out equations.

"It will definitely take longer than past pairings of this type because we are starting with a much larger population. I would estimate that we are starting with ten times the population this time around in Tier 1, meaning approximately fifteen million people who are able to reproduce starting today. Considering that Tier 2 population is always dropping, that increases the overall percentages. If we factor in an average reproduction rate in Tier 1 of 1.8 with each generation reproducing between the ages of 18-25," he says to himself. "Then we factor in— well, let's say we find one percent of people who match, so 150,000 people or 75,000 pairs," he continues, mumbling under his breath.

He is in his own world now. Even though most of this goes over my head, I don't want to break his concentration, so I quietly watch. His eyes flit between the numbers, excitedly moving from one result to the next. He has a bit of a mad scientist look about him with hair slightly disheveled and a rumpled shirt, from Bentley's body resting against him earlier.

"Based on our initial scans, that might be a long shot, but let's pretend," he continues, writing a few other numbers down. "If those TSG matches reproduce at a rate of two or three, in one generation we would hopefully see an almost *two percent* increase in overall population resistance," he proclaims, looking at me expectantly. "In the next generation, assuming all of those factors remain equal, we would see that number rise to over five percent of the population with resistance," he says. I can tell I am not giving him the reaction he wants, but it's so much to process.

"Over just a few generations, we would not only see a drastic increase in population, but also a radical decrease in cancer patients. Of course, that's as long as we can find, at a minimum, one percent of people who match." He exhales loudly, suddenly looking unsure. "That's a big 'if'," he admits. "These genetic variations are few and far between. We ran an initial pairing filter for our community and only found eight pairings."

"Eight total?" I say incredulously, tuning in. This I can understand.

"I know. It sounds completely unrealistic with that number. Assuming that the scans are similar in other communities, our regional number would be 378 pairs. That's a far cry from 75,000."

"Each community has slightly different genetic variations," I say hopefully. "Maybe you will find more in other communities with those scans. And, even if our regional numbers are small, when you add that to all of the regions in the territory, then the numbers from other territories, you may have more than you think."

"True," he concedes, his lips pursed in contemplation.

"What's worst case scenario? That you only find 15,000 pairs and it takes a few more generations to see that effect? That's a pretty good worst case." He nods.

"I know. I guess I'm just impatient."

We retreat to the living room and splay ourselves out on the couch. Lying back, I rest my legs on his.

"You also have to consider that, as our nutrition continues to improve and toxin levels are reduced, cancer levels may begin to decrease organically, as well. That, combined with this genetic selection...we may be able to see stronger results sooner," I muse.

"That's wishful thinking, but I like it," Eric says as he leans across my outstretched body and kisses my cheek. "Though I'm not convinced that levels are going to be coming down anytime soon. After everything we've done, we've hit a plateau. Unless new technology is somehow created, we are somewhat limited in our ability to lower the toxicity levels of the water and soil. It's just such a slow and costly process."

"I'm hopeful that it will happen." I nudge him. "Maybe Bent will figure something out."

"I wouldn't be surprised," Eric laughs.

"You know this is going to become an ethical issue, though," I caution.

"That a seven year old discovered how to sustainably clean water?"

I smack his shoulder, teasing. "No, the pairing for TSG's."

He chuckles, obviously amused with himself.

"It was one thing to force pairings when there was a need to rebuild the population from the ground up, but now? How do we allow people to pair organically if we are giving them 'options' of only a handful of potential genetic pairs? Can we justify that? Given the population growth we have experienced in the last few centuries?" I ask.

Eric leans his head back, staring silently at the matte ceiling. "I know. There were so many options for selection originally. I considered suggesting that we pull all of the pairs together as a territory to allow for more instinctive selection within our pairing groups, but I didn't. I knew Berg wouldn't go for it."

"Hmmm."

"They are still conducting research in our communities, and if we suddenly mix it all up, we could prevent future discoveries. And, our populations could become too homogenous. It's unlikely with *that* low of a population percentage, but still a risk."

"So. These people are kind of stuck."

"Right."

The front door slams open and we hear Bentley sobbing, his wails fracturing our peaceful moment.

"Guess the bedroom will be way later," Eric teases, moving my legs to the floor and springing up to help. "Bent, what's wrong, bud?"

"Dad, I fell off the slide. I am bleeding really bad," he splutters.

"Let me check it out. Where are you bleeding?"

I move quickly to the cabinet in the kitchen that contains all of our medical gear.

"Does it look like a spray will do it?" I call, assuming that the initial description was an over exaggeration on Bentley's part.

"Yes, thanks. That will be great," Eric replies. "It's almost stopped bleeding on its own."

I grab the slender steel canister and walk over to them, witnessing the small scrape for myself. "Here Bent, let me spray them." I reach out, but he wiggles away.

"It's going to hurt!" he complains, protectively wrapping his arms around his knee. I suppress an eyeroll, slightly frustrated by his dramatics.

"Bud, remember, this is the good stuff. Can you tell me what it does?" He sniffs.

"It cleans my skin and makes a shield so nothing bad can get in."

"You got it. It doesn't hurt at all. Let me see." I gently move his leg towards me and quickly spray it on his skin before he can flinch away, and he immediately begins to settle down.

"See? All better," I say, pulling him close, my fingers unintention- ally ruffling his gossamer hair. Reaching up, he smooths the misplaced locks, shooting me a scowl.

"Do you want to play longer, or should we call Tal in for bed?" Eric asks and Bentley lifts his head.

"Is Tal the only one who has to go to bed?" he questions hopefully, tears still resting on his cheek. Eric chuckles.

"No, you both need to."

"Then I am going to go play." He wipes his nose on his sleeve and walks glumly back out the door.

"Ten more minutes!" I call as he closes the door behind him.

CHAPTER 5

ERIC and I sit on a wooden bench in the courtyard after meeting with Tal's instructor, Mr. Dane. The ancient willow tree next to us gently waves in the breeze, its low hanging branches sweeping the native grasses in nearly silent communion. An ant wanders over my toes, and as uncomfortable the sensation is, I don't disturb it. I like watching it meander.

As a parent, I often find myself bristling slightly when I receive suggestions from the boys' mentors or instructors. I know this feeling comes from my own insecurities—my own worries that I am not good enough. More than that, though, it stems from a deep, gut-wrenching place where I wonder if they might know something about my child that I don't. It is completely unrealistic to think that I would be able to have a monopoly on knowing a person. But I still secretly want it.

Mr. Dane, as expected, wasn't worried about Tal's questioning in class, but he did feel like it was an indication of his need to be working with a more advanced peer group. I hadn't realized that he was hitting a developmental stage earlier than many boys his age, nor did I understand that this would mean making adjustments to his conditioning. Being a first-time parent is hard. I am way out of my depth.

"What are you thinking about?" Eric asks.

"Just Tal. How big he's getting. How much I want to keep him safely in the little box I've created in my mind for him." I exhale slowly. "How incompetent I am at doing this parenting thing right."

Eric laughs, settling his arm across my shoulders. "You and me both."

"Even though we've watched other parents raise kids to adulthood, I wasn't really paying attention," I murmur.

"What do you mean?"

"I wasn't listening when they talked about the struggles they were having or the feelings they had during transitions like this. I have only ever tuned in to things that were relevant for me at the time. I missed out."

"I think that's pretty normal," Eric muses. "I also don't recall having *that* many opportunities to talk with people who have been through this before. Don't get me wrong—I love Matt, but I have often wondered if it would have been more beneficial to match with a mentor who had the opportunity to have children."

I nod. "That's a good point. Do you think they will ever adjust that? Shari gets me, but there have been times when I haven't been able to fully open up because I knew my parenting struggles wouldn't resonate with her." I shift closer to him, resting my head against his shoulder.

"I think it's definitely something that should be considered. It's difficult though, because when we match up with mentors, we don't necessarily know who is going to pair and who isn't. The question would really be: could we match with a mentor later? When we know what an individual's trajectory is potentially going to be?" he postulates.

"But then we would miss out on those early years, which, at least in my case, were extremely beneficial," I interject.

"Exactly. Me too."

I play with the cuff of his sleeve errantly, remembering those early days with Shari. All of the questions—some of them embarrassing enough that I didn't feel comfortable asking my parents. She always answered me, making me feel like I was uniquely mature to be looking beyond my current life as a child.

"Do you think it's odd that neither of us entered the program to be mentors?" I ask.

After a few moments, Eric answers, "No. Maybe the people who don't feel inclined to mentor are those who are more likely to pair and have children. I know that's why I didn't feel drawn to it. I knew I wanted kids and felt like there was a high probability that it would happen."

"You were that confident, hey?" I tease. Eric grins, gripping my hand in his.

"I think we're doing alright," he says gently, and I squeeze his fingers.

"Are you saying I can keep Tal in my box?"

"Maybe just a slightly expanded one. For now," Eric says, rubbing my shoulders as we stand and find the path that will take us home.

Approaching our lane, I am taken off guard by the hoard of people coming and going from our neighbor's house. Leaving Eric, I walk forward quickly, my eyes searching for Fay, but I don't find her familiar face. Come to think of it, I haven't seen her or Cameron at all lately. They have been our neighbors ever since we settled here. Their children are older, and we are on opposite schedules with our work assignments, so our paths don't often cross. Still, it's strange that I haven't seen anyone puttering around in the flower bed over the last few weeks. What kind of neighbor am I that I didn't even notice?

I approach one of the strange men as he exits the house. He is dressed in a crisp blue collared shirt, navy blue tie, and khaki pants. Though he is engaged with something on his display and doesn't acknowledge me, I tap his shoulder.

"Excuse me, we live next door and I couldn't help but wonder what all the fuss is about. Is everything ok?" I ask, smiling apologetically for the interruption.

"The couple here has been reassigned, that's all," he answers curtly.

"Reassigned?"

"Yep."

"Can I ask what type of reassignment would require re-homing?" I am met with a blank stare. "I have never heard of anyone having to leave their home when changing service assignments," I try to clarify.

"Some changes require that. You could ask at your next training meeting and I am sure they could give you better info. I am not privy to the particulars of this situation."

I thank him and retreat to our house. It seems odd that Fay wouldn't have said anything before leaving. She was such a support to me when the boys were born. Maybe the change just happened too quickly? They could have sent a message at the very least, though. The whole thing leaves me feeling strangely hollow and disappointed. That connection must have meant more to me than to her, I think.

Upon entering the house, Eric motions excitedly for me to join him. The boys are already perched on stools next to his display.

"What's the rush?" I ask, kicking off my shoes.

"Our scan results are in!" Bentley shouts, and I run over to join them.

The images are vibrant and beautiful. It's breathtaking to see the inner workings of the brain, and especially those of brains we have created.

"Why do Bent's and my scans always look different?" Tal asks.

"You guys have slightly different genetics. And you are the oldest," Eric says absently, engrossed in the images. "Bent is the youngest. That gives you divergent social experiences, as well."

"I know that. I mean why do you always spend more time looking at Bentley's scans over mine?"

Oh. I didn't realize he had noticed that. I look at Eric hoping he has a good explanation for this. His expression tells me he's not sure what to say either.

"Well, we spent more time on your scans when you were younger, too. But you're right. We do have to spend a bit more time when it comes to Bentley," I admit.

"Is there something wrong with me?" Bentley asks worriedly.

"No, bud. Not at all," Eric assures him. "It's actually a lot of good things that are responsible. Every scan from the time you were born has shown a really advanced genetic and social profile. Do you understand what that means?"

"It means he's better than me," Tal mumbles, his body deflating.

"No way. That isn't true, Tal," I interject. "It means that you have different needs. Do you think you are better than the kids whose brains haven't developed as quickly as yours?"

"No, but— "

"It's the same thing. Mr. Dane is adjusting your conditioning based on your needs, not because you are better or worse. There is no judgment there."

"But why aren't Bentley and I the same?" he asks earnestly.

"Dad and I were able to have kids because we both have viable profiles, so of course our children would enjoy those same benefits. You and Bentley are the same in so many ways. But, unless we specifically farmed my eggs and Dad's sperm to get the exact progeny profile we wanted, there were going to be variations in what ended up matching naturally."

"Why don't they just do that for everyone? Then you'd get the right thing every time," Tal says. Bentley is wiggling and almost falls off his stool. Luckily, Eric grabs his arm and stabilizes him without losing his train of thought.

"People tried that before the Crisis. It did give people exactly what they wanted— "

"And made corporations a lot of money," I add.

" —but there were plenty of unintended consequences," Eric finishes calmly, giving me a wink.

"What are unintended consequences?" asks Bentley, putting his face closer to the shifting colors.

"Things people didn't know would happen. Usually bad," Tal answers.

"Right," Eric agrees. "Parents would pay to create these perfect embryos, but the chances of them actually being viable inside of the mother and living until birth were small. They also didn't have the testing to be able to match up all of the needed markers to create a well-rounded, healthy child. Many of the variations they were looking for—like blue eyes, height, or gender—were actually also linked to disease and negative personality markers that they weren't aware of."

"And it was a huge waste of resources that really only favored the rich. The Committee decided against it," I finish.

"But now you are left with one son who is not as 'viable' as the other," he chides.

"Again, not true," Eric corrects. "What do you think would happen if all of our gene variations were the same? Or really similar?" He turns and faces him.

At this point, Bentley has proven completely incapable of successfully remaining upright on the stool. I lift him down, placating him by offering to read stories in the other room. Between lines in the book, I try to catch snippets of the conversation still taking place in the kitchen.

"In the great green room..." I read softly, almost a whisper.

"...our world and our bodies are always adapting and changing. What if some new virus appeared tomorrow that targeted some system in our body that we've never paid attention to in the past? If all of our genes were too similar, the human race could be wiped out. We need that variation..." Eric is explaining.

"...and a bowl full of mush..."

"So Bentley needs special stuff because of his genes and I'm here as a safety net?" Tal asks, pretending to be offended.

"...and a quiet old lady who was whispering, 'hush'..."

"Yep, that's why we had two kids. We got the safety net first and then decided to try for one that had a real chance of success," Eric says soberly. It's silent and I hold my breath.

"Of course not!" Eric continues, his voice laden with affection.

"Mom, keep going," Bentley reminds me.

"Sorry, bud. Good night, room. Good night, moon..."

"...both of you have incredible potential. Your path might be more traditional than Bentley's. I don't know! We have to kind of make things up as we go, using and learning from other people's experiences to create the opportunities he needs..."

"...Good night, noises everywhere," I finish. Bentley is still, and my guess is that he internalized more than just the book. I kiss him gently, tucking his miniature frame beneath the blankets.

CHAPTER 6

I WALK into the main Berg campus center on time. Normally this reception area is buzzing, but tonight it's quiet and still. The sound of my shoes against the tile echoes around me. This place always feels somewhat sterile, but this evening it seems especially hygienic. I guess I can't expect anything more when geneticists are in charge of building design. The entire campus is entirely utilitarian, which I appreciate, but also helps me resonate with our predecessors obsession with carpet and upholstered chairs.

I should have asked Shari where we were meeting specifically, but assume it will be in one of the smaller rooms next to the main auditorium. I head that direction and begin peeking through windows. A small group of people sits huddled around a table in one of the classrooms. Though I can only see the backs of their heads, I would recognize that short brunette bob anywhere.

My hand closes around the circular handle and the door swings open. All eyes turn toward me. Finding Shari's face, I smile and make my way to an available chair across from her. Gratefully, my footsteps don't sound nearly as abrasive in this space.

"And here I thought I was on time. You are all overachievers," I say jokingly and hear a few chuckles in response.

"We had a couple of things to discuss before you arrived," a woman responds, her voice high and clear. She must be the group leader. Though I have no previous experience with these commit-tees, I immediately wonder what they would need to discuss without me being present. I let the thought slide, taking my seat.

"Kate, my name is Grace, and I am here to give assignments for the ceremony this year."

Grace looks to be about my age, perhaps a little older. My eyes are drawn immediately to her jet black hair, twisted up in a tight bun. Her every movement exudes professionalism and poise.

Nodding, I open my tablet and steal a glance around the table at the rest of the group. The man across from me looks disturbingly familiar. He is young, probably early twenties at most. How would I know him? My brain starts scanning through all of the potential options, trying to puzzle it out.

"Kate? Does that work for you?" Grace asks.

"Could you repeat that? My mind was distracted." I flush, whip-ping my head to attention, focusing again on Grace.

"Of course. I was asking if you would be willing to work with Nick on introductions this year. Since you both have some relationships with the candidates transitioning, we thought it would be comforting for them to see you up there. It should be easier to write the introductions with some personal knowledge of them anyway." She smiles at me, but it isn't a warm expression, rather an assiduous one.

I don't dare dissent, despite my hesitations. "That makes sense," I respond meekly. "I don't know who Nick is, but I am happy to help."

"Nick, why don't you introduce yourself," Grace commands, gesturing to the man I had previously noticed. He shoots out a hand and I reach across to shake it.

"Hey, I think we have worked at Washington Park together a couple of times but haven't officially met. Though I did smack into you by the washroom one time." He smiles and it seems to envelop his entire face. Of course. The moment comes rushing back to me, causing my extremities to tingle, going slightly numb.

"It's funny—when I sat down," I stammer, "I thought you looked familiar, but I must have blocked that awkward experience out. I didn't recognize you all cleaned up and out of context," I explain.

"I'll try not to be offended that I didn't make an impression," he teases.

My cheeks burn and I change the subject. "I hope you don't mind me asking, but aren't you a little young to be a health consultant?"

Everyone around the table laughs, making me question whether I have missed something. Suddenly becoming aware that my hand is still in his, I quickly release it, blinking rapidly.

"I don't mind at all," he replies, grinning, his eyes rich with youthful energy. "I am a little young, definitely, but I was fast-tracked through a lot of my conditioning because my results were...abnormal. I am just happy to be serving here instead of taking more classes."

Interesting. I didn't even know that was possible to such an extent. Is that what it will look like for Bentley? When Doctor Harmon mentioned accelerating, I was thinking by a year or two. Maybe this guy is an extreme outlier? He does have incredible skin and bone structure. Above-average musculature...thick, wavy hair... Probably an anomaly. I clear my throat.

"That's impressive. I'm surprised our paths haven't crossed more at Washington Park. How long have you been stationed there?" I ask.

"Not long. My first day was actually just a couple of weeks ago. I am still fully riding the learning curve." He smiles, turning his attention back to Grace. "Why don't I go with Kate to the office so we can look over the files for the ceremony. Does that work?"

"That would be great, Nick. Thank you both for being here."

"Grace, just to clarify," I stall, "Nick and I will be presenting the candidates at the ceremony, but what specifically should we focus on in our introductions? I haven't attended one of these in years, so I want to make sure that we are on the right track."

"Oh, Nick has all of that information. I will let him give you the checklist. Any other questions before you go?" She looks at me unblinking, another smile not quite reaching her eyes.

"No, that's great. Thanks so much." I look over at Shari questioningly as I shuffle my tablet into my bag. Grace is already starting in on seating logistics with the others. Shari waves me off. Why did I need to attend this meeting if I would be leaving immediately to receive my instructions from Nick? Couldn't we have met separately and he could have explained everything? I'm hopeful that Shari will call me after training and we can talk about it then.

I hurriedly follow Nick out of the room and down the hall. Though I pass this way regularly, I have never actually entered the office. I watch him rummage in his pocket for a key and smoothly insert it into the lock. His head nearly reaches the top of the doorframe, a detail I missed during our initial harried interaction. I want to ask him more about his conditioning, but maybe that would be weird? I resolve to simply receive my instructions tonight and then finish my portion at home. There will really be no need for me to interact much with him in the future, anyway. Though, I guess that may be an argument for being willing to make a fool of myself?

Nick sits down at the desk and pulls up the display. All six candidates appear in front of us. I immediately recognize Cassidy and Max, another candidate I worked with earlier in the year. Not knowing the others, I assume Nick must have some connection.

"Alright, why don't you show me the checklist, and we can determine which candidates should be assigned to each of us. I can put something together at home. Training starts in ten minutes," I say abruptly. Nick looks at me, amused.

"Oh no, this will be in place of training tonight. Grace already let our groups know that we won't be available. We will actually be writing these intros together," he says nonchalantly as he stretches back in the chair, reminding me of a cat, lazily extending after a nap. "We all thought that might make them more cohesive and consistent. I'm sorry you weren't there when we were discussing this. I think Grace felt like I needed some extra instruction since I'm completely new to all of this, but I hope it didn't make you feel excluded."

"No, I mean... I did find it a little odd that everyone was there before me, but I am not overly concerned about it. If we are doing this instead of training, though, I need to quickly message my pair. I told him I would save him a seat. Do you mind?"

"Of course, go ahead. I'll pull up the focus list while you do that." His fingers deftly begin scrolling through files on the tablet.

I step into the hall, noticing people beginning to trickle in through the front doors. Eric may be a few minutes late since he has to get the boys settled. Tal's mentor, Stephen, always watches them for us when we have training, but sometimes the boys still insist on me or Eric reading them stories before we leave.

I quietly speak into my sensor: "For Eric. Hey, this meeting is actually taking the place of training, so I won't be able to save you a seat. So sorry! Hope the boys aren't being too clingy. Let me know what I missed? Love you."

I wait to confirm that it sent, then reenter the room. Nick has pulled up the document on the display and is scrutinizing what seems to be a personal message when I walk back in. He closes his window, turning toward me.

"All good?" he asks cheerily.

"I hope so. We have two boys, so sometimes getting both of us to training is a little tricky." I see a thought flicker across Nick's face, but then he is back to his perky self.

"That must be tough. I'll avoid taking up too much of your time so you can get home," he says. My tablet clatters on the table's smooth, wooden surface as I set it down.

"Nick, can you tell me more about how you were fast tracked? I've never heard of that happening. We recently had our annual scans, and my almost-eight-year-old son showed some results that might require some acceleration. It makes me nervous. I have always been taught that we need certain experiences over a specific amount of time for our brains to really develop. For us to truly embrace the values needed to fulfill all that is required of us in Tier 1. Aren't you worried that you will somehow have problems later on? Or burn out?"

I don't mean to pry, but I am extremely curious. Being Tier 1 is a big risk with high reward, not only for the individual, but for society, as well. Years ago, when we split to a Tier system, it wasn't because the system was ideal, but because it was necessary. The world population only had so many resources, and a decision had to be made on how to allocate those in the best possible way for our survival. Tier 1 was created to ensure that survival.

Those who had the highest chance of life and successful procreation were given top priority, to guarantee that the next generation would be as genetically viable as possible. It was thought that a group with clean DNA and consistent, positive social input could produce generations of stable individuals who could then learn, discover, and serve society as it healed. And it's working. Here we are, almost 275 years since the Crisis, and all we have seen is success. Our average lifespan has increased by almost 20 years, infant mortality is less than 5%, and we have significantly reduced suffering during old age. Why would we, all of a sudden, alter a proven system?

Nick rolls back on his chair and turns toward me. He isn't grinning as widely anymore. "It's actually terrifying," he says quietly. "When I was younger, my parents were informed that my responses to conditioning were far beyond age level. They knew that, genetically, I was completely clean. I mean, no markers or variations besides something as benign as motion sickness."

I cough. He pauses.

"I'm sorry, I just...well, nobody with motion sickness would describe it as being benign," I explain. "Go on, sorry. That was completely involuntary."

Nick laughs. "I guess mine isn't that severe." He gives me a mock disapproving look. "Before I was so rudely interrupted, I was saying that besides the completely debilitating motion sickness that I deal with, I am genetically perfect." He holds up his hands. "I know, it sounds pretentious, but that's what they tell me. After my conditioning results were abnormal, our local committee—of which Grace is a member—petitioned to the regional and then territorial leaders at Berg to push me forward. As far as I know, this hasn't happened in the past. But I guess there are a couple of other people around the region who are in my same situation, all of them men. So, long story short, yes. I am scared. I don't know what to expect, and I don't think anyone else does either. But I was plateauing in conditioning. It all just made sense. I meant what I said back there. I am really glad to be actually contributing to the world, and I guess I hope that it will all work out the way Berg expects it to." He lifts his arms behind his head again and leans back. I try to stay focused on his face. "Any other questions before we actually get to work? Home to your children, remember?" he teases.

"Yes, sorry. My curiosity got the better of me. No more distractions." I pick up my tablet and turn on the display when I feel his hand brush my arm.

"I think curiosity is a good thing. Ask me anything, anytime." He's looking at me intently. It feels strangely intimate, and I pull back.

"Thanks." I pull my hair up and words begin to awkwardly tumble from my mouth. "Should we start with Cassidy? She is the one I know best. Unless you have someone you'd like to discuss. I assume you know some of the others."

I can feel my face flushing. Pull it together, Kate. It's been so long since I talked extensively with any man besides Eric. It really doesn't help that Nick is so physically appealing. Despite the fact that I am paired and in every way fulfilled, my body and mind can't help but respond to the perfect symmetry of his face, his angular jaw, and his broad shoulders. I am tempted to reach out and trace those lines. Not because I want to be with him, but because I want to make sure that he's real.

I have spent a lot of time studying physical attractiveness as part of my health training. The history of it is fascinating. It has changed so much over the course of human history. Especially for women. From buxom to stick thin, back to curvy, and then muscular. Usually society favors signs of health, but with the influx of technology before and during the Crisis, girls and boys were inundated with unrealistic images that exaggerated certain characteristics before they fully matured physically or mentally. Large-breasted women with tiny hips and waists, faces coated in products to make people look flushed and youthful, men with arms and chests so large that their arms couldn't even rest against their sides naturally, hair treated with chemicals to make it look shiny, and the list goes on. It became impossible for people to actually gauge true attractiveness, and people were constantly stressed about being appealing to others. They mutilated their bodies in search of an ideal that didn't exist—which, ironically, made their genes less viable.

Our society now values *true* health and viability. We didn't have time or resources after the Crisis to fake it, and to do so now would be completely socially unacceptable. In my position, I must be able to assess a patient's outward appearance—their skin elasticity and pallor, muscle tone, eye clarity, bone structure. It isn't just an indication of genetic potential, but also of their general nutrition and physical fitness. If someone were to artificially boost their performance or appearance during those appointments, how would it serve them? They would only be hurting their future possibilities. Not worth it. I give myself some credit: it is my responsibility to notice people. Of course I would notice Nick.

"Sure, let's start with Cassidy," Nick says.

The rest of the meeting is all business. Nick explains how the goal of the introduction is two-fold. We need to provide information that will promote acceptance within Tier 1 while also building up self-confidence in the candidate. Acceptance into a group requires both the existing members of the group and the new addition to accept the relationship inherently. We discuss different ideas on how to accomplish this and make good progress with a few of the candidates. Nick is extremely thoughtful, and I am surprised by the depth of his insights at such a young age. He is in the middle of another thought when I realize I desperately have to use the restroom. I glance down at my sensor and see that it is almost 9pm. Training must have ended an hour ago. I also see that I have five messages from Eric. Nick notices that I am distracted and pauses.

"I had no idea how late it was. I really need to get home to my family. I'm so sorry to cut you off." I hurriedly stand up and slip my tablet into my bag. "Do you think we can finish up in one more meeting next week sometime?"

"Definitely. I will message you to set that up. Thanks Kate, it was great to meet you."

"You too." I rush out and quickly head to the car. I can't believe I stayed so late. Eric must be worried. I send him a quick note letting him know I am on my way home.

In the car I quickly call Shari. I only have five minutes before I get home, so hopefully she is available. Her face comes into view.

"Took you long enough. Were the kids up when you got home?"

"I am barely *on* my way home."

"Wait, what? I thought you were only meeting during training. What happened?"

"I don't know! We were passing ideas back and forth and the next thing I knew it was nine o'clock. I am almost home, so I just wanted to call and say that was a really weird initial meeting. Why did they even have me come? I could have just met with Nick and received instructions there. I felt really out of place."

"I know, it was strange. Grace is interesting. I think she just really likes to see everything organized. She wanted all of our faces in the same room. Thanks for hanging in there. I really think you will do great. And Nick. Right?" She gives me a knowing look and an eyebrow raise.

I laugh. "I'm glad I'm not the only one who noticed," I admit, relieved. "I'm actually really excited."

Shari laughs.

"Not about Nick," I scoff, "about the ceremony! I haven't gotten up in front of people in a long time, but this is important. Helping these candidates feel at home in Tier 1 is so crucial to their success."

Shari winks conspiratorially, and I roll my eyes, glancing out the window. "I'm pulling in now. Sorry for such a short call."

"Have a great night Kate. We can talk more in depth at our next session. Friday, right?"

"See you then. Enjoy your eight hours." I wink and she is gone.

CHAPTER 7

I STEP into the house and slip off my shoes. Every movement sounds deafening in the silence. Hanging my cardigan and bag on the hooks by the door, I tip-toe into the kitchen. Gently, I open a cupboard and slide out a glass. Turning, I notice the top of Eric's head sticking up on one side of the couch. After filling my glass with water, I quietly navigate around the furniture, noticing that his eyes are closed and he is breathing deeply. I can't help but snuggle in beside him, setting my water on the wood floor. He sighs, wrapping his arms around me and pulling me close. This is home.

"Late meeting?" he mumbles.

"Yep. Sorry to make you worry."

"Oh, I wasn't worried. Just excited to have a night as a bachelor. I'm only tired because I partied so hard," he says groggily.

When he doesn't continue, I check to make sure he didn't slip back to sleep.

"Mm-hmmm. Your messages say otherwise," I tease.

"I had to send those. So you wouldn't be suspicious."

I kiss him then, softly. "I love you. I'm sorry I was so late. How was training?"

"I'll tell you tomorrow. Let's go to bed. My shoulder is cramping from being on this couch."

"You're getting—"

"Old, I know." He pushes me off the side and I fall to the floor. Laughing, I push myself up and follow him into our bedroom. Shedding my clothes and crawling under the covers is a relief. In the dark, I feel that Eric is already there. My feet find their usual place between his calves, and I am asleep as soon as my head hits the pillow.

Drenched in sweat and gasping for breath, my eyes fly open. I flinch when a hand reaches out and brushes my arm.

"Same dream?" Eric asks softly.

"Mmm-hmm," I mumble, still trying to calm my heartrate down.

"How often is it happening these days?"

"This is the first time in awhile," I say, dazed. "I think Bentley was still fairly young when it happened last. I know Shari seems to think it happens more when I am under stress..." I trail off. I don't feel stressed. Maybe it's just because of my assignments with the Ceremony and the fact that I was out late.

"Is it always exactly the same or are there slight variations?" he asks, pulling me close to him.

"Pretty much identical, I think. I am always sitting in the garden. The air is cool and everything moves slower than usual, even my hair seems to blow in slow motion, it's hard to explain. My mom rushes out the back door yelling for me and time seems to speed forward. Almost violently. Something is pulling her back inside and I can't get to her," I explain, tears filling my eyes. "She is always wearing the same thing—her favorite loose, linen skirt—and her hair is down, whipping around her face." I wipe a tear from my cheek. "I'm sorry, it's just so disturbing. I don't know why my mind is conjuring up that image. What am I supposed to take from that?"

"Our dreams are usually random synaptic responses," Eric says. "Sometimes they can be indicative of our fears or concerns. Maybe you have always subconsciously wanted to know more about your mom."

"Maybe." My breathing settles. Glancing at my sensor, I realize it's close enough to our normal waking time that there is no point in trying to go back to sleep. Instead, I lie on my floor mat, beginning my stretches, and changing the topic of conversation.

I fill Eric in on my assignment while he gives me details on the training I missed. Most of it seems theoretically intuitive, but I will need to go into my consultant software to become completely familiar with the upgrades. Eric makes tea while I cook up some greens to go with our eggs. I hear the door open to the boys' room and see little, disheveled heads making their way down the hall.

Today is Family Day and we have all been looking forward to our hiking plans.

Bentley sits up to the counter first.

"Morning," Eric says as he gives him a big hug. "How can I serve Master Bentley this morning? May I procure some eggs, greens, and tea for the gentleman?"

"Dad. I don't even know what you're saying," he giggles and yawns.

"But you like it, right?"

"I just want breakfast."

"Hear ye! Hear ye! Master Bentley desires breakfast!" Eric whirls his hands in the air and moves around the island with a flourish. He dramatically dishes up Bentley's food and places it in front of him with a bow. "Will this suffice, sir?"

Eric has always been a little silly and childlike. Not immature, just full of energy and exuberance for life. That's definitely why I was drawn to him. His goofy, whole-body laugh whenever he sees something ridiculous happen is contagious. Like when a squirrel jumps and misses a branch. Or someone misjudges how fast a door will close. Bentley grins at his antics.

"Thanks, Dad," he says shyly.

Tal, who made a pit stop in the washroom on his way to the kitchen, sits up next to Bentley at the counter. "Dad, please don't. If you are going to be weird, I will get my own breakfast."

Eric looks at him skeptically, feigning offense. "I love you, Tal. I will not be weird, I will simply dish up your breakfast and not say a word."

I slap some eggs on a plate and pass it to Eric so he can add the greens. He, in turn, places it in front of Tal.

"Kind of boring, right? I bet you wish you asked for weird," Eric teases.

Tal rolls his eyes and begins cramming his mouth with soft egg. After the boys finish up and clear their dishes, they ask if they can play for a while with their robotics kits. We acquiesce, grab our mugs, and head to the porch. I figure we can leave right before eleven and still have plenty of time for our hike. I am grateful we picked a short one so we don't have to force the boys to rush, especially since they seem to be playing nicely.

Eric and I sit down on the porch swing together. The wood gently creaks as we rock, the air fresh on our faces. A spiderweb catches my eye, dew shimmering in the delicate web, and my gaze shifts to the house next door.

"What's on your mind?" Eric asks, causing me to jump at the unexpectedness of his voice.

"You ok there?" he laughs and I feign annoyance, slightly embarrassed.

"I still think it's so strange that we haven't heard from Fay or Cameron," I say, ignoring his continued amusement.

"Oh," he says, suddenly serious. "I actually asked about them at training, I forgot to tell you."

"You did? What did you find out?"

"Not much, just that they had gained new responsibilities that required them to move territories."

"They moved to a completely new territory? Have you ever heard of that happening?"

"Honestly, not really. Do you know what their work assignment was?" Eric asks.

I am reminded, yet again, how one-sided our relationship must have been. I know virtually nothing about them. Information about their family, yes, but nothing about their personal life. I was always so impressed that they were still in such good health with children entering young adulthood. I wish I would have learned more from them while they were here.

"No, I don't," I admit, exhaling slowly. "I wonder when someone else will move in there."

"You would think it would be soon," Eric muses.

"Moving territories. Your research would never require that, would it? In some ways it sounds exciting, but..." I trail off. I am not quite sure how to verbalize the emotions rushing through me as I consider change of that magnitude.

"Do you remember the stories we explored in conditioning about travel?" Eric asks as he puts his arm around my shoulders.

"Yes, how could I forget? I remember wishing so badly that I could go to a beach. That picture of the waves breaking on the rocks is still fixed in my brain," I say wistfully.

"I wonder what it would have been like to randomly jump on a plane and be somewhere else in a couple of hours."

"Probably amazing. But also terribly wasteful. I don't know that I could enjoy it, understanding the societal cost." I take a slow sip of my tea.

"I don't think anyone back then knew what the cost actually was. They simply paid for their ticket and went. Ignorance is bliss," Eric says, almost longingly.

"Do you wish we were ignorant?" I ask, surprised at his tone.

"Sometimes," he considers, "but mostly I am just happy to be alive at this time, doing what we're doing. I think travel probably exacerbated the general feeling of dissatisfaction in society then. The idea of an exciting trip—escaping from the mundane, repetitive tasks of normal life—would have served as a constant distraction."

The edge of his mug meets his lips, his two-day-old stubble accentuating his masculinity. I watch his eyes close as he inhales the earthy smell of the chamomile.

"That's really it, isn't it?" he continues. "The whole idea of vacation seems odd to me. If your life is set up in such a way that all of your needs are fulfilled, why would you need to escape it? That was their downfall."

"Travel?"

"No, escaping. Everything they did was to escape. Through entertainment, virtual experiences, travel, food, everything. Such an unhappy people. Or at least not a people at peace," he concludes, leaning over and kissing my forehead. "I am going to go put our day packs together. Is there anything you need in yours besides the usual?"

"The usual is perfect, thanks," I say as he rises to return inside. "Eric, we are at peace, right?"

He looks at me intently and smiles softly. "Always."

CHAPTER 8

My MEETING with Shari is today and I have been high-strung all morning. I have so much to talk about and really want to hear her opinion on Eric's research. She has more experience than I do with Berg, specifically with gene sequencing. One of her parents was actually involved in troubleshooting the new pairing software when it was released.

My initial excitement fades a little as I consider the final topic on my mental docket for today. I am slightly more hesitant to discuss the alert. Or more specifically, the reason for the alert. I haven't been able to get it off my mind and have been obsessively researching it in my spare time. Nothing about it makes sense. There isn't any documentation of even a *single* incident of Tier 3 violence instigated by individuals approved for work assignments. A report for this specific alert is also still forthcoming, which is extremely odd. Normally, we receive a debriefing after even the slightest interruption to a service assignment. The whole thing simply isn't sitting well with me, and Eric is sick of hearing about it.

I arrive at her door and walk in. We are way past knocking.

"Shari?" I call, moving down the long hallway. Her house feels infinitely larger than ours with the vaulted ceilings. I know it isn't *that* much bigger, and that she has roommates, but it still seems almost frivolous to have such an expanse of wasted space.

"In here! Just making my menu for the week. Do you mind if I finish it up while we talk?" I follow her voice into the kitchen and find her, bent over the counter, working. Her coral shirt seems neon in comparison with the white cabinets and tile.

"Not at all," I answer. "What are your levels at?"

"Well, it's my first week with these new portions," she explains, setting her tablet down and standing upright. "My mapping last month showed some deterioration in my folate one-carbon metabolism pathway. I don't have any markers for dementia or cardiovascular disease, obviously, but we are trying to adjust my diet to get that cycle on track. Just lower my risk as close to zero as possible. Pretty boring stuff. Involving lots of vegetables."

I laugh. "Not boring. I'm taking notes so I know what to do in ten years when I'm in the same boat."

Shari returns to calculating the nutrition values in her recipes. While she writes, my shoulders begin to tense, not sure where to begin. This isn't like me to feel unsure around her, and I hate it. I wait, hoping some easy transition will come to me.

"I'm guessing you want to talk about Eric's research," she says a few moments later, shooting me an excited smile. I mentally sigh in relief.

"You know details already? Word got out fast."

"Oh, everyone knows. The whole lab is abuzz with it. You do realize that this represents the first successful match in over two hundred years, right?"

Goosebumps begin to rise on my arms. "I do. It seems surreal. On one hand, I am ecstatic, but on the other, I am a nervous wreck," I say, running my hands through my hair. "What if this is a fluke and can't be replicated? How are they going to work with this information if it *can* be replicated? Eric says the pairing in the general population is incredibly low. So what then?" I let my hands fall down to the counter a little too quickly and it stings my palms.

"Whoa, ok. Let's take this one at a time. Here, let's go sit out on the patio. I'll finish this later." Her loose cotton pants, tied above her hips, sway as she moves through the kitchen. Hair falls loosely around her neck, and I notice she is wearing her glasses again today.

"Are you wearing glasses full-time now?" I ask.

"Almost. I can still see just fine, but my eyes feel more fatigued when I try to ignore the fact that I need them."

"Are you going to do the laser enhancement?"

"Yes, as soon as I officially qualify. I think another six months should do it," she says, raising her eyebrow surreptitiously.

I laugh, following her through the backdoor. "I'm sorry I'm so discombobulated about all this. My mind has been cycling around and around since I heard the news. Eric doesn't have any answers, so I don't want to stress him out by asking or expressing my doubts," I complain. Shari pulls out a chair for me and we sit in the warm sun. Maybe a tad too warm, I think. Before I have a chance to say anything, Shari puts up an umbrella.

"I can completely eliminate your first concern. The experiment has already been replicated by other researchers. Twice. With exactly the same results."

"Wow. Eric didn't tell me that."

"He couldn't have. The results were just posted last night. So let's talk about your next concern, which, yes, is completely founded. The initial scans only show a handful of matches in the entire region."

"What exactly are they matching? I know I could ask Eric, but he has been slightly overwhelmed the last few days."

"I can give you the shorthand version. Basically, they are looking at specific allele matches on the short arms of chromosomes three and nine. You already know that the sheer number of genes they are dealing with, along with all of the possible allele variations, creates nearly infinite possibilities. They have been shuffling alleles around for years, finding that some do better than others, but then this. Their combination worked."

She lifts her legs, stretching them out to rest her feet on the chair across from her before continuing. "This pairing scan is looking for individuals with genetic code containing a specific sequence of alleles that, when paired during meiosis and mitosis, will create progeny with that exact winning sequence. The reason this process is so difficult is that they also have to take into account the past matches we already have on file. So, these people not only need to have variations consistent with this research, but also the sequences for diabetes, heart disease, auto-immune function, and so on."

"But wouldn't most people already be consistent with the past matches? Considering that all of us are already Tier 1?"

"Yes, most people in Tier 1 are at that point now, but the matches are specific enough that it's difficult. The Committee isn't willing to make any exceptions. A couple of pairs were discovered with a sixty percent match on the original 25 markers and a perfect match on the five TSG variations and they threw them out." My eyebrows shoot up and Shari nods. "I know, eighty percent or higher is the minimum with exact TSG matching. So. You can imagine the difficulty."

"That does seem like it would be limited. Given that—okay, here's my biggest concern—" I gulp in air.

"Ethical ramifications when it comes to pairing?" Shari says before I speak, and my breath escapes me in a relieved huff.

"Exactly! If there are so few matches, can Berg even move forward? How would that work? We have to allow people to pair organically. It wouldn't be socially responsible to force two people together. How would that allow for a similar life experience for bonding? Courting and building up trust takes time, and our minds and bodies have to be in sync to create bonds for child-rearing. It won't work if we force it—" I pause, noticing Shari's demeanor.

She places her index fingers to her lips and taps them. "Why not?" she asks calmly. "Why couldn't people still court and build up trust over time if they were paired by Berg? Doesn't everyone put their genetic information into the database after a first date anyway? Wouldn't this be basically the same thing? They wouldn't be the ones scanning, but they would be the ones connecting. The only difference is that they would have the information ahead of time. Years ago, marriages arranged by parents were actually extremely successful."

"I would say that's up for debate," I argue. "Cultures that had arranged marriages were also extremely restrictive. How do you know that they were successful because they were *actually* good marriages? Maybe they simply couldn't end them in a way that would be socially acceptable."

Shari shrugs, letting it go. This conversation likely won't go in a positive direction and I figure now is as good a time as any.

"Hey, I have actually been meaning to ask you: have you heard anything else about the incident the other day? When we had to evacuate Washington Park?"

She looks at me, entirely puzzled. "I honestly haven't thought much about it," she answers. "Why?"

"I still can't wrap my head around it and I have been unsuccessful in finding any helpful information. Besides the fact that there hasn't ever been—"

"What are you concerned about?" Shari interrupts, her eyebrows drawn together.

"I don't—"

"Do you think that Berg just made it up? That they randomly asked you to evacuate?"

"No, I—"

"Could there be some sinister reason for the alert? Is that what you are getting at? Kate, at this point, you should be convinced of the fact that Berg has nothing to hide. Eric is involved with everyone in leadership. If there was a problem, he would know."

"I know, I know, that's not what I am saying. I'm sorry, I haven't been able to stop thinking about it, but it's probably my own issue," I backtrack.

Shari is unnervingly still. "Kate, do you remember when we went over your gene sequencing? When was the last time we looked at that?"

I slump over and rest my forehead on the table that sits between our two chairs. "I don't remember," I mumble.

"Ok, stop being pathetic. Let's go look at it again. I think it will make you feel better."

I force myself to follow her, but every cell in my body wants to get in the car and go home. What is wrong with me? Why am I pushing this? And, while I'm at it, why am I so against assigned pairings? Of course people can build a relationship even if they are put together by Berg initially. Is it because I love my own story

with Eric? How ridiculous that I am projecting personal experience as the ideal. And why does having unanswered questions
make me so darn uncomfortable? Within my head, these thoughts
swirl, creating a toxic concoction of self-doubt. It's difficult to focus
as Shari pulls up my file on her display, but I watch obediently as
she zooms in on one section of the strand.

"Do you see this here? Let me pull up mine so you can see the
difference." Her chart appears and she places it next to mine on
the display.

"I see that they are different, but I don't necessarily know what the
significance is. I mostly deal with disease markers. I'm not as
familiar with this section of the sequence." My brows furrow as I
try to find something that I recognize.

"These markers are all associated with loyalty, and these," she
scans further up on the DNA strand, "are associated with questioning. Can you see which alleles are completely opposite on our
charts?" I can. Several variations differ slightly, but two are
completely different. I point to the display.

"These don't look like they are in any way similar. What does that
mean?"

"It means that even though you and I share ninety percent of the
variations on these personality markers, we aren't completely identical. I know that sounds obvious and redundant, but I wanted you
to see it. Look how opposite we are in these areas. You have to
allow your brain to soak this in so you can reframe the internal
conversations you are having. When you push back, it's because
you are coded to push back. It's who you are. It's actually prefer-

able that Tier 1 individuals have a fair amount of curiosity. How are we supposed to find new solutions or work hard to build others up if we don't? Pros and cons, Kate."

"I see that. And I hear you. But...I don't feel like I have ever questioned anything," I blurt out,. "I have always done what was expected of me. Maybe it's age, but I am growing increasingly uneasy. I want to make a difference!" I exclaim. "How am I supposed to question and find solutions when my life is so straightforward?"

"You only perceive it as straightforward because you are in it. To me, you are problem solving all the time. I don't know how you do what you do. Stop viewing your impact as something you have to force. You are living it, Kate! Every small moment with your kids, every person that you touch in Tier 2. That is the biggest impact any of us could hope to make. And, if you remember, recognizing that is one of the specific goals of your conditioning." She raises an eyebrow and smiles.

"Great. Let's find more ways I am failing, shall we?" I joke. Shari laughs and beckons for me to move closer, wrapping her arms around me.

"Kate, you are building strength now so that when opportunities for growth and responsibility come your way, you'll be ready to shoulder them. You're perfect the way you are. Except for the 10% that's not me. You could work on that."

I laugh, squeezing her tightly. Then a thought occurs to me. "Shari..." I pause, pulling back. "This is random, but do you remember anything from when I was around Tal's age?"

She gives me a quizzical look, and I rush on to explain. "I remember specifically when I first met you and I have so many feelings about that time—I remember liking certain things, feeling content. I remember the way my mom's eyes squinted when she smiled, my dad's laugh. But, I can't bring up specific instances. Eric seemed to think that was strange. I know you view it as normal to forget certain times in life, but I just wondered if...well, if maybe hearing you describe an event would trigger it for me. You're the only one left who knew me then—"

"Of course I remember," Shari cuts my sentence short. "I remember one time when you were so intent on creating a play—a little show for your parents. They didn't really want you to waste your time on something so frivolous, but you were determined. You would act it out when we were at the park and force me to be all of the extra characters. It was surprisingly fun."

I giggle in spite of myself. I do remember loving stories and creating shows. Still. I don't remember this particular experience with Shari. Not wanting to hurt her feelings, I hold my thoughts back, feeling disappointment well up inside me. What was I expecting? Some magical moment where everything would click?

"Thanks," I say.

"Hey, we are doing something for your birthday, correct?" she asks, thoroughly changing the subject. I had completely forgotten about it.

In Tier 1, we don't really do much to celebrate birthdays. Except for people over 50. Those years garner a lot of attention, and rightly so. When I was five or six, I saw a family celebrating a birthday in Tier 2 while I was helping my mom at the distribution center. Entranced, I sat watching the family place a string of flowers around an older woman's head and sing to her. I was supposed to be refilling the wheat bucket, but when I looked over ten minutes later, it was already done. From that day on, my mom always had a flower crown sitting at the table for me on my birthday. As an adult it seemed silly, and I insisted that Shari stop the tradition after my mom died. Now, we usually just get together with my old roommates and take a picnic to the park.

"I can't believe I forgot. I didn't set anything up this year," I say, disappointed.

"Don't look so dejected! *I* didn't forget. I told the girls to plan on Thursday night. I didn't see anything on your calendar. Will that work for Eric?"

I give her another hug. "You're the best. I'll ask him and get back to you tonight."

We say our goodbyes while I gather my things and practically float to the door, feeling lighter than I have all week.

CHAPTER 9

NOT ONLY DOES Eric approve of my birthday plans, he all but pushes me out the door when five o'clock rolls around. I walk down to the gardens where Shari expressly asked me to meet her, and I see three women sitting on a blanket in the shade of a large oak tree. It looks like Shari recruited both Alyssa and Tess and my heart swells with gratitude. Alyssa and I lived together for a year and a half, and Tess overlapped with us for eight months of it. That time was intense, fun-filled, and formative for me. These women supported me while I transitioned from my youth to adulthood. We supported each other. Despite the fact that we hardly see one another now, that bond is still as strong as ever.

Alyssa paired shortly after I did. She and Jordan both work in agricultural innovation, and they have three children around the same age as ours. Tess paired a couple of years after. She is insanely skilled with computers and was on the team that programmed our current sensors. I actually haven't spent much time at all with Rob, Tess' pair. He seems like a decent guy. They have two boys, like us, but they are significantly younger. Both couples have service assignments that take them away from our community frequently, which works well for them, but is unfortunate for me.

All three of them turn and see me coming and run up to greet me. I haven't seen them since my birthday last year and the sheer act of embracing them pulls me into deep nostalgia. Though we have sent each other messages on and off, that is hardly enough correspondence to stay up-to-date on each other's lives. Momentarily, I long for the days when we had hours each day to compare experiences and connect. Friendships haven't come easily since pairing and procreating. I kick off my shoes and sit down to join them.

Shari, as always, has chosen an ideal spot. The grass is soft under the blanket, and all I can hear besides our laughter is the hum of cicadas in the trees. I release my hair from the clip that was holding it back, allowing it to fall loosely around my shoulders as I stretch out my legs.

"Dish!" Alyssa exclaims. "I want to hear everything that has happened since our last picnic." I laugh.

"I don't know that I have anything dish-worthy to tell! You are the one who should be dishing. Someone let slip that you may be expecting again? Is that true?" I tease. Shari told me a couple of weeks ago, but I had forgotten to call.

"It is true and, Shari, I will not be trusting you with a secret again," she says, pointing accusingly in her direction. "But we'll get to that later. Seriously, I want to hear what has been going on with you, Kate!"

"Okay!" I hold up my hands in defeat. "I'll do my best, but it might be horribly disappointing." I sigh, trying to determine where I should start. "Obviously the boys are now a year older and that has presented certain challenges..."

"Like..." Tess eggs me on.

"Like Tal suddenly has a lot of opinions on things. He doesn't just take our assessment of a given situation as the final word anymore. I know that's a good thing, but it's kind of scary." I see Alyssa nod. She has a nine-year-old. She knows. "Eric and I are still doing great. He actually just had a huge break with the research he has been working on for years." I look at Shari. "Did you already spill that secret, too?"

She smacks my leg in mock horror. "How dare you even suggest such a thing?"

Alyssa and Tess laugh and my head whips in their direction.

"She told us," Tess admits, "but I would love to hear it from you."

"Well, I don't want to repeat anything. What do you know already?" I say, feigning annoyance.

"I only know that he made a discovery, that's it," Alyssa assures me.

"You know Eric was working on TSG's, right?" I ask and they both nod. "He and his team have been working for years on finding a genetic variation that would be strong enough to overpower cancer cells. One of them worked. I don't know much more than that, but it looks like they are moving forward fairly aggressively."

"How so?" asks Tess.

"I mean, Berg wants to run pairings. Move forward with actually creating these variations in the population. That's how compelling the results are."

"Wow," Alyssa sighs and leans back against the tree. "So what does this mean for you and the kids? How involved does Eric need to be at this point?"

"That. Remains to be seen," I say hesitantly, opening up one of the reusable containers and peeking at its contents. Shari begins opening the others. She has put together an impressive spread: fresh bread, vegetables from her garden, dried fruit, and—I look up at her abruptly. Oranges. There are oranges in this sack.

"How in the world—" I ask, not even able to finish my sentence.

Shari laughs. "You know that one of my special skills is getting my hands on contraband."

"But seriously, how? How did you get these?"

"I can't give away my secrets," she says mysteriously, looking away.

"These have got to be from the southern territories," Alyssa says in awe. "Unless they have started growing citrus in our greenhouses?"

"I would think you, of all people, would know about it if they had," Tess interjects.

Alyssa shrugs.

"I am literally speechless, Shari. Thank you so much," I say intently as I reach out to pick one up.

"Wait!" Tess says. "I need to add the pièce de résistance!" She reaches behind her back and pulls out a small package, delicately placing it in my hands. The brown paper crinkles as I pull back the edges to reveal a soft, white rectangle. The shape isn't immediately identifiable, but the smell is.

"Oh wow, Tess. What kind is it?"

"Herbed goat. I made it three weeks ago so it would be ready. Can you believe I actually remembered to start something on time?"

"Can you believe I'm the only one who forgot about my own birthday?"

Laughing, I use a fork to dig in immediately. My mouth explodes with flavor as the creamy slab melts over my tongue. The subtle gaminess of the cheese is perfectly tempered by the rosemary and oregano. My eyes close in enjoyment and Tess beams.

We fill our plates, saving the oranges for last. As I press my finger-nail into the soft peel, a fine mist of citrus sprays into the air. For a second, I just breathe it in, allowing it to transport me to the past.

My dad worked in agriculture innovation like Alyssa, but he was mostly focused on trade. After the Crisis, Berg was focused solely on local agricultural production. They wanted to help each community become self sufficient, using only the resources they produced themselves. It took a long time, and still isn't always sustainable in every Tier 1 zone. Certain geographic locations can only produce specific resources efficiently, and those resources don't always align perfectly with the needs of the people.

Because of this, Berg has perfected a minimalist trade system between Territories, but there was a time when they experimented with diversifying the foods that were available to everyone. My dad hit the tail-end of that project. The research Berg collected during that time didn't show a statistically significant increase in quality of life based on the increased diversity of food alone, so the project was terminated. While my dad was working on it, though, he would travel between territories looking for potential varieties of produce that could be efficiently and sustainably traded. When-ever he went south, he would always bring me back an orange, or a lime, or something else completely exotic. I would savor them, eating one piece at a time until it couldn't possibly last any longer.

I don't think I have the self-control to save it this time. I pull back the rest of the peel, exposing the fruit, and pop a sliver into my mouth.

"This is so divine," I say. "Best birthday ever."

Shari grins, and I can tell she is overly pleased with herself. Despite the awkwardness of our last few interactions, moments like this remind me where her loyalties lie. I need to do a better job of trusting her judgement.

"You didn't answer my question earlier," Alyssa says between bites. "Do you really not have any idea what this discovery means for you and Eric? Haven't they given some idea of what will be expected?"

"Not yet. I think right now they are just trying to figure out what the initial pairing will look like. My hope is that he will be able to bow out and start in on a new project once Berg takes over. But," I admit, "I am also gearing up to do whatever is needed. This is such a big deal. I have really struggled with how I can make my biggest impact with all of the resources we have been given. Maybe my impact is supporting Eric so that he is free to do this. I don't know." I put another slice of orange into my mouth. "Enough about that, though. I want to hear about this new baby! Are you nervous to have another one?"

"Of course. Yes! Totally nervous. But also really excited," Alyssa smiles.

Tess reaches over and gives her belly an ostentatious rub. As we reminisce about our birth stories, I notice that Shari checks out a little bit. I try to change the subject as soon as it makes sense.

When the sun begins to set, we say our goodbyes and promise to get together again soon. I know it won't likely happen for a long while, but it feels good to show that we all would ideally like to commit to more time together. I walk home exhausted, full in more ways than one.

Gently, I open the door, trying not to wake anyone. I slip off my shoes and flick on a light temporarily so I can see where I am going. My hands trace the walls as I move through the hall. Our bedroom is dark, so I toss my clothes near the closet, not wanting to wake Eric by opening drawers, and I try to use the washroom as quietly as possible.

Slipping between the soft sheets, my head hits the pillow. I immediately sit back up, having hit something cold and pointy. I reach down and pick up a lightweight rope of some sort. Not immediately recognizing what it is, I pad back to the washroom, shut the door, and turn on the light. A delicate flower crown made of fresh-picked columbines drapes around my fingers.

CHAPTER 10

It's Saturday, and our request to visit the holding and rehab center was approved. We are planning to take Tal over this afternoon while Bentley spends the afternoon with Shari. She felt like she needed some kid time so she could better appreciate her time alone this next week. That's what she told me, but I know she loves spending time with the boys. Especially Bentley. He is still full of wonder and energy and she needs that in her life.

Initially, we talked with Tal about taking this day trip, he was hesitant. While Tier 1 contains a fair amount of genetic diversity, all of us have similar personality markers and social inputs. This means that all individuals are working toward the same goals and have a somewhat homogenous outlook on life. Tal hasn't ever met someone who has a significantly different viewpoint. He hasn't ever seen anyone do something that is drastically against the rules. He sees people act and he sees their consequences, but even the negative consequences that he has observed are pretty tame.

Consequently, his anxious feelings at the prospect of visiting the rehab center are expected; he simply has no idea what to expect.

I remember being extremely nervous the first time I went. Honestly, I still feel on edge physically being in a facility like that. I hope that for Tal, this will bring his understanding to a new level and deepen his commitment to fulfilling his potential. It's difficult to avoid recognizing your own strengths when the limitations of others are laid bare.

Shari comes to pick up Bent and, after waving goodbye, the three of us hop onto our bikes. We don't have to go far. There aren't any holding centers in Tier 1, so we are headed to the closest one on the Tier 2 side of the city. A part of me wishes that we could go to a Tier 3 center, but from what I've heard, that would only be appropriate for adults at this point.

The trail whizzes by beneath our pedals and the soft whir of our tires is the only sound besides the soft chirping of birds overhead. Tal hasn't said a word, so I try to lighten the mood.

"Your turn," I say to Eric. "Where would you go if you had one plane ticket anywhere and knew you were going to die in a week?"

"So this is the last place I will ever see?"

"Yep."

"Am I still in full health, or am I old and decrepit?" Eric mimics an old man with no teeth.

Tal grins but doesn't laugh. He must be more nervous than I thought.

"Full health. You just know in a week you will keel over and die," I say.

"Hmmmm...I think I would go to one of those remote islands way out off of the Pacific coast."

"I thought those weren't even habitable anymore?"

"They aren't, but if I'm dying in a week, who cares? New islands are cropping up in that same belt every year and Berg is doing some really incredible biological research there. I would fly to the islands and live out my week experiencing the ocean, the wildlife, not worrying what I was going to eat or drink. It would be amazing."

"Good choice. I like your logic."

"What about you?"

"Well, your idea sounds really good, so now I am second guessing my choice."

He laughs. "What is it?"

"I was thinking I would go to one of the northern territories. I would be there in the perfect transitional week to see the leaves in full color, and then the first snow. My death would be perfectly timed so I could see both."

"You didn't tell me I got to pick the timing of it."

"Would it have changed your pick?"

"No," he responds confidently and I laugh.

"What is it about nature that is so alluring? We have so much beauty here, and yet I long to see something different. Maybe travel before the Crisis was more about that than just escaping?" I postulate.

"I think for some people yes, but the extensiveness of the travel is what makes me think it was escapist. If you want to see something, just see it. Experience it. Be present and soak it in. They were bouncing around endlessly. It was like they could never fully enjoy something because they were always on the lookout for something better."

"True," I admit, realizing that we are getting ahead of Tal. Me feet slow on the pedals and Eric mimics me. "Do you think the fact that I love to envision these places means that I am looking to escape?" I ask, and he ponders this for a moment.

"No. I honestly think you are seeking the beauty of it. You would soak it in and let it add to you, still happy to be in your own life."

I nod, but question the truth of that statement. Would I be able to come home and feel satisfied if I knew that exciting, first time experiences were still out there?

We pull up to the center and afix our bikes and helmets to the parking stalls. My legs feel rubbery as I begin to follow Eric and Tal toward the entrance. We are greeted by full body security scanners. By the look on his face, I don't think Tal has ever done this before, but he follows Eric through without hesitation. We leave our sensors in the security boxes and enter the main court-yard. Our guide, a Tier 1 rehabilitation specialist named Talia, intrudes herself as soon as we enter.

"Hi Tal," she says smiling, reaching out to shake his hand. "You have my nickname. This might be a little confusing today."

Tal smiles, though he is already looking around at the people around us, processing what they are doing. What they might be here for.

"I assume you already know what we do in this facility?" she asks.

"Yes," he nods.

"Tal, tell us what you know already," Eric encourages.

"I know that when people are breaking the rules, they have to come here."

"Kind of," Talia responds. "It's actually more specific than that. If they are just breaking the rules in a way that creates negative consequences for themselves, we allow them to work through that and learn. If they are creating negative consequences for those around them, for society, or simply infringing on the rights of others, they have to be removed and rehabilitated. Take, for example, that woman over there."

She points across the yard to a tall woman with short black hair. "She wasn't treating her child well. She had been cleared to procreate, but then her birth was unexpectedly difficult, and she wasn't able to function appropriately during that first year of her child's life. She was neglecting to fulfil the level of care expected. We had to remove her from the home and help her heal."

"How long has she been here?" I ask.

"About six months."

"Will she be able to return back to her family?"

"It doesn't seem likely. Especially because at this point, it would be more traumatic for her child to go through another transition."

"Where is her baby?" Tal asks.

"Great question. Her daughter is with the father and his new pair. It is so important that children have both parents in the home, especially during those formative years."

Tal's eyebrows furrow.

"It's nothing that could have been predicted. She is healing now, and she will have the chance to re-pair if she wants," Talia explains.

"Can she have another child?" Tal asks.

"No, it would be too risky for her and the child." Talia answers, shifting our attention to a stout man playing frisbee with another specialist.

"This man is here because he was stealing from the resource center."

Tal looks up sharply. "Why would someone steal when they are receiving all that they need?"

"Some people in Tier 2 don't feel like they *are* getting everything that they need. Remember Tal, they are genetically, and often socially, limited. The resources we are able to give them now are much better than they were in the past, improved from even fifty years ago. Their social conditioning is getting better and better, but this man was actually the product of an uncleared pregnancy.

Genetically, he is barely qualified to remain in Tier 2. If he continues to make progress, he can continue here. Otherwise, we will be transitioning him to Tier 3. We do the best we can, but at a certain point, we need to use our resources for people that are making the most progress."

"So what would happen to him in Tier 3?" Tal questions.

"Everyone in there has their basic needs met, but they are not able to enjoy the freedoms that we do. Their ability to act and react in societally-appropriate ways is limited. Some of them do really well with structure, like having a job for example. When they are able to serve and contribute in society, that earns them extra freedoms and privileges."

"Like what?" Talia starts leading us around the back side of the yard to another building and Tal's question hangs in the air.

"Like more variety in food," she answers a few moments later. "The opportunity to attend a conditioning enrichment class during the week. Some of them even get the chance to pair."

Tal nods, seemingly satisfied with this response. Then his face pulls together, his eyes squinting. "I don't understand why this system is better than punishment," he comments, taking quick steps to keep up with our long ones. "It seems like prison would waste fewer resources on people who aren't going to be able to go back into society anyway."

Eric and I meet each other's eyes, waiting to see how Talia will respond.

"That is actually the exact reason why prisons used to exist before and during the Crisis. Society, at the time, thought that it was both the proper consequence and the cheapest way to deal with the problem. They were actually dead wrong," she says, a hint of disdain creeping into her tone. "Obviously we know that people don't 'deserve' punishment. They act the only way they are able to, given their genetic coding and social inputs. If we want to change the behavior, we change the variable that we have control over."

"Social inputs," Tal repeats.

"Exactly. What kind of social inputs do you think people were receiving in prison?"

"Probably not good ones."

"Not good ones. You're right. They were learning to look out for themselves or to rely on those stronger and more hardened than they. They were taught to be invulnerable, therefore avoiding relationships and distrusting authority figures. They absorbed the message that society despised them. Which...well, they weren't wrong," she mutters, scanning her sensor to unlock another door. We follow her through. "Given that information, can you start to see why prisons would also not be the cheapest option?" Talia pauses, awaiting his response.

I glance around, taking in our surroundings. We are in a long foyer. Light shines through a vaulted skylight in the center of the hall, refracting through the glass and forming miniature rainbows on the white tile ahead of us.

"It seems like that conditioning would lead to more misbehavior. And apathy," Tal responds finally.

"Right on," Talia says approvingly. "Inmates in prisons were not willing to serve. They gave nothing back and required more and more resources to keep them in check. It was a constant drain on society."

We walk down a hallway behind the skylight and I am in awe of the bright, open layout. It is so luminous that I involuntarily squint.

"This is our conditioning area. We spend a *lot* of time on physical conditioning in this center. Typically, if we can help our patients feel corporeally strong, and build habits of success with fitness, we often see dramatic improvements in their ability to stick to nutrition and mental health regimens."

"What is the success rate of your program?" Eric asks. "By that I mean, what percentage of patients are able to go back into Tier 2?"

"Almost eighty percent of our high-functioning patients are able to integrate within three to six months. This group usually consists of people who are self-serving and engaging in behaviors like manipulation of their pair or their mentor, using more resources than they are allotted, or being verbally or emotionally abusive to others. Typically, with some consistent education and practice, we can reverse those behaviors."

"What about the group that isn't high functioning?" I ask.

"That is usually closer to fifty percent."

"And the fifty percent that don't rehabilitate...they move to Tier 3?" I assume, based on her earlier comments.

"Yes. As long as we are seeing progress, we will continue to work with them, but when they become stagnant, we have to move on."

We walk into a room with a display and an odd-looking machine with two electrodes hanging from the side. Tal immediately approaches it.

"This is our reversal therapy machine. Brand new for us this year," Talia virtually coos.

"Wow," Eric exclaims. "I didn't think that Tier 2 had access to this technology."

"The Berg Committee approved it a few months ago and we are thrilled to have it. Using this has exponentially increased our ability to treat mental illness and reverse habits in behavioral pathways."

"How does it work?" asks Tal.

"Would you like me to show you?"

He backs away, looking skeptical.

"Sit in the chair and I will do a small procedure so you can feel it," she suggests.

Tal steps back quickly, running into Eric, and I laugh.

"It's completely safe, Tal," Eric says.

"You don't have to do anything you don't want to," Talia assures him. "I was planning to simply activate a pleasant memory so you can see how it works."

Tal looks at me questioningly. I shrug my shoulders, a smile on my lips. He pauses for a moment, then walks forward again and sits down tentatively in the chair. The machine hums after Talia flips a switch. Tal sits stock still as she uses a swab to clean a small circle behind each of Tal's ears, then places the electrodes to his skin.

"During the Crisis, scientists had access to these electrodes; they were able to stimulate outer tissues of the brain without surgery. However, in order to stimulate deeper brain tissue—like the areas where emotions and memories originate—their only option then was using implants. Due to the many, obvious risks involved, these implants weren't a great option, so researchers were really limited in what they could do. With this machine," she pauses and moves behind the display, "we are able to use a high frequency current that does not disrupt normal neurons to penetrate deep into the brain tissue. We angle the electrodes so they will intersect in the region of the brain that we are activating. Where those currents cross, they cancel each other out almost entirely, leaving only a low-frequency wave that the brain interprets and understands, causing neurons to fire in response. So Tal," she says as her fingers frantically dance across the keyboard, "I am specifically activating a section of your hippocampus. I have access to your brain scans and am able to be fairly specific in what I stimulate here. Let me know what you feel."

She presses a button, and Tal's eyes close. He looks as though he is sleeping. Talia flicks the switch and the humming dissipates. Tal sits up.

"So?" she asks expectantly.

"Oh, that was the best dinner ever," he sighs. "It was my birthday."

"What did you get on your birthday?" she questions.

"I had creamy macaroni and cheese and ice cream."

Talia laughs. "That is your best dinner ever?"

"It is his favorite, definitely," Eric chuckles.

Tal looks to us, his eyes wide. "That was amazing. It was like I was there again." He turns to Talia. "Can I do it again?"

She laughs and moves toward him to remove the electrodes. "Unfortunately not, though you can probably see why we have to be really careful with how we use this. I'll let your parents discuss addiction with you later," she says with a smirk. "Usually, we are removing unwanted memories, so slightly different than what you just experienced."

Tal sighs.

"It is also really effective in helping people open up new pathways. To dust off the cobwebs, so to speak," she continues, cleaning the electrodes with sanitizing swabs.

"What about people who don't want to do it?" Tal asks.

"What do you mean?" she asks as she drapes the wires back on the machine.

"If you are using it to help people that have mental illness, are they always willing to do this? I was kind of scared to sit down. It seems like some people wouldn't want to. Does it still work?"

"That" she looks at him pointedly, "is a great question. Yes, it does still work, but definitely not as well as when someone is open to treatment. When someone is fighting off an incoming signal, they are creating a signal of their own. Those two currents conflict and make the treatment less effective—less powerful. So, yes, it still works, just not as well."

Tal nods. "For people that are willing," he says slowly, "does it always work perfectly?"

"What do you mean?" Talia asks.

"Like, do you always get the results you want? And do the results last?"

"Another great question." Talia looks impressed. "We do always see immediate results, but your second question is a little bit harder to answer. The brain is constantly in flux. Most of the therapy we do is minimal, but in the odd circumstance that we need to eliminate memories or feelings more extensively," she pauses. "Think about it this way. What usually triggers you to think about your mom?"

"Pretty much everything."

"Right. Now, what triggers you to think about, say, your conditioning instructor from first year?"

Tal thinks for a minute. "I really only think about her when I see a full moon. She always told us when those were happening."

"That's perfect. So, if I needed to remove the pathways for that instructor, it would be incredibly easy to do right? If I had to remove pathways for your mom or dad, not so easy. The risk increases that we would miss a trigger and cause a lot of confusion and frustration for the patient. Does that make sense?"

Tal nods. It's pretty fascinating. And also good to know that this therapy has its limits.

"This concludes my tour." She winks at Tal. "I always save the best for last."

We thank her, and she walks us back through the courtyard to the security area where we retrieve our belongings. I find myself still trying to accept that Tier 2 will have access to reversal therapy now. I have so many questions that I should have asked, but was too distracted by Tal to think of. Will it be used for more than rehabilitation? That could vastly improve the likelihood of Tier 2 individuals moving up to Tier 1.

Tal is quiet the entire ride home, but I can visualize the wheels in his head turning, too.

CHAPTER 11

BOTH ERIC and sleep have eluded me for the last few days. Though Eric's absence is explainable, I have wracked my brain for potential areas of stress to rationalize my insomnia, to no avail. The dreams have become inevitable and, even when I am lucky enough to be sleeping deeply, my body has embraced a pattern of waking regardless; my heart hammering for no apparent reason. I am afraid of something, that much is obvious. But what? Could it simply be the unknown? The fact that Eric is doing something I don't understand and it is taking him away from me more frequently?

That night, I suggest to Eric that it may be helpful for me to go into the lab the next day. Perhaps, if I see everything with my own eyes, my subconscious could be persuaded to release the fear. Giving the boys more information on Eric's research couldn't hurt either. He agrees, and we set a time for the afternoon.

It occurs to me that I haven't stepped foot in his lab for over a year. A pang of guilt hits my stomach, making me extremely aware of the lack of interest I have shown in his work prior to this discovery. Much to my surprise, frustration follows the guilt like a tethered pet. I am upset at Eric, I realize. Upset that he did something that could potentially change our trajectory. Without even realizing it, I have created an entire picture of what our life will look like: Eric will do research during the week, I will work with patients, Tal and Bentley will grow up and be successful in their paths. We will chug along happily, forever. The end. How have I become so complacent? So content to sit in this comfort zone. Our life has been completely predictable, but now. Now I don't know what to expect.

Of course, I recognize it's ridiculous to be frustrated. How could I possibly hold negative feelings toward Eric for being *too good at his job*? It's completely irrational. I know change is always supposed to be difficult and transformative. I hear people talk about it regularly. It's just...it's been theoretical for me up to this point. Pairing, having kids—those were changes I wanted and expected, which meant they weren't really changes. More like planned adjustments. This is truly unexpected, and I haven't quite settled in to acceptance yet.

The next morning, I wake to find Eric already gone. He doesn't typically have to go in early, but every once in a while it does happen. Usually he gives me *some* notice. I pull my arms high above my head, reveling in the release I feel in my lower back and neck as I stretch. The lack of solid sleep, and contorted sleeping positions resulting from it, is taking a toll on my spine.

During last night's predicted restlessness, I scrolled through some old files to pass the time. Using the same rationale of 'unknowns' causing stress, I wondered if Eric was right—that the dreams have been stemming from a desire to know more about my mom. I didn't necessarily find anything new, but revisiting details about her life gave me comfort, and I was eventually able to rest. Though it seemed to increase my positive affect in the moment, the downward cycle of exhaustion and irritability is already in full swing, and I don't expect that I can rely on reminiscing to solve it.

I force myself to leave the coziness of the bed so I can wake the boys and get breakfast going. We have a lot to get through before we head to the lab. While they are eating, I casually mention the need to finish our reinforcement tasks before embarking on our laboratory outing. This week, the boys have been focusing on coding and reading comprehension. Coding is never the issue, but reading has always been hit-and-miss with Tal. I am already steeling myself for the push-back.

"I hate it," Tal groans.

"The lab? Like Dad's lab?" Bentley asks excitedly.

"Tal, it won't take too long, and yes Bent. Dad's lab."

"What will we get to see there?" Tal asks. I can tell he is gauging whether completing his reading assignment is worth it.

"It's not optional," I sing, giving him a knowing smile.

It takes an eternity for them to finish. Seems almost purposeful. Tal is making goofy faces, and Bentley can't stop laughing long enough to swallow. Hearing their laughter—Tal's lower chuckle and Bentley's higher, out of control giggle—makes me begin to laugh, my annoyance nearly forgotten. It won't be long before Tal is over funny faces. I give them a few more minutes to be silly. Eventually, I nonchalantly place myself between them so that Bent can focus. After clearing their dishes, the boys are quick to put on comfortable clothes and we wipe down the kitchen together.

I'm pleased with how quickly we are able to move on to our tasks. The boys each take turns coding commands into their trial sensors, making mistakes and trouble shooting along the way. They will likely graduate to something more challenging soon, but this is appropriate for now. Their faces light up each time their sensors display colors, or make various sounds in response to their commands. I sigh, dreading the quickly approaching moment where I will have to remind Tal about his reading.

"Tal," Bentley says, as if reading my mind, "can I read with you today?"

"Sure," he shrugs, tapping his sensor to pull up the assignment.

Bent shoots me a sideways glance, and I swear I see him wink.

We arrive at the lab that afternoon to Eric standing in the entrance, waiting to greet us. He looks a little disheveled, but his grin stretches from ear to ear. Ushering us in, he scans our sensors, and we follow him down a lengthy, barren hall. We pass door after door, finally reaching the right one. Eric pushes it open, allowing us enter ahead of him. Researchers are abuzz, transferring samples in and out of the coolers, washing petri dishes, and measuring samples in test tubes. Eric leads us past them to a table near the back. He has his own samples set out, along with a microscope. I cringe as Bent comes dangerously close to knocking it off the counter. We get them situated on the step-stool and then back off, allowing them to experiment with the magnifying dials.

"I missed you this morning," I whisper, finally having a moment to stand still.

"I know, so sorry. I didn't want to wake you. I had a couple of things I needed to take care of so I could be available to show you guys around." He shifts his attention back to Tal and Bentley. "Boys, what do you know what you are looking at?" They both stare at him blankly. "I'll give you a hint: it is a result of the research I have been doing," he prods, sitting down on a stool next to them.

"Well, you are studying genes," answers Tal.

"Yep," Eric answers, "any idea what could be in the samples?"

"Not really," Tal says, and Bentley shakes his head.

"Well, let me see if I can explain it." He picks up a small vial. "They each contain a sample of DNA. Not even a full DNA sample, but a specific piece of DNA that we have selected for. Obtaining that section is an incredibly difficult process, but once we have isolated the piece that we want, it comes here."

He motions to a petri dish in the center of the table, picks it up, and places it gently under the microscope. "Knowing that, look in there, Bent, and tell me what you see." Bentley gets up on the stool and lowers his eye to the viewfinder.

"It looks like a big piece of snot." he says, disgusted and I snort in surprise.

"That's a great way to describe it," Eric chuckles. "Tal, do you want to see?"

Bentley moves over to allow his brother an opportunity to observe.

"These are tumor cells," Eric continues. "Tumors are just normal cells in the body that, for some reason, decided to continue growing and changing in ways that harm the body's healthy tissues, or just take up too much space. Our goal was to find specific DNA pieces that, when paired with other variations of the same piece, could begin to shut off these tumor cells."

"Snot cells," Bentley corrects.

"Yes, of course—snot cells," Eric repeats.

"So, did you find it?" Tal asks.

"We think so," Eric answers excitedly. "We don't know all the ins and outs of how this is going to look long term, but so far, it seems like the match we created is continuing to do its job."

"Guys, isn't this amazing? Your Dad is the first one in hundreds of years to find something like this," I say excitedly.

"That long?" Tal seems skeptical.

"Yes, that long," I answer, ruffling his hair.

Eric reaches out for another petri dish and slides it in, replacing the previous sample under the microscope. The boys immediately scramble to get the first look.

"This is a battle," Eric says, and both of the boys are immediately entranced. "The matched DNA pieces are taking down the snot cell." I stand there and watch them. Their eyes widening and heads straining forward to catch a glimpse of the new samples Eric shows them. In this moment, seeing them engaged and growing together, my fear dissipates. For the important things, there aren't any unknowns here.

CHAPTER 12

My last meeting with Nick is tonight. The goal is to finalize everything and submit our notes to Grace for approval. We had intended to meet a few days ago, but Tal was ill and I felt like I needed to be home with him. We won't have as much wiggle room now for making adjustments, though the ceremony is still three weeks away. Plenty of time.

Tal and Bent did not get along well today, so walking out the door and leaving bedtime to Eric was a welcome relief. He was a good sport about it, though I could tell his day at the lab wasn't much better. Even just these few moments walking in the still evening air allows me to literally and figuratively breathe more freely.

I am positively buoyant as I walk into the office to find Nick waiting. He grins at me as I close the door.

"Hey Kate, how have you been?"

"I'm doing well, thanks," I say cheerfully, walking toward him and setting my bag on the table. "I really appreciate you being flexible on the timing for this. Having kids is always an adventure."

"No prob. My evenings are basically free at this point."

"I don't know if I believe that. With 'perfect genetics', you must be inundated with dating requests," I tease, and he chuckles.

"Not as of late. You are the only female on my calendar this week."

"Well, I'm not sure how that's possible, but I will allow myself to feel privileged." I curtsy as I sit down.

He rolls his eyes, amused, and motions to the display. "I think we left off on Max here. Do you know what you want to add for him?" he asks, and we dive into the remaining candidates, trying to find the perfect balance of making them sound impressive, but also approachable. Most importantly, we overemphasize their similarities to all Tier 1 individuals, to avoid people feeling intimidated. When you have lived as Tier 1 all your life, it's tempting to feel like somehow these individuals who are transitioning are encroaching on your turf. I have suggested multiple times that the Committee release real-time resource counts. Even monthly would help. If we could see how well we are doing, this particular concern would likely dissipate.

We finish up and send the file off to Grace, thankfully ending at a much more reasonable time than our previous planning session.

"Well, that's that. Thanks so much, Nick," I say, packing up my things. "I am sure we can message about any updates or changes we need to make, once Grace gets back to us. I will probably just plan to see you at the ceremony, if that's ok?"

He nods.

"My next two weeks are a bit busier than normal. We are meeting Bentley's mentor this weekend and have some activities planned to promote bonding the week following," I expound.

"That's exciting," Nick exclaims. "Bentley must be turning eight? And how old is your other son?"

"Yep, he turns eight in a couple of weeks. My oldest, Tal, is ten."

"Wow. That's wonderful, Kate."

"Thanks. We've kept them alive this long, so I guess that's success?"

Nick laughs. "I'm sure you have done more than purely keep them alive," he flatters, then speaks more soberly. "What is it like being a parent?"

"You don't need to ask me," I retort. "Go find yourself a girl and get going! With your gene sequence, you probably only need to find a low-level match on disease markers. You could practically pick anyone off the street and start having babies within the year," I smile, quickly realizing that Nick isn't sharing in the jest. I clear my throat. "I'm sorry Nick, I was just giving you a hard time. I don't know you very well and shouldn't have jumped into personal territory."

"No, it's fine," he says, his shoulders relaxing, and he exhales slowly. "I did find someone I was interested in last year, but she decided to...go in a different direction. Because of my coding and my ability to respond to social conditioning, I have more responsibility. Well, at least, I feel like I do. I want to contribute more and she—" he pauses and takes a deep breath. "She wanted something simpler."

My eyes widen at this revelation. How could somebody have turned him down? "Nick, I'm—so sorry. That must have been really hard," I stammer.

"It wasn't the most fun ever," he admits as he starts to gather his things. "If I can write introductions to make other people seem approachable, you would think I could somehow find that balance for myself."

"I guess I have a hard time understanding her reasoning. She would have had the opportunity to have as many children as she wanted *and* push society forward in so many ways. Why would anyone say no to that?"

"Those are the exact reasons why it didn't work." He shrugs. "It doesn't make sense to me either."

I put my jacket on and reach my hand out to open the door. It's shocking to me that somebody in Tier 1 wouldn't share those priorities. We are conditioned *specifically* to be ready to shoulder responsibilities of that magnitude. My interest is piqued, and I crave more details, but decide that asking wouldn't be appropriate. Or kind.

"Kate," Nick says quietly, "nobody has asked me about this before. Everyone thinks that I must have my life perfectly planned out. I feel like I don't have any clue—" He stops mid-sentence and looks down. "Anyway, thanks for asking. It was really helpful to share that with someone."

"Anytime, Nick. I should have just answered your initial question. I'm sorry it's been difficult finding a pair. Are you still actively looking? I know you said you don't have dating plans this week—"

"I'm honestly kind of burned out at this point, but I'm sure I will get back out there. I'm focusing on training and all of that right now," he concludes, obviously trying to convince himself that this is a better option.

I nod. "Not a bad strategy. I have no doubt that you will figure it out." Picking up my bag, I force myself to smile. "I guess I'll see you at the ceremony? Thanks for all of your work on this."

He waves as I walk out the door. At home, I know Eric is waiting for me, and I don't want to be late this time.

I walk in and the smell of garlic wafts over me. A smile crosses my lips involuntarily at the unexpectedness of a special meal that I didn't have anything to do with. Does garlic mean 'special'? I laugh to myself at how pathetic that is. After hanging up my things, I follow the intoxicating aroma to find Eric grilling on the patio. Grilling is special, definitely. My assumption feels much less pathetic now.

"To what do I owe this delicious surprise?" I ask, wrapping my arms around his waist from behind.

He immediately places his spatula on the side of the grill and hugs me tight. "It's actually a peace offering."

"A peace offering? For what?" I lean back and look up into his face.

He sighs deeply. "I have to spend a couple of days down at Headquarters South. I just received the assignment this afternoon. I will be working on training some researchers at their lab on the different variations we are looking to match."

"And that takes a couple of days?"

"I know," he says apologetically. "It seems like it could be done in a few hours, but they want us to be really thorough. I think they are also planning to give us more information on how Berg plans to move forward with everything." He pauses to check the temperature on the grill. "And...I have to go again next week."

"What? That seems a little over the top. Why two weeks in a row?"

"They are flying in a couple of those pairs we found in our screening. We are going to do some advanced sequencing and just make sure that our information is correct. Then, we will sit down with them and discuss their future. I really don't know how it's going to go. You understand how sensitive this is."

"I do," I say soberly. "I still don't know how I feel about you moving forward so quickly."

"It has been made very clear to me that my opinions are not needed on the matter," Eric mutters, moving toward the grill. As he opens the top, I notice that he is searing trout. My mouth waters.

"Really? How so? Wouldn't they want all of your opinions, since you are the lead researcher?"

"Not necessarily. They need me to train, but even then it would be easy to have one of my team members do that. If I want to be involved, I need to toe the line."

"That seems ungrateful. And out of character."

"No, just efficient. With a breakthrough as big as this, they don't want to waste any time. I, however, feel like it would be okay to 'waste' some time to make sure that we are doing this the right way. It's simply a difference of opinion."

"I'm sorry, Eric. I will support you in whatever you need to do."

"*I'm* sorry I have to be gone. I haven't had to be away from you and the boys in years. I can't say I'm looking forward to it."

"Where are the boys? I haven't seen them since I walked in."

"I put them to bed early." He leans in and kisses me. "There may have been some bribery involved."

I kiss him back. "You mean, bribery that I have to pay up on since you won't be here?"

"Nope. I told them I would bring them back something cool from the trip."

"Something cool from headquarters? Good luck with that."

He traces my cheekbone with his finger. "You seem a little distracted," I murmur. "I think the fish is done."

He turns back to the food and transfers the filets to a dish on the side of the grill.

"We will eat, I will clean up while you relax, and then I vote we spend the rest of the evening not wearing clothes."

"Are you bribing me now, too?" I laugh as he pretends to be offended.

"The cleanup is out of the kindness of my heart, I don't know what you're talking about."

"Well, I'll take it. And thanks for dinner. Seriously, this is a great surprise."

He smiles and takes the trout inside. I turn up the heat on the grill, watching the leftover skin sizzle and fall to the flames below. Then, I follow him.

CHAPTER 13

THE NEXT FEW days are a blur. Between making a few changes for Grace, keeping up with my work schedule, and preparing for Bentley's first mentor meeting, I hardly have a moment to miss Eric. Yet I still do. Bentley has taken advantage of the situation to finagle his way into my bed each night. This morning I find both boys in my room; Bentley is strewn across the bed sideways, and Tal is curled up on the floor with a pillow and a blanket.

I try to get out of bed without waking them, but Bentley stirs despite my cautious exit. Tiptoeing into the washroom, I hope to at least pee in peace.

"Mom?" Bentley calls.

"Hey bud, I'm just in here washing up. Did you sleep well?" I say as quietly as possible, while still allowing him to hear me through the door.

"Yes," he says, sleepily.

After washing my hands, I walk back into the bedroom and resume my position under the blankets. Tal is awake now, too, and he jumps up on the bed to join us, pushing Bentley out of his way.

"Tal! Stop it! I just woke up. I don't like being messed with when I'm tired."

"Hey, there's plenty of room for all of us," I correct. "Bent, here, you come next to me. Then Tal can have all the room he wants." I pull him close and kiss his forehead. "Tal, did you sleep well?"

"I ended up on your floor. What do you think?"

"That you love me so much, you just couldn't stand being in the other room?"

"Nice try, Mom." He lets his face flop into the pillow. "I had a really bad dream."

"Oh, man. I'm sorry. Those are the worst. Do you want to talk about it?"

"I've mostly forgotten it now, but it seemed really real."

"I know, I have had some like that before. They can be truly terrifying." I reach over and push his hair off of his forehead. "What do you boys want to do today before Daddy gets home? You don't have conditioning today since we are meeting Bentley's mentor tonight. Dad gets home around 2pm, I think."

"Mom, am I going to like my mentor?" Bentley asks hesitantly.

"I like Stephen," Tal says as he rolls over, stretching and yawning simultaneously. "You like him too, right?"

"Yeah, he's nice. I just don't know if mine will be nice."

"Bent, he is going to have so much in common with you. I think you'll definitely click," I assure him.

"But, you don't know for sure." Bentley looks skeptical.

"Mom, why do we even have mentors?" Tal asks. "I already have a mom and a dad and a brother. Why do I need Stephen, too?"

I shift Bentley over to my other side so that I am between the two boys, putting my arms around their growing shoulders.

"Do you remember learning about what it was like waaaay before the Crisis?"

"Like way before? Like when dinosaurs were on the earth?"

"Not that far back. More like when the United States first became a country," I answer, amused.

"What is the United States?" asks Bentley, tracing freckles on my arm. His soft touch sends shivers up my spine.

"That's what this whole region was called before the Crisis," I clarify.

"It was called the United States? That's weird."

"It was actually the United States of America. And it was a lot bigger," Tal says, reaching over to my nightstand and drawing a squiggly shape in the dust. I am now aware that I haven't been keeping up on cleaning lately.

"This is what our region used to look like. And this," he draws a thinner shape next to it, "is what it looks like now."

"Why is it so much smaller?" Bentley asks quizzically, looking between the two shapes.

"You have to imagine that all around these shapes are oceans, Bent," I expound. "A long time ago, the top and bottom of the earth were covered almost entirely with ice. Now there's just a little bit. All of that extra water flowed into the oceans and lifted the sea level above where the land used to be."

"Yeah, and lots of people died," Tal interjects.

"Tal, enough," I warn. "He will learn more about that when he's older."

"Fine. Anyway, now our region looks like this, and this right here," he draws a large rectangle, "is the Midwest Territory."

"That's us!" says Bentley excitedly. "Where is our house?"

"Right about there," I point. "But, back to my original question. What was life like then?"

"I know people were farmers. They had to start from scratch in a new land," Tal says.

"Right. Once they set up communities, did children grow up and move somewhere else in the country?"

"No, the same families lived in the same place for a long time."

"Yep, for generations. What do you think that looked like for a kid, say Bentley's age, in a town like that?"

"That kid would have lots of relatives," Tal jokes.

"Exactly. They would have their parents, their grandparents, their aunts and uncles. If they were having a hard time, they would have lots of people to talk to."

"And lots of people to tattle on them," he mutters.

"But that's a good thing, too," I say, raising my eyebrow. "It might not seem like it now, but when you are older and have your own kids, you will be *so* glad to have extra eyes and ears around."

"I doubt it," he grins.

"That's specifically why the mentor system was instituted after the Crisis."

"For tattling?" asks Bentley.

I laugh. "No, silly." I tickle him and he thrashes wildly. "Because once the world started getting more populated and new technology allowed for people to just up and move all the time, people became disconnected. They ended up living in places where they had no family. Nobody to help them with kids or to support them and teach them how to navigate the tough times in life. Kids and parents ended up self-medicating all the time with entertainment or substances. It was a mess. So, as soon as they were making societal decisions, they instituted the mentoring program to foster more connection."

"So we have more people to turn to," says Tal.

"Exactly. And people who are genetically similar, just like family."

"But why not only have family?" he asks.

"I think it would be ideal to have family around. Maybe we will have the option of doing that in the future, but it won't work as of now."

"Why?" asks Bentley.

"Because. People don't live long enough. Do you really even remember my parents?"

"I do," says Tal. "Barely."

"The last time you saw them was when you were five years old, Tal. Grandma died when she was 44, and Grandpa died six months later at 46. So," I sigh, "we keep families together as much as possible, but there's only so much we can do. Mentors are still a great option, for now."

"I'm hungry," whines Bentley.

"Are you bored with this conversation?" I tease.

"I am," says Tal.

"Hey, you are the one who asked!" I reach over and poke his ribs.

"You didn't warn me that the answer would take five years!" he laughs.

"Alright, sorry. Let's go have breakfast. You guys still haven't told me what you want to do today."

"I want to go to the duck pond!" yells Bentley as he runs to the stairs. Pants. I still need to find that kid some better pants.

. . .

After breakfast, I spend some time looking over the plans I received for Bentley's new conditioning routine. They were sent a couple of days ago, but I haven't had a chance to review them. I notice right away that he will be advancing in both math and social ethics. Advancing is the wrong word, rather he will be shifting focus. I think immediately of my conversation with Nick. I know that Bentley will be much more entrenched in experiences and education that will solidify the social responsibility pathways he has already formed. I know he will have much more expected of him, but I hope he won't get the same societal pushback that Nick has.

"Help me out, they're attacking!" I hear Bentley's voice filter down the hall.

"Bringing reinforcements," Tal answers in an official tone. I pause in my task, just listening. It is rare these days to hear Tal engaged in imaginitive play, and I don't want to miss it. Eventually, their voices lower enough that I can't make out what they are saying. I return to the report, a smile still on my lips.

It looks like Bent's math will be much more experiential, and he will have a new instructor. Most of the kids in his group will be at least three years older. I check to see if Tal is in the same group, but he isn't. Makes sense. I don't think that would be a good situation for either of them. My eyes widen when I notice Bentley's time requirement has gone up; he will be as busy as Tal.

Signing the form, I turn off my tablet. This year is going to be a shift, and I'm not sure I am ready for it. Again, the unknowns of Eric's service create instability where there wasn't any before.

How can I prepare to handle this when I have no idea what it will look like? The constant weight on my chest feels a little heavier this morning. As boys are still playing happily, I take a few moments to meditate; I close my eyes, enjoying the momentary peace and quiet.

CHAPTER 14

THE BOYS and I are waiting in the community room of the Mentoring Center when I see Eric walk in. Finally. I was honestly worried he was going to miss the meeting. I shoot up from my seat and walk quickly to him, trying not to make a scene. We embrace, and something in his kiss feels desperate.

"I missed you so much," he whispers.

"Me too."

"Dad!" the boys yell as they jump off their bench and run over to hug his legs.

"Hey, I missed you guys!" Eric laughs, bending down to wrap his arms around them. He pulls out two miniature objects. I can't see exactly what they are, but the boys' faces light up.

"They're programmable," Eric says. I guess I shouldn't have knocked finding something cool at headquarters. The boys are ecstatic. In that moment, I hear our last name called across the room and see the receptionist looking in our direction.

"Ooh! Guys, it's our turn. Grab your water bottles and let's go!" I direct. The boys run to gather their things, and we walk, as a family, toward the meeting room.

"Is this Bentley?" the woman asks. Bentley smiles shyly.

"I'd like to introduce you to someone. This is Nick."

I stop dead. Nick? My Nick? That's ridiculous, he's not my Nick, I mean *that* Nick. I look over and see that it's him. I flash back to our conversation that first evening. How could he be matched up with Bentley? How could anyone have high enough markers to be a suitable match for Nick? After shaking hands with Eric, Nick squats down to greet Bent. When he stands up, his eyes meet mine. He smiles, unsure, and gives a small wave. My body unwillingly moves toward him, my mind still reeling, and I cannot coax my hands from my pockets.

"Hey Kate."

"Hi." I look to Eric. "Nick has been my partner for creating those introductions for the ceremony," I explain.

"Oh, you're that Nick? It didn't click when we walked in." Eric doesn't meet my eyes and seems distracted. Something has been off since the moment we met in the waiting room, but I can't put my finger on it.

"I'm sure there are lots of Nicks," he says, then directs his attention to me. "I didn't find out that I had been selected as a mentor until earlier this week, otherwise I would have said something when we last met."

The woman who first brought us in speaks up, "Technically, it wouldn't be considered protocol to give that information before this initial meeting, anyway."

"Of course. I wouldn't have dreamed of it," Nick says, winkin in our direction, then squats down. "So Bentley, tell me a little about yourself."

Bentley sits in a chair next to him and begins talking about all of his favorite things. Nick, noticing Tal's boredom, pulls up a game on his display and hands it to him. Based on Tal's expression, this scores him major points. Eric and I, lost in observation, eventually notice that we are being summoned. The women at the desk waves us over to sign approvals. We are reminded that it is recommended for new mentors to have contact with our family at least four days a week for the first month or so. They need to bond with everyone, not just the child. We nod and listen, though having gone through this process with Tal makes it less important to absorb every detail. We know the drill. After talking with Bent, Nick agrees to come over the next day, after conditioning, to spend some time with us and have dinner at our place.

On the way home, I am eager to hear how the boys felt about it. Perhaps that can solidify my unsteady experience.

"He seems cool," Tal says nonchalantly. "Can Stephen come for dinner tomorrow, too?"

"Sure, I don't see why not," Eric answers. "I will message him and see if he's free." To me he says, "I think that Stephen might be pairing with someone. I have seen him with a blonde woman quite a few times over the last month."

"That's great. It's about time." I turn my head toward the kids. "Bentley, what did you think about Nick?"

"I like him," he says, observing the trees along the road.

Sometimes it can just be that simple. I wish it were for me. Granted, I haven't had much time to process. On one hand, I am excited to have Nick as a resource; he may be one of the only people who can help Bentley on this journey. Plus, I know he is a good guy, so that's a relief.

We got so lucky with Stephen that I didn't even explore the possibility that we could end up with someone who didn't fit our family naturally. When I messaged Alyssa this morning and mentioned where we were headed, she referenced a slightly disconcerting experience they had with their oldest. Nothing terrible, but plenty of awkward family dinners. Though I assume she wasn't trying to make me nervous, she did. Now that I know it's Nick, I don't necessarily see it as a negative, but I have so many unanswered questions.

After the typical dinner, kids in bed, clean up routine, Eric and I take a much-needed break on the couch together. I find myself mentally avoiding the whole mentoring situation, so I opt for asking about his research instead. We still haven't had a chance to catch up from his trip.

"How did the training go? Tell me about your last few days," I say as I lean back into his chest and rest my eyes.

"It was good. Same old, same old."

"Same old, same old? Seems like this is the first time you've ever done anything like this. How could it be same old?" I nudge him, teasing.

"It is a new situation, but I just showed them the same thing we've been doing for years, so it feels 'same old' to me."

I was expecting to have Eric return energized and excited to share. Usually this stuff is so fun for him.

"So...that's all I get? I was hoping for more detail."

"I don't know what else to say, Kate," he says, sighing, obviously exhausted. Maybe he is just overtired? This is definitely not the conversation I was expecting, but I try to summon compassion.

"You sound tired. Maybe we should go to bed? Or we could just spend some time together without...talking?" I stand up and pull on his arms good-naturedly, but he doesn't respond.

"I think we should go to bed. I am really tired."

He stands up and pats my shoulder, then walks down the hall. He's been gone for three days and I get a pat on the shoulder? Seriously? I stay in the living room for a few minutes, seething. We never fight. I don't even remember the last time I felt the urge to yell at Eric, but right now, I have it. I know part of it is that I feel overwhelmed by the whole mentoring situation, but thinking of that makes me even more frustrated. I need to talk it over with someone, and my go-to person isn't available.

I force myself to take a few deep breaths and start naming facts to help my logical brain take over. My expectations are most likely the problem here, I rationalize. I thought he would come home, we would talk for hours, we would fool around, and all would feel like it was back in its proper place. I shouldn't have built up his return in my mind like that. I walk to the bedroom, ready to apologize to Eric, but when I get there, he is already asleep. So I stand there. Desperate. Apparently I had expectations for my apology over having expectations.

CHAPTER 15

CONSCIOUSNESS DAWNS the next morning and I roll over to Eric's side of the bed. Finding it empty, the night before comes crashing into my mind. My schedule follows. I have to go to Washington Park today and plan tonight's dinner with Nick. Based on the dim light barely creeping in through the window, I am positive that it's early—my alarm isn't close to going off yet. Having no faith that I will fall back asleep, I leave the bed to practice yoga before I have to wake the boys. I need to clear my head.

When I enter the living room, I hear a hushed voice, and see Eric outside, leaning against the patio door and talking on his sensor. I immediately move to go to him, but stop myself. Instead, I lower myself slowly to my mat, the cool fabric soft on my skin. Connecting with my body, I begin to flow and breathe.

It is at least another fifteen minutes before Eric opens the door and comes back inside.

"I'm so sorry. I didn't mean to wake you," he apologizes.

"It's fine. Is everything ok?" I ask, standing from a warrior pose.

"Yes, that was someone from Regional Headquarters. They needed some information on how to proceed with an issue we are having with one of the pairs we met with."

"At 5:30 in the morning?"

"It's 6:30 there." He smiles.

"Eric, I'm really sorry I was pressing for information last night. I don't know anything about how this process is going. I was curious."

"It's fine. I was tired and a lot of the information is classified."

He still seems cold to me. Distant. I can't place it, and I feel a slow panic rumbling deep in my chest. We are having a normal conversation, but it feels like we are strangers. Is it me? Am I am being dramatic? Trying to avoid starting another misunderstanding, I walk over to him and give him a hug. And now I am positive it's not all in my head. This embrace is a sad excuse for comfort.

"Well, I'm glad you're back," I say curtly, turning on my heel.

He moves moves to the kitchen and starts busying himself with breakfast. "What do we have going on today? Do the kids have conditioning?"

"Yep. We need to get them off at nine this morning. They are done at two, so I thought we could all go for a hike or something before Nick comes over for dinner."

Eric stiffens. "I forgot that was tonight."

"Is that ok? Do I need to reschedule?"

He cracks an egg and sighs. "No, it's fine. I need to stop over at the lab at some point. Maybe I will go with the boys at nine. Are they just at their usual spot today? It's not much farther to the lab from there."

"That would work. How long will you be? I am planning to pick up our groceries. I assume our amounts will be slightly smaller this week since you will be heading out again. When? I don't think you told me what day."

"I'll be leaving again on Thursday, actually."

"Thursday? But that's in two days. I thought we would at least have you for the weekend."

"Me too. I'll get back Monday night, possibly afternoon, depending on how the weekend goes."

I am quiet. Was it only a week ago that I was feeling so stable? So safe? This thing that is supposed to be so exciting and wonderful is sucking the life-blood out of me and my family. And it's only been a week! Literally *nobody* in our lifetime has been through this, so it's not like I can simply search up a support group. I need to talk to somebody. And I need to not be kept in the dark.

"Can I come with you?" I blurt out.

"What?" Eric looks at me quizzically.

"Can I come with you? I could find a place for the boys, maybe split time with Shari and Stephen? I could come and see the training you are doing. I know I wouldn't be privy to all of it, but I bet they would at least let me see some things, right? Maybe tour the facility? I haven't left our city boundaries in almost four years."

"I can't bring you with me, Kate. I'm sorry." A look of pain and tension briefly flashes across his face, but then he laughs under his breath.

My heart aches. I can't read him. "Why not? Why is this being kept so hush-hush?"

"I don't know." He sits on a stool and runs his hands through his hair. "I think we just really don't understand what we're dealing with yet. We already know we need to start the process of pairing immediately, but with so few numbers, it seems even more critical. Who knows if those matches will stay consistent over time? Or if they will even have time or ability to procreate if we wait? We made the decision to move forward, and I have to be a part of it. I mean, I don't *have* to be a part of it...but I have to be a part of it. You know? It's my life's work."

"I get it. But I feel like ever since you got back, you've been distant. Have I done something wrong? Is it me?"

His face softens. "Kate, no. You haven't done anything wrong. There are just some things that I need to accept and work through on my own. I'm sorry I can't talk more with you about it. I...need a little bit of space to process."

Again, this is not the response I was expecting. Space to process? I feel my chest start to feel tight. I need to eat something. Or get some fresh air. Really, anything to distract me from this moment.

"I could help you process," I plead.

"I don't want you there, Kate," he says sharply. I smile tightly at Eric, grab a plum, and escape to the front porch, tears streaming down my cheeks as soon as I turn from him. He doesn't follow.

Nick rings the doorbell at four o'clock on the dot. The boys are helping me chop vegetables for the salad and Eric is out grilling the chicken. I open the door, trying not to touch it with my cucumber-covered fingers. Nick is standing on the step with a bouquet of tulips. They almost distract from how handsome he looks, freshly showered and wearing a loose, button-up linen shirt.

"Hi Nick, come on in. We are just finishing dinner preparations. Almost ready to eat," I say warmly.

"You brought us flowers?" shouts Bentley excitedly, seeing what Nick is holding.

"I sure did. Do you like this color?"

"I like every color!" he says. "Bring them in here and we can put them in a big cup, so they don't dry out."

I grab a vase from the cupboard below the sink. "Here you go, bud," I say, handing it to Bentley. Nick helps him trim the stems and arrange them. They are simple and stunning.

"Well that made his day. Where did you get these?" I ask as he puts them on the table.

"I cut them from my garden. They're all in full bloom right now." I cock my head in surprise. I didn't visualize Nick as a gardener.

Bentley rushes over and grabs Nick's hand, pulling him intently to the playroom.

"Is Stephen coming tonight?" Tal asks from the couch.

"He should be. He said he was planning on it, but he may be a bit late. He had to work a little later than usual. Do you want to go play with Nick and Bentley while I finish up?"

He gives me a skeptical look.

"I mean, do you want to go hang out with Nick and Bentley while I finish up?" I revise, grinning. I have to remember that 'playing' is not something Tal is officially interested in anymore.

"I guess." He washes his hands and heads back to the playroom. In a few minutes, Nick returns to the kitchen.

"How did you escape? Didn't Bentley immediately rope you into helping him with his block city?"

"He did, but then he and Tal started blowing up buildings, and it seemed like my services weren't needed anymore," he laughs.

"Is it weird for you, just being thrown into a family like this?" I pause mid-chop. "And, how is it possible that you and Bentley are a match, anyway? From what it sounded like the other night, it didn't seem like anyone would be similar enough to you to qualify for something like this." When he doesn't answer right away, I ask "Why did you even want to become a mentor? You have been fast-tracked and have the whole world ahead of you—"

"Ok, that's a lot of questions," he says, cutting me off as he sits on a stool. "I'll try to answer them all, but let me know if I missed something."

"Sorry," I say.

"No, it's ok. We didn't really get a chance to discuss anything the other day. Do you want to wait and discuss with Eric here, too?"

I look longlingly toward the patio. I do want to have Eric involved in the conversation. I really, really do.

"It's ok, I'll fill him in later," I say, hopeful that it isn't a lie.

"First, yes, this is incredibly strange to suddenly be a part of a family. I am an only child, so I don't know what it's like to be around kids. I feel like I'm intruding, but it's also really interesting and fun for me to see what having a family is like," he says, pausing. "Bentley and I are not actually ninety-percent matched," he admits.

I exhale loudly and he holds up his hands defensively.

"We are pretty darn close, though! I wanted to mentor because I was sick of only focusing on myself. When I officially accepted my place in Tier 1 as an adult two years ago, I took that oath seriously. I want to give back, to serve my fellow human beings and I want to make society a better place. I will continue to strive for that in every aspect of my life, but this is the only option available to me now. Yes, I am a health consultant, but it doesn't allow me to actually dig deep and be a part of my patients' lives. That, along with personal things I've been going through, is why I asked to be a mentor. I felt like something was missing for me. Bentley was the closest option, and the committee approved it. I'm really grateful to be here, Kate. I hope it's helpful for you, too. I know Eric is busy with all of his research and you must be feeling a bit overwhelmed."

"How do you know about Eric's research?"

Nick pauses. "They gave me a briefing on your family before we were introduced last week. Sorry, was I not supposed to know?"

"No, I'm just surprised that they told you, when it's still so new." I finish with the salad and mix it all together in the bowl. Eric walks in with the plated chicken. When he sees Nick, he pauses slightly, then continues walking toward us.

"Nick, glad you could join us." He sets the chicken on the counter and shakes his hand gruffly.

"My pleasure. Thanks for having me." Nick says, avoiding his eyes. His confidence suddenly retreating. Am I missing something? Eric has only met Nick once and it seemed to go fine. I don't understand men.

At dinner, everything is delicious, and the boys do most of the talking, which is helpful because I don't really feel up to making conversation. Thankfully, Nick heads out shortly after we finish cleaning up, and I jump at the opportunity to put the boys to bed. Exhausted, they nearly fall asleep before I finish reading our story. I know I should attempt a discussion with Eric, but instead, I lie on their floor, watching their eyes flutter closed, listening to their breathing.

CHAPTER 16

I START AWAKE a few hours later, my body stiff. It takes me a moment to take in my surroundings. Standing up groggily, I make my way out of the bedroom as quietly as possible. I brace myself against the wall as the evening comes rushing back, and my heart starts to pound. As usual, everything feels more dramatic in the middle of the night.

I doubt that I will be able to fall asleep right now with all of this negativity and adrenaline pulsing through me, so I backtrack to the kitchen and put some water on to boil. Maybe after a cup of tea, I will feel more relaxed and be able to bring this fear and apprehension back to normal levels. Even though I'm conscious of the magnifying effect night has on my emotions, they are still hard to shut down. Right now my mind is going a mile a minute, pulling out every worst-case scenario with Eric, Nick, the boys' conditioning—you name it. All of my deep-seeded concerns splayed out on repeat.

I pick them apart one by one, until I get to Eric. I have nothing on that. I am completely baffled and hurt. Even during other stressful times—and we have been through many—he has never treated me this way. He has never felt distant. It feels oddly personal.

Glancing at the clock, I see that it's nearly one in the morning. I tap my sensor, sending a message to Tess. She has young kids, but she has always been a night owl. I hope that she is either up, or that her sensor is on silent so I don't disturb her.

My heart leaps as my sensor dings, relief flooding through me. The call connects and I escape to the porch.

"Hey Kate, what's up?" she says brightly. Way too cheery for this time of night.

"I'm so sorry to bother you—I didn't wake you, did I?"

"Look at me. Seriously? I never go to bed before two." She does look completely awake and put together.

"How, Tess? You have a toddler!"

"She wakes up around this time most nights. It's always a bad dream, needing to go to the washroom, being thirsty, or some other random night-time need, so I figure I may as well wait up. I take a nap in the afternoon."

"You are my hero," I joke.

"I know you didn't call me to ask about my nightly shenanigans. What's going on?" she asks, more seriously.

"I..." I don't know what to say. Why did I call? Where do I even start? "I think Eric and I are in trouble," I say in a rush, tears springing to my eyes.

"What?" she asks, obviously taken off guard. "What do you mean?"

"Don't say anything to anyone, please," I blurt out. "I don't even know what I mean. He just came back from this training, and he feels so distant. He didn't hold me like he normally does, and he won't tell me anything about what is going on—he *patted my shoulder*, Tess!—he hasn't said one thing about what he did down there-"

"Whoa! Kate, slow down," she interrupts. "Take a deep breath and go through that again." She waits for me to compose myself. "So, Eric came back from a training?"

"Yes, sorry," I say, swallowing. "He went to this training and has been acting strange since he got back. He says he is tired, and I'm sure he is, but this feels...different. I know tired Eric. Tired Eric is still kind and funny. He doesn't fall asleep without even saying goodnight."

"Obviously, I literally know nothing about the situation, but just throwing this out there—has he ever been in *such* a stressful position before? Before you answer, let me clarify. I know that having kids is stressful and all of that, but I mean stressful like 'I am now in charge of a societal shift'. Has he ever had to travel? Train people he has never met? Make decisions that could affect people's lives long-term?"

I hesitate. I hadn't thought about it like that. "No, not really."

"Not really?" she echoes.

"No, not ever. He has always just plugged along in the lab. Some of his research has resulted in extra training that he has had to oversee, but only locally."

"Do you think this could just be a completely different type of stressor, and he might be responding differently than you have seen in the past?" Tess asks gently.

"Yes, maybe? I hadn't considered that. I kind of assumed that stress is stress. I am sure the pressure he feels is really intense. It all seems theoretical to me, but, I guess, he is actually living it."

"Kate, I don't want to take anything away from what you are feeling. If you feel like something is off, go with it. I just know that for me and Rob—well, when he is acting like that, it's usually because he is hurting, you know? Think about Eric. He is missing out on that closeness, too. What would compel somebody to pull away from the person he cares about most?"

I stare blankly. The only image I hold in my mind is Eric, years ago, looking pained after I asked him to leave. I had just given birth to Bentley, and my mom was struggling with her health. I was overwhelmed and hormonally all over the place. I didn't want to see or talk to anyone in that moment. I was haunted by his expression even then, but I couldn't force myself to call him back. I do understand being in so much anguish that you don't physically have the energy to allow someone else to help you out of it. Which then, in turn, makes you feel more desperate and alone.

I am completely selfish. I have made this all about me and haven't thought about where Eric is in all of this, not really.

"Tess, I think you are right. I might be a terrible person."

Tess laughs. "Yeah, ok, Kate."

"I am serious!" I say, attempting to imbue my voice with indignation.

"I know you are, but you are also wrong. It's not terrible to be afraid of losing something that means so much to you. It's not terrible to feel stripped raw at even the slightest hint that something might be awry. It's pretty amazing, actually. You guys have something that is so meaningful to you that you are terrified. And, it's not terrible to need an amazing friend to help with a little perspective shift." She winks at me.

I roll my eyes. "Alright, alright. I am not terrible, just a bit dramatic."

"Easy to do at 1 a.m. I guess it's 2 a.m. now. Time for me to be on the lookout for Little Miss Bad Dreams."

"Thanks, Tess."

"I love you, Kate. Talk soon?"

I nod, and the display goes dark. Returning to the kitchen, I realize that the water has been at a full boil long enough to reduce down to almost nothing. I turn off the heat and move the pot to the cool side of the stove. I don't need tea after all.

CHAPTER 17

I AM on my way to Washington Park again this morning. It has been a couple of weeks since my last assignment there, which means I may see some of the same patients that I met with last time. I am more stable in the light of day, though worry still subconsciously laces every moment. My talk with Tess did me good. Walking my usual route, I find myself looking for Nick. I don't see him, but I do spot Lily. There are still a few minutes before we hit our first appointments, so I stride over to her. She looks involved in something, so I patiently wait, scrolling through a few patient files. She eventually glances up, noticing me.

"Kate! Oh my goodness, it's been too long!" she exclaims, and we embrace warmly. "Shane told me that you two ran into each other a couple of weeks ago."

"We did. We were only able to chat for a few minutes, but he filled me in a little bit. Sounds like you are both up at Highlands? Or at least he is, and they are transitioning you there as well?"

"Yes, his most recent scans and blood work suggest that he needs to be exercising in the mornings. It made more sense to swap his schedule rather than change all appointment start times here."

I laugh. "I don't know, changing all of the times sounds completely reasonable to me."

She smiles. "Right? I don't know what they were thinking."

"He said he is really loving it."

"We both are. Change brings different challenges, but I think it's a good thing. It stretches us. We see a lot more uncleared pregnancy up there. I think that's the hardest one for me."

"Oh wow, really? How is that happening? I thought Tier 2 pairings were sterilized after one child?" I question. "I don't see many patients these days, and most of mine are either older or working to transition and, therefore, putting off pairing. Am I out of the loop on policy?"

"It's a little more complicated than that now. Policy has always required sterilization after one child for Tier 2 qualified pairings, but the timing has changed. Ever since Berg organized the Tier system, we have been doing these procedures at the time of delivery. Over the last sixty-five years, Berg has consolidated more research on patients who have had these procedures done. Some of the statistics are pretty concerning—specifically for the mother. Breastfeeding was more difficult in sterilized women, likely because the body was under so much stress, and recovery was longer than would normally be expected."

"That makes complete sense."

"It does. For years, they have been weighing pros and cons of waiting versus doing the surgery immediately, because there are obvious risks involved either way."

"Like uncleared pregnancy," I repeat.

"Exactly. Waiting gives couples enough time to either purposefully or accidentally become pregnant before the procedure. Two years ago, it seemed that we had enough evidence to justify waiting six weeks to allow the body to heal."

"Why couldn't they sterilize the father immediately?"

"Berg actually tried that, but it takes a good six months to be sure they are clear, and it left the mother with very little support while she was recovering. Pros and cons. Eliminate risk on one side, but increase the risk of depression, mental breaks, and lack of care for the infant on the other. They also thought about requiring the father to go through that procedure before delivery, but sometimes the pregnancy doesn't go full-term, and then the couple is left without recourse."

"What about birth control for the mother?"

"Again, that almost eliminates the risk, but the most effective options we have are not considered fully safe for breastfeeding—"

"Oh, for sure, that's too important to mess with," I agree. "That's quite the conundrum. So, how often are you seeing these pregnancies? Is it becoming a huge problem?"

"Not a *huge* problem. Most women's bodies don't start ovulating again until at least six weeks after delivery. Especially if they are breastfeeding. Many pairs are also extremely conscientious, making sure to use birth control and take precautions. But we do have some that see it as an opportunity to bypass the rules."

"You don't think they are accidents?"

"Some are, definitely. But some are...not."

"So, how do you deal with that?"

"The same way we deal with any pregnancy: support, nutrition, and education. The frustrating thing is, I know some members of Tier 2 look at pairs successful in seeking out a second child and start thinking about it themselves."

"It seems like people would recognize that getting pregnant so soon after delivery is a risk in and of itself."

"Right. And I honestly think if the numbers start going up, Berg will institute policy changes to discourage and condition that behavior."

"You don't think they would force abortion, do you?"

"No, I don't think they would go that far. But, they have been gathering all genetic information on the pairs that are attempting this. If they notice common threads, I wouldn't be surprised if pairs with those markers are not able to have children at all."

I whistle. "Back to the beginning."

"Well, it's important for qualified Tier 2 individuals to recognize that the only reason they are able to have one child in the first place is that we have enough resources to allow for it. It used to be that only Tier 1 individuals could procreate. Period. If the general population becomes diluted again by disease markers because of uncleared pregnancy," she sighs. "Well, they may not have that privilege anymore."

It's harsh, but true. I start as I realize that it is a few minutes past my first appointment. "I wish we had all day to chat! I have so much I still want to talk about. I didn't even get to ask you about the kids or life outside of work. We should get together again soon." I give her another hug.

"I know, I have missed seeing you all the time. Remember when we had lunch together every day?"

"Of course I remember. I only had Tal then."

"We were babies," she says. We both laugh, and I wave as I head over to my station. A couple of patients are already lining up, and I prep my display with the few screens I will need access to. I pause when I notice the procreation panel, realizing I haven't had to open it in years. After talking with Lily, my service suddenly seems incredibly straightforward.

CHAPTER 18

I DREAM AGAIN. That same linen skirt, the same terrified eyes on my mother's face. I wake up in a cold sweat and reach for Eric, like I always do. I am actually surprised to feel him there. It's a rare occurrence these days. I suddenly feel vulnerable. Old me and Eric would cuddle up and talk, but I don't know what to expect now. He doesn't stir, so I surreptitiously slide closer to him, running my hand covertly across his chest and down his side. My body shudders in response. His soft skin prickles under my touch and I hold my breath when his hand gently moves over mine. He pulls me close and kisses my cheek, then pauses, suddenly moving away and sitting up. Tears spring to my eyes and I quickly brush them away.

"Sorry to wake you," I say, hoping to salvage the moment. "Did you get in late?"

"It's ok. I did."

"How long will you be here this time?" I ask, not allowing myself to break.

"Two days. They wanted to make sure I had some time with the boys before I head out into outlying communities. I am not sure how long I will be gone this time around."

"Outlying communities? More training or more pairs found? Both?"

"Both. Everything is moving along well. It's just busier with more pairs. We have more work to do."

"Makes sense. Do you have plans today? I didn't know you would be here, so I scheduled for us to go visit my mom's Tier 2 distribution center. I know the boys always love serving there. I'm sorry if that's not ideal—"

"That works. I just want to spend time with them. Happy to do whatever."

Time with *them*? What about me? Heat rises to my face. I slide off the opposite side of the bed and hurriedly turn on the shower, making a point to undress near the bed, right in front of him.

In the shower, I mentally cling to anything that was good, trying to convince myself that I'm not crazy, and I am drawn into one of my favorite memories with him.

A few months after we met, he somehow got clearance for us to drive out of territory together. I knew that we were going to officially pair at some point, but the anticipation of when and how was deliciously agonizing. Eric showed up at my room and asked me if I had any plans over the next couple of days. I listed off my mundane training tasks.

I remember him saying something like, "If I told you that I was going to take you somewhere for a couple of days, would you be able to skip all that?" I wish I could say that I threw caution to the wind, jumped into his arms, and went to the car right then. Instead, I blinked far too many times and stuttered out my concerns, saying that I would love to, but didn't know if that would be approved. He laughed and put his hands on my shoulders.

"I was trying to surprise you. I already got clearance for both of us. It's all approved," he said smiling. That's when I remember jumping into his arms. He carried me down to the car, and I realized I didn't have any clothes or necessities packed. He smiled and said he had already taken care of it. I found out later that Alyssa had helped him pilfer some items earlier that morning when I was exercising.

We sat in the back of the car getting to know each other. Much better. My heart begins pounding just thinking about it. We refueled, talked, slept, and ate food that he had packed. When we arrived at our destination the next evening, I remember feeling completely filled. My whole being was alive and tingling. And then we stepped out of the car. To this day, I have never seen something as breathtaking as that view. We were looking out over the sheer edges of the Grand Canyon. I had read about it and seen pictures of it, but none of that even came close to doing it justice. The colors in the stones were breathtaking— oranges and reds turning to purple as the sun set. My brain couldn't comprehend the sheer magnitude of it. I felt compelled to run through it, to touch it, just to convince myself that it was real.

I got my chance when we did some hiking the next day. Then, arriving back up to the rim, Eric took my hands in his and asked if I wanted to pair with him. It was the best moment of my life up until that point, probably still in my current top three. I still have no idea how he was able to get us clearance, or approval for the extra fuel and mileage. Every year or so, I ask him, and he always grins, giving me some ridiculous answer. I doubt I will ever know the real one. Now, I wonder if I will ever get the chance to ask again.

I chastise myself for being so quick to jump to conclusions. If this is a season of intense stress for Eric, it will pass. I steel myself to support him and stop allowing his icy demeanor to send me into personal crisis. It will pass. It has to.

We don't say much to each other the rest of the morning and I get the impression that Eric is purposefully avoiding me. With frustration ever present in my currently aching heart, it makes things easier for me. The boys eat breakfast and are so excited to go to the center, they rush through their morning tasks so that we can leave sooner—despite the fact that I have repeatedly announced an eleven o'clock appointment time. Finally giving up, I decide to leave early. If they can accommodate us, great. If not, there is a fun little park on the corner where we can burn some time. Eric plays cards with the boys on the way down. All the while, the boys pepper him with questions about his research. He answers. Every single one of them. I stare out the window, seething, tears burning in the corners of my eyes.

We do end up spending some time at the park, but I can't even begin to enjoy watching Eric run around with the boys. Luckily, I brought my tablet, allowing me to work and distract myself. When our appointment time draws near, I gather up the boys and we walk over to the distribution center. As we enter, the comforting effect it has on me is immediate. Every part of this place reminds me of my mom. The shelves are stacked with raw goods, scales dot the counters, and scanner stations are on the wall. Just as I remember. People haven't arrived yet to start collecting rations, but there's still plenty to do. Noticing the pod out back, I ask if we can begin unloading. Receiving the go-ahead, we begin to pull out all of the fresh produce. Tall, leafy kale, crisp Jerusalem artichokes, radishes, and garlic scapes fill our boxes as we take load after load.

Every week, distribution centers like this one open their doors for Tier 2 individuals and families. It's much like ours, but the options aren't as widely varied. People go to their assigned center, scan their sensors, and receive their portions for the week. According to my mom, Tier 2 portions used to be much smaller than those in Tier 1, but they have been fairly similar since I started serving here. Another sign that our system is working; we have enough to take care of Tier 1 and provide plenty for those in lower Tiers. Though I haven't ever seen a Tier 3 center, I assume it's similar. I make a mental note to plan a time to serve there and check it out.

Tal and Bentley only lose a couple of items from the pod onto the road. For the most part, they are extremely careful and meticulous, understanding how important it is to avoid waste. Once we have finished, we close the pod and send it on its way. Then, on to organizing and preparing for pick-ups. Eric works right alongside us, talking to the boys all afternoon. I get nothing from him, so I throw myself into connecting with the faces in front of me, filling orders as quickly and efficiently as possible.

A woman in line casually mentions her service years ago at a Tier 3 center and I tune in, but am somewhat disappointed. She isn't sharing details, just commenting on the fact that she feels more gratitude at receiving her own portions now, after being assigned there. I ruminate on this while measuring out oats for the next order, my scoop plunging into the wide bucket. I have never thought much about what Tier 2 individuals do to serve and it sparks my interest. Cassidy could be a good resource there. I have always been so focused on helping them progress that I haven't ever taken time to understand their lives.

Moving swiftly between orders, I don't even notice Tia in the line until she calls my name and waves. I put down my bowl and go around the counter to give her a hug, figuring the boys can cover for me for a second.

"Tia, how are you?" I ask grinning.

"I'm ok," she says. "Last week I found a lump in my armpit."

My heart sinks. Please be just a swollen lymph node.

"The Doctor says it's cancer. I'm starting treatment this weekend," she elaborates.

"Tia, I'm so sorry. How is your family taking the news?"

"They are hopeful that treatments will work." She smiles wanly.

"I am, too. They are making huge strides in many areas. Hopefully yours will respond."

"All I want is to see my grand baby. That's at least a year and a half away. My goal is to last that long."

"I think you are determined enough to make it," I say, rubbing her shoulder. "I have to get back to help, but what number are you? I'll go fill your order now."

She smiles and thanks me while I measure her portions. I wave, watching her go, and feel Eric's eyes on me. I turn, not looking up, and process the next order.

CHAPTER 19

ERIC IS GONE. He's been gone on and off for three weeks. I am waiting at a table for Shari, who is meeting me for lunch while the boys are out with Nick, Stephen, and Stephen's friend, Liz. At first I wasn't sure how I felt about that arrangement, but I figure if Liz is going to be a part of Stephen's life, we may as well get to know her sooner rather than later. At least Tal seemed to connect with her right away.

Shari walks in and I motion for her to join me, embracing her when she arrives at the table.

"Wow, are you ok? That hug was intense." She laughs.

In that moment, my facade cracks and I can't help it. My face contorts and tears spill onto my cheeks.

"Ok, whoa. What is going on, Kate? You didn't seem upset when we talked on the phone."

"I don't know," I stall, realizing I may not understand how to describe my feelings to someone who hasn't experienced a long-term pair for themselves.

"Eric has been really distant and I don't know what to do. Shari, he is basically a part of me—we talk about everything and now...I have honestly never felt so alone. He is completely shutting me out; he hasn't told me anything about the work that he's doing, he barely says two words when he's home, and he isn't ever home!" I say, exasperated.

"I knew he was going to headquarters a lot, but I didn't know that he was having a hard time."

"He's gone again until Monday, and I don't know if *he* is having a hard time, necessarily. I definitely am. Do you—do you think he wants to un-pair?" I say, a little too loudly, then lean toward her and lower my volume, my hands gesticulating wildly. "I can't even believe I am even thinking that. But seriously, do you think he does? Maybe he has experienced this whole new, exciting life, and coming home to us is dull? Maybe he—" I stop, bile rising in my throat, "—met someone else?" I force the words out and look at her pleadingly. Please say no.

Shari's tone is even, not impacted at all by my hysteria. "I really don't know, Kate. This is all new information for me. People do choose to break pairings sometimes. Usually it's when their kids are older and they feel like they can give more to society individually than as a pair, or their responsibilities don't make it possible to stay paired. In Eric's case, his work responsibilities are becoming really intense. He could simply be really stressed. Or," she sighs, "maybe you're right and he feels like he has to move in a different direction."

I look at her, aghast. "But, we have built a life together, Shari. We have two kids, and they are *not* older. They are still little boys. How could he ever feel like work demands were more important than that?" I ask, the knot in my stomach growing by the second.

"Kate, I don't know if he does. Just speculating here. Being Tier 1 means sacrifice. We are the hope of humanity and all that," she says melodramatically. Then, seeing the look on my face, she says more seriously, "We are given all of the best resources and opportunities, and in turn, we commit to making the best decisions for the whole. Not just the best decisions for ourselves. I know Eric wouldn't ever put work above his kids, unless it meant that his work was going to benefit society as a whole more than his work within his family. What he is doing is life changing. He is at the start of completely new possibilities. To think about eradicating cancer? Come on, Kate. You have to see how huge that is. No more suffering, no more pain. Families having grandparents again. Think about it, who do you know that *hasn't* had a parent die of cancer? I am 38 years old, and I am staring all of that in the face. I know that in the next few years, my chances of getting some form of cancer are incredibly high. If I knew that something I could do would spare a percentage of individuals in the next generation, more in the next, and eventually clear the human race? How could anyone say no to that?" She takes a long drink of her water. I am transported back to when I asked Nick the same question about the woman he considered pairing with. Suddenly, I see that situation in a different light.

"I know. I get it. But, he made a comment a few weeks ago that is just not sitting right with me. He said that he needed to "toe the line" if he wanted to still be involved. Wouldn't that insinuate that his involvement is optional? That Berg could move forward without him? Couldn't he be at home with us, knowing that he made his contribution and let someone else take it from here?"

"I don't think that's how it works, Kate. It may have felt that way to him, at first. He was in complete control during the research phase, but after their discovery, Berg took over. That must have been really hard for him. I am sure he felt like he wasn't imperative anymore, but they do still need him and will keep needing him until this first phase is complete. They don't know exactly how this is going to look when those first alleles match. New pairs will need to be trained, embryos tested for the entire nine months, and then they will continue to scan, watch, and compile data on them over the course of their *entire lives*. Then hope that those progeny have enough genetic diversity to pair again. This is just the beginning."

My body seems to slump lower with ever sentence and as she finishes, I am completely deflated. What does this mean for me? For the boys? Are we just left to pick up the pieces and figure it out?

I stumble over my words. "I don't even know anyone that has been through this. What do I do?" The tears start to well up in my eyes again. With as much crying as I have been doing lately, my eyes feel permanently irritated and puffy.

"I think you need to talk to Eric. Ask him how he feels and what his expectations are. Who knows, maybe this does have an endpoint and he is only overwhelmed."

This has all happened so fast, and again I chastise myself for jumping to conclusions so quickly. But I *have* given it some time and I can't keep ignoring my gut. I can sense that he is done, that he is purposely driving me away, but I can't imagine living life without him in it. Why *should* I have to imagine that? 'This life requires sacrifice', I get that. In this situation, though, why can't we make both ideals work? This discovery is huge, yes, but it will be generations before the benefits are realized. My two boys are also going to be contributing to future generations. How can we not find a way to take care of both sides?

"Kate. Are you going to say anything?" Shari asks gently.

"I don't know what to say. I think I was hoping I would come here today and you would just tell me that my fears are unfounded. That everything will go back to normal in another week or two. I didn't expect to have to think about changing every expectation I have had for my life."

She reaches across the table and squeezes my hand. "Trust me. I know all about changing expectations. It's no fun, but you do become stronger through the process."

I, out of habit, squeeze back, though I find no comfort in it. My body craves to be home, but even as I think it, I realize that my 'home' doesn't exist right now. Eric is my home. Anywhere I go feels empty without him there. Without all of him. This shell of a person in my house is not Eric, and I don't know how to get him back. I am empty, and there is no place I can go that will fill this void.

CHAPTER 20

Nick sits next to me on a park bench, watching the boys play tag with their friends. He is still breathing hard from being 'it' and, without meaning to, I pay attention to the heat diffusing from his body, filling the few inches of space between us. With Eric gone, I have really appreciated having him around. It was strange at first, spending time with a man who isn't my pair, but Nick is easy to talk to. It really beats feeling sorry for myself all the time.

"You seem to be in your own little world over here," Nick teases.

"I kind of am." I smile.

"What are you thinking about?"

I don't want to talk to him about Eric, and I don't know how to express gratitude for his company, so I talk about my mom. When I was file scrolling again last night, I happened upon more of her service assignments and records. I fill him in on the most interesting parts.

"I remember as a kid, I used to see people from Tier 3 all the time. My mom worked with them. When she wasn't working in the Tier 2 distribution center, she was in charge of managing resources for their district. I remember going with her a few times and being fascinated and scared all at the same time. Theoretically, they seemed so different from me, but in person..." I trail off. "I don't know, I guess I was mostly surprised at how much we had in common. I realized last night that it's been a really long time since I interacted with anyone in Tier 3. Just got me thinking."

"I don't know that I've *ever* seen someone from Tier 3," Nick admits.

"Really? How is that possible?"

"I spent all of my time either conditioning, testing, or in the medical center with my dad."

"What does your dad do?" I ask.

"He is an ER doctor for Tier 2. He doesn't work much anymore. He mostly helps support the new doctors coming in. He's forty-six and counting."

I gasp. "Forty-six? Wow, that's impressive. I am sure you still saw a lot. Your mom was okay letting you be there with him all the time? That must have been pretty shocking for a little kid."

"She knew I loved it, but I don't think she would have approved. She died when I was 7."

"Oh wow, Nick, I am so sorry." I had no idea. "How were you able to fasttrack your conditioning with that kind of trauma to work through?"

"My dad opted to do reversal therapy on my limbic system. Just some slight adjustments to make everything bearable and allow my rational brain to function without being overpowered. It was really helpful. Even now, I view that time as being tender, but not painful."

I haven't ever known someone who has been through reversal therapy to that extent, though I know the basics of how it works. Witnessing it in action at the rehabilitation center the other day made it even more tangible. By referring to a persons' scans before and after trauma, they can actually achieve complete removal of pathways formed by the event. Typically they don't erase all of them; it seems to be more effective to simply weaken them. Humans learn through pain and emotional stress, but only to a certain point. That same stress that allows us to grow can quickly become debilitating, if left unchecked. Partial removal allows patients to feel the amount of pain that is helpful, but ensures recovery and healing.

"We actually saw a reversal therapy machine the other day in Tier 2. Do you remember what it felt like when you were undergoing the treatments? I've never talked with someone who has lived through it."

"I was really young, but I remember it feeling warm. Like a soft blanket was being wrapped around me. My dad actually had to cut me off because I wanted to go until I couldn't remember—" he stops himself, running his hands through his hair. "Well, until I didn't feel any hurt at all."

"I am sure. As a kid, that would be tempting not to have to feel anything."

"It was. But I'm glad we stopped where we did. I would regret not remembering my mom, and I think my memories are more focused because of the therapy. I'm grateful for that."

The boys are darting happily around the playground. I can't imagine leaving them without a mother at this age.

"Are you ready for the ceremony this weekend?" Nick asks, changing the subject.

"I think so. It feels like so long ago that we wrote those introductions. We get to read them on displays, right?" I laugh.

"Definitely." He grins. "You can even download them to your sensor, just in case."

"I will do that tonight. Thanks for the tip."

Nick slides lower on the bench and leans his head back, content. He closes his eyes and soaks in the evening sun. The silence makes the children's laughter more vibrant, and I notice the rustle of the leaves in the branches above us. I don't mean to watch his broad chest rise and fall, or his hair gently moving in the breeze, but in that moment, I am transfixed.

Later that evening, I walk with Nick and the boys to our co-op. It's our night to tend the garden beds, clean up the livestock areas, and harvest the vegetables and fruits that are in season. Everyone in our neighborhood is assigned a couple of days each month. It isn't practical for each of us to have our own gardens and food-production animals—not only logistically, but because space and areas with approved soil are limited. Our neighborhood co-ops allow for sustainable food production for all. Another side benefit is that we have the opportunity to interact with microbes in the soil, ensuring the health of our guts and promoting ideal immunity. Digging in the dirt every few weeks is enough to gain the maximum benefit while not infringing terribly on our other societal responsibilities.

Tal and Bent look forward to our assigned days every month. They love collecting eggs, picking raspberries, digging up carrots, and especially snitching and snacking on anything they can get their hands on. Tonight we need to milk the goats, which is, admittedly their least favorite task, and pinch off the side shoots on the tomato plants. We have the opportunity to harvest greens for the distribution center, as well. Handing the boys their scissors and canvas bags, I send them off to start cutting greens. They know the drill. I watch them carefully remove a third of the leaves from each plant, allowing for future regrowth.

I pick up a clean bucket and ask Nick to grab a small pail of grain. Reaching under the fence, I snap off a handful of weeds to add to the pail.

"What do we need this for?" Nick asks.

"We," I hand him a sanitizing wipe, "are going to milk the goats."

Nick stares at me blankly. "That's a thing?"

"You've never milked a goat before?"

"I have never been given that assignment, no," he laughs.

"What is your typical assignment?"

"I am usually turning over soil or repairing equipment and shelters at my co-op."

It makes sense that he would be used for manual labor. Harvesting and milking take knowledge and skill, but not necessarily muscle.

"Well, you are in for a treat," I say with a smirk.

I let him lead our first doe up onto the milk stand. I laugh as he awkwardly pushes and pulls, fighting against her locked legs and swinging head. When she is in place, I gently pat her head and offer her the weeds and grain, which she happily accepts.

"You can milk her now," I say. Nick looks so taken aback that I laugh out loud this time. "Here, let me show you," I say, walking over and motioning for him to move close. I show him how to clean the teat, then help him use his fingers and palm to start expressing the milk. His fingers move awkwardly at first, but his face lights up as a thin stream of milk hits the bucket, making the metal sing. He continues until the udder appears wrinkled and empty, and I rest my hand on his to let him know he can stop. He quickly turns and sends milk spraying past my face.

"I missed!" he laughs, letting go and moving back before I can smack him.

"You are lucky you missed," I tease. He picks up the bucket and we repeat the process with the other four goats. By the end, our bucket is completely full. Being in the evening air and doing something repetitive has calmed my senses. As we gather our things and walk back to the main shelter for clean-up, I feel more centered than I have in weeks.

"Thanks, Kate," Nick says softly.

"For what?" I laugh. "You're a natural."

"For letting me be with you guys today. I loved it. I haven't felt this, I don't know, comfortable, I guess? Really ever. It's nice."

I smile. We meet up with the boys and finish our tasks. I felt fairly comfortable today, too. For that moment, I don't allow the 'buts' and 'what ifs' to enter into my experience. I give myself permission to have a nice moment, no strings attached.

CHAPTER 21

THE CEREMONY IS TONIGHT. I have spent all day with the boys, making sure to have enough face time together so they won't be upset when I have to leave before dinner. They are playing happily now, and Stephen should be here in about a half an hour. Just enough time to get dressed and make sure I present myself well. I fuss with my hair for a few minutes, becoming frustrated when I can't get it to sit right. Why am I stressing? I have my introductions downloaded, and I am good at public speaking. I take a few deep breaths to calm my nerves. I probably should have showered, I think. My hair is flat. My eyes stare back at me from the mirror, and for a moment, I see a scared, pleading little girl. I am acting as if I have something to prove, that somehow looking beautiful will solve all of this. My heart drops, and I brace myself, hands firmly planted on the counter top. I haven't gone out with Eric in months; we had previously been too busy to plan anything, nor did I understand that it was time sensitive. Now, I haven't had any attention, or felt loved by anyone in weeks. Well, anyone over the age of ten, that is.

This thought crushes me. My body aches to be held, to be wanted. I wipe away an errant tear that has trickled down, along my cheekbone. I force myself to breathe deeply and look at myself squarely in the mirror. The face I see is hollow, a shell of a person right now. That won't be fixed in the time I have left. Eric isn't going to be there tonight, so it really doesn't matter how I look. Then, the thought crosses my mind that Eric might not be the only one I'm trying to impress. I quickly finish up and exit the washroom. This will be fine, and I am being ridiculous.

I walk into the kitchen to grab a snack. A boiled egg and blueberries will have to do. Berg will serve an actual dinner at the ceremony, so it doesn't have to hold me for long. My sensor dings, just as the soft white hits my teeth. I attempt to chew and swallow, but boiled egg is not the easiest thing to get down quickly. Quickly downing some water, I head to the door to let Stephen and Liz in.

"Hi, sorry, I was eating and it took me a minute to get to the door." I wipe my finger across my lips, just to make sure I don't have any pieces of egg stuck there.

"Wow, Kate. You look beautiful," Liz says, admiring my dress. I really like having another girl around. The compliment makes me blush, again confirming how desperate I am for someone to notice me. My stomach turns. I am not someone who struggles with confidence and I know who I am. At least, I thought I did. Maybe I only know who I am with Eric.

"Thanks, Liz. I appreciate it. I am feeling oddly anxious about tonight."

"I've heard you speak before," Stephen says. "You will do great."

Stephen's hair has gotten long enough that he is able to pull it up in a small bun at the top of his head. It suits him. I give it two weeks before Tal decides he needs to start growing his hair out.

I usher them in, and the boys peek their heads out of their room to say their hellos.

"Looks like I won't need to pry them off me tonight. They seem pretty happy to keep playing," I laugh.

"Perfect." Stephen smiles. "Get out of here, before they remember you are leaving."

"Sounds good. I'll sneak out. I shouldn't be too late, but I'll message you if something changes."

I head to the car and hear a pitter-patter of feet behind me. I turn around to see Bentley running down the hall. He collides with my legs and squeezes tight.

"I love you, Mom," he says, running back to play.

The contact was so brief, and yet it filled my soul to the brim. I blink back tears, not even worrying about his slipping pants, and walk out the back door.

The Capitol Building looks especially regal tonight, it's broad columns lit up, dropping dramatic shadows along the veranda. A true relic of past civilization. I step out of the car and walk up the steps, making my way to the ballroom entrance. My arms wrap protectively around each other, somehow trying to disguise the fact that I am entering alone. As soon as I walk through the main foyer doors, I see Nick. My breath catches, taking in his tan skin against his grey suit. He looks incredible. I have never seen him in anything but a button-up shirt and jeans. As he walks over to me, I suddenly feel awkward, not knowing whether to shake his hand or give him a hug. In typical fashion, I decide on nothing.

"Well, you certainly clean up nice," I say.

He smiles and his eyes shine, reflecting the lights overhead. "I could say the same about you. C'mon, I'll show you where we are sitting." He gently places his hand on the small of my back, causing instant heat. At first, I walk a little faster instead of settling into it, but as we enter the ballroom, I stop. It's breathtaking. It reminds me of old videos I have seen of award programs, honoring celebrated public figures. Being so frugal with our resources now, events like this are extremely uncommon. I suddenly feel foolish for not attending the ceremony in the past. And my heart hurts because now, I am experiencing it without Eric.

Nick points me toward a table in the middle of the room where I find my name tag and take a seat. Having looked over the schedule earlier this week, I generally know what to expect. Some of the initiates will be seated at our table, which will allow us to put them at ease. Hopefully, focusing on them will have the same effect on me. Dinner will be served, and then the ceremony will begin. Grace will be introducing Tier 1 and, after she finishes, Nick and I will do our portion. Last week, while Eric was gone, I distracted myself by putting together some photos to display during our presentation. Should be a nice touch.

Feeling a tap on my shoulder, I turn around and freeze, trying to process the person in front of me. It's Eric. I jump out of my seat, almost knocking it over, and embrace him. He kisses me. Not softly. His hands grip my back, and heat rises through my body, leaving me breathless. I pull away and search his eyes. There is an intensity there that makes me want to ditch this dinner and walk out with him right now.

Nick clears his throat. "Eric, I thought you were down at head-quarters?" he says, looking awkwardly at his hands.

"I wasn't supposed to get back for a few days, but I just couldn't miss this. I know Kate has worked so hard on it. I will have to fly back down tomorrow."

Knowing he only has one night makes me want to escape even more desperately. I know I can't, but it can't hurt to imagine it for a minute. Nick's voice brings me back to reality.

"Since we weren't expecting you, I don't think we have a seat available."

"I know, I talked with Grace just a few minutes ago. I will need to sit over there." Eric motions to a table in the back corner. "You both have work to do, and I don't want to be a distraction. Just wanted to come say hi before it started."

"You should say hi like that more often," I whisper. He smiles, and I feel his hand move slightly below my waist.

"More later," he whispers, moving a stray strand of hair behind my ear. To the group he says, "Can't wait to see the introductions. See you both after the ceremony." I release his hand slowly and watch him walk toward his table, all of my fears melt away in his path. *That* felt like Eric and me—the real version of us. I sit down, almost giddy. My hands are restless, so I reach into my purse and pull out some lip balm. As I'm applying it, I look at Nick, who is staring at me with a grin on his face.

"What?" I ask, grinning back.

"What was *that*?" he asks, with raised eyebrows.

"That? That was me not seeing my pair for a month." I grin sheepishly.

"Are you guys doing ok?" he asks more gently. I can't figure out how to give an appropriate answer. I don't know that I want to talk about it with Nick, but it feels wrong not to give him some information, when we have been spending so much time together.

"I mean, yes? *That* felt ok." I laugh. Trying to avoid a serious answer.

"I'm guessing it did," he chuckles uncomfortably.

"No, honestly, I don't know. Eric has been so absorbed with work, and we haven't really talked in weeks. I don't know how things are going to work out or what is going to happen in the future."

I really don't. I have been whipped back and forth this last month. One day we were normal, the next completely backward. The catalyst was obviously Eric's discovery, but the excuse of intense stress still doesn't sit right with me. There has to be some other explanation.

"I didn't expect any of this. I had life all mapped out and now...I don't know." The worries gain traction, my chest constricting, and a little bit of giddiness seeps out of me. I cling to that kiss.

Nick doesn't get a chance to respond as we see a couple of people making their way toward us. One of them is Cassidy. I wave to her, and she smiles nervously. When she is close, I rise from my seat and embrace her warmly.

"I have missed you! I need to hear all about how the last month has gone," I say.

"It's been crazy, but so good," she grins.

"Are you at our table? I haven't even had a chance to check the name tags." I start glancing around at the cards. Nick finds it across from us and motions for her to sit.

"I'm so glad we will get to catch up!" I say, lowering myself back into my seat. Cassidy hangs her handbag on the back of the chair and sits down.

"Fill me in before our table fills up," I say conspiratorially, leaning toward her.

"There's not much to tell, really. I packed up my approved items, spent as much time with my mom as possible, and then moved into my new place," she says, positively glowing.

"Do they have you on any of your new programs? Diet, exercise, conditioning?"

"They usually start with diet first, then move on, one by one, over time," Nick pipes in.

"Yep, that's how it's been for me so far," Cassidy agrees.

"Are you liking it?" I ask. It must be so strange to suddenly move to a more restrictive setting. It's really more freedom in the long run, but I wonder how it feels to someone coming in cold.

"I am. It's actually so much easier. I love having things spelled out for me. I have obviously been eating really deliberately for the last few years as I have been trying to heal, but I structured most of that myself. I had to make the menus, and I had to work with the foods that were available to me. Now I just go and pick up my food for the week, and I know exactly when and what to eat. Maybe some people would feel restricted, but I feel like a weight has been lifted off my shoulders. They are still doing some testing to find my ideal macro and micro nutrient values, but I think we are in the right range. I feel great."

"I think that's the whole point," I say. "The goal of Tier 1 is to provide needed resources to help people function at their best, which leaves more brain space and energy for innovation, creativity, efficiency, and social responsibility. I am sure Grace will talk more about that tonight." I smile.

"I love it so far," Cassidy says.

Servers are setting salads at our table now. Two more people are behind our table, waiting for the food to be placed so they can sit. Nick recognizes them and helps them find their seats. From here on out, it will be small talk. I am grateful and slightly disappointed at the same time.

"Hey, Cassidy, can we get together at some point in the next week or so? I really would love to learn more about Tier 2, and I felt like you would be the perfect person to ask, if that's ok."

"Absolutely. I have some things I wanted to ask you about, too. Let's do it," she says, as she reaches for her water.

Nick hasn't said much since Cassidy arrived. I put my fork to my lips, observing, and allow the others to take care of the introductions. Glancing back at Eric's table, I catch his eye, and we exchange smiles. In that moment, I sense Nick looking my direction. Lowering my head, I continue picking at the lettuce on my plate, pretending I am none the wiser.

CHAPTER 22

A FEW MINUTES after we receive our main course, Grace takes the stage. She moves to the side of a large display and addresses the room.

"Thank you so much to everyone for coming tonight. We are especially pleased to welcome our new initiates." At that, the room erupts with applause. Grace is smiling and nodding at the initiate tables. "I wanted to take a few minutes to talk about Tier 1 and what you are accepting and receiving by joining us here. I know some of this information will be familiar to many of you, but now that you have progressed to the point of transitioning, we feel like we can be a bit more candid." A large chart appears on the display.

"This chart reflects real resource counts at the time that the Berg Committee was asked to take control of the government back in 2091. Obviously, the entire world was in flux, so this is the best data they had at the time. The first thing that the Committee did after quarantining those affected by the virus was to take inventory of all available resources. People were terrified. They were dying, starving, infected, or scared of becoming infected. There was no time to waste; they simply had to act." A large map appears with three highlighted areas.

"Those who had not been exposed were immediately set up in safety zones, and people from around the world were rapidly migrating to what then constituted the Central United States, Southern Italy, and Central Asia. These safety zones were instituted through the help of the UN and world military leaders. The world population was decreasing dramatically every day. Anyone wanting to come in or out of these safe zones was tested for exposure. Individuals who had been exposed had to wait weeks to be cleared, before entering. Unfortunately, many people from around the world did not have the time or resources necessary to reach these zones. The virus had a death rate of over sixty percent, and it quickly spread to every corner of the earth. Global travel at the time made it impossible to contain. The Committee tried to assist people, but again, in a crisis situation, there was only so much that could be done." I hear some errant chatter throughout the room. Grace waits for silence before continuing. A picture comes into focus, showing queues of people receiving food at a rations table.

"Available resources were few. People couldn't risk going outside of the safety zones for months. The Berg Committee immediately initiated testing on the virus that had been released. They needed to know more about the replication cycle, possible mutations, and potential treatments. Life expectancy during the Crisis was already low, due to the unhealthy habits we know all too much about, but the decrease of inoculations in the general population left people particularly weak, and therefore susceptible to this virus. Berg was tasked with not only learning the weaknesses of the virus, but also determining how to strengthen immune systems in the survivors and those fighting the infection. In the meantime, people within the safety zones needed food, water, and places to sleep."

Numbers appear on the display. "In the two weeks after the virus, we went from a world population of 8 billion people to approximately 3 billion. Our world was absolutely devastated and in chaos. I am sure you can imagine the fear and widespread panic."

She clicks ahead to the next image. "Weeks after that, we were left with an estimated 1.8 billion total population, many of those on their own and unable to seek help. Our Central United States safe zone held only 3 million people." The display goes dark and the room is eerily silent.

"With limited resources, the Committee had to determine a way to allocate them. Who should receive food? Water? Medical help? These were not determinations that Berg took lightly. With initial data collected in the safe zones, they projected that 90% of individuals residing there were age 9-28. As we would expect, the virus had affected those beyond their physical prime most severely. Using the available genetic data and research, Berg put together a proposal for resource allocation. Individuals who were clean, the top disease markers absent, and who were within the age range of 9-18 years old would be given first priority to ensure survival of the species. Some of you may recognize this as the original Tier 1. Tier 2, comprised of those ages 9-24 who had no more than ten disease markers, or those age 19 or older who were clean, would receive up to seventy-five percent of the resources they needed. This, of course, would be limited by availability after Tier 1 received their share. Tier 3 was anyone outside of these limits. They would receive the remainder of available resources."

I scan our table to see how the initiates are receiving this information. Tier 2 is taught this history, but I doubt they have heard it in such depth. Cassidy is completely engrossed, her body leaning toward the podium, lips slightly parted.

Grace continues. "As you know, this system was successful in that it allowed for repopulation and growth. Years later, after the safety zones were dissolved, the decision had to be made whether to keep this Tier system or go back to the way things were previously.

The Committee debated and reviewed their research extensively, ultimately deciding that continuing on was the best way to avoid the pitfalls that had created the Crisis in the first place. By centralizing resources, Berg could ensure low waste, sustainability, environmental healing, and specific practices to begin healing our own bodies and minds. They could also ensure that those who had the greatest chance of living healthy lives, contributing to society in meaningful ways, and creating viable offspring would receive society's greatest assistance."

Pictures begin slowly sliding across the display. Families. Farms. New technology. Nature.

"We are still a healing society. We don't have all the answers. Yet. But our numbers have increased dramatically in the years since these events. Our careful and precise organization of resources and terrahealing projects have resulted in increased resources and opportunities for all. We are still fighting to live longer, healthier, more meaningful lives. Tier 1 is where you will have the opportunity to continue to progress, not only individually, but together as a community. By committing to live within these proven patterns of success, you will be given resources and opportunities to truly become your best self.

Your core needs will be met so that you can focus on serving others and reaching your highest potential. This, in turn, serves society not only in the obvious, tangible ways, but through what you create, what you think, and who you become. We are thrilled to have you here tonight, and we are committed to your continued success. Our programs will allow us to support and mentor you, as you learn and develop. Thank you for taking this important first step in a beautiful new path." Grace smiles and steps back from the podium as the room applauds enthusiastically.

When the noise dies down, she says "I would like to invite Kate Bailey and Nick Standeford to come forward and introduce each of our new initiates this evening."

This is it. I stand, and Nick touches my elbow to steady me as I navigate around the chairs. I remind myself that this is a service I am providing and nothing more. There is no reason to feel nervous in front of my friends and peers. The reframing works. Kind of.

We had agreed that Nick would go first. He is charming, as always, and begins with a couple of jokes that pull a good response from the crowd.

The first initiate is an eighteen-year-old with very impressive scans. The pictures I arranged are slowly scrolling on the display as Nick talks. I look toward the back of the room and see Eric giving me a thumbs up. Nick continues to work through the other initiates on his list, but then I hear his last sentence, and know it is my turn.

My heart begins to race. That went a lot faster than expected. I take my place next to him and begin with Max, a 32-year-old man whom I have gotten to know fairly well over the last few years. I show examples of his expertise in engineering. Max is grinning at a table below, and I see many others in the audience sharing glances, obviously impressed with his work. He will integrate in no time.

Eventually, I make it to Cassidy. I see her shift in her seat uncomfortably as her name is mentioned. I begin talking about her ability to nurture and serve, how strongly she is inclined towards caring for others and being a mother someday. I smile inwardly.

Before the Crisis, these characteristics wouldn't have been so highly regarded. I think of my mother. She taught me through word and example that these humble qualities are what society needs. More people who were selfless, who understand that their neighbors are extensions of themselves. Individuals who are willing to put in the work to watch someone, or something, grow.

As I finish, people begin to applaud and some rise from their seats, looking toward the initiates. I will have to ask Shari and Eric how it came across, but based on that reaction, I think we did our part to begin their transitions on good footing.

Grace retakes the stage and asks us to exit through the side door. For a moment, I don't move. While speaking, perhaps triggered by Grace's earlier historical account, I was overwhelmed with a thought that hadn't crossed my mind before. I haven't ever felt criticized or 'less-than' for following this path. I have never lacked for anything. My life involves sacrifice, yes, but not like Cassidy. Not like Max. My commitment to serve with all that I am is again deepened and rolls through me with intensity.

Nick nudges me and we walk together behind the curtains. Then, in the dark, we somehow have to find our way back to the ballroom. We probably should have practiced this part. It's pitch black and we giggle like children, feeling our way around looking for the entrance. Suddenly, Nick's arms are around me and before I can react, he spins me toward him. His face is inches from mine and his energy is electric.

"Kate, you did great. I just wanted to tell you before we go back out there. I know Eric is here and you will go with him and—well, I won't get a chance to talk to you privately. I have loved these last few weeks. I love talking with you and hearing what you think. I love watching you with the boys. I love your food," he laughs. "I know you're paired, but hearing the heartache that you are going through has brought up...I guess, I have just been thinking a lot. You shouldn't be alone. I want you to know that I will always be there for you." My skin is tingling and the air feels slow and thick. I have to remind myself to breathe. He lets his arms fall to the side and I am at a complete loss for words. I have enjoyed the last few weeks, too, and I feel close to Nick, but my desperation for human contact and affection makes it impossible for me to think rationally.

If Eric hadn't kissed me earlier, I would be in real trouble right now. I have probably given Nick some strange signals with Eric being out of town. Has he wondered if we are splitting as a pair? Is he interested in me like that? Does he think I am interested in *him* like that? I can't be. I'm paired, and I love Eric. I love him deep in my bones. Sure, Nick is attractive to me and fun, but that doesn't come close to the intimacy that grows from years of growth and perseverance together. Serving side by side. Knowing every piece of a person.

I step back. "Nick, thank you. I appreciate you and all that you have done for our family. I am so sorry if I said or did anything that gave you the impression that Eric and I aren't planning to stay together. Our boys are so young— "

Nick cuts me off. "No, you haven't given me that impression at all. I just...I know how difficult things could still be for you in the future with all of this pressure on Eric. I need you to know that you have me. I'm all in." His lips brush my cheek and he walks out the side door that is now, obviously, right behind me. All in!? What does that even mean? All in for Bentley? All in as a supportive friend? I stand there, steeping in my confusion for a minute, attempting to compose myself.

Standing alone in the dark I realize that I am not going to be able to figure this out in the next five minutes. Meanwhile, Eric is out there waiting for me. I hear the initiates on stage taking the Tier 1 oath. "...accept that where much is given, much is required...". I burst through the side door and walk briskly down the hallway to enter the ballroom near the back. I sigh when I see him. Eric.

CHAPTER 23

As soon as he sees me, he rushes my way, smiling. We embrace, and in that moment I forget about the recent turbulence and all of the uneasiness that has become commonplace over the last few weeks.

"What do you say we get out of here?" he suggests, raising his eyebrow.

"Yes." I agree immediately. "Do you have a different car here, or can we go together?"

"I was dropped off. I was hoping to catch a ride home with you."

"Done," I say, already walking toward the door, grabbing his hand and pulling him along. We are stalled a couple of times by people thanking me or recognizing Eric and wanting to discuss his research. Eventually we make it out and head down the stairs to the car request. I feel more nervous now than before I spoke. It feels like I am on a first date, but we've already used up all of our conversation starters. My blood feels electric, and my jaw is chattering despite the perfectly comfortable air temperature. Every move he makes sends my heart racing. Eric and I stand there, holding hands, and staring into the street. The car arrives, and Eric opens the door for me. I settle into the seat as Eric jumps in on the other side. As soon as the door shuts, he unbuckles my seatbelt and pulls me onto his lap. I laugh and then hear the sensor alarm, announcing that I am unbuckled. Eric reaches around me and re-buckles my seatbelt, then throws his bag on the seat to simulate body weight. He swiftly enters a code into the drive bar to manu-ally indicate unsafe driving conditions. The car immediately slows down by 35 MPH. Looks like our drive home will be taking a little longer than normal. I don't have time to speak before Eric is kissing me.

When we arrive in the garage, we quickly re-dress, giggling like teenagers, and try to make ourselves look presentable. It's not really possible, but we make our best effort. Stephen and Liz give us a sidelong glance as we walk into the kitchen.

"Eric! I didn't know you were back, man," Stephen says and gives him a hug, clapping his shoulder.

"It was kind of a surprise for Kate. I have to fly back tomorrow morning after breakfast," Eric says, grinning.

"Well, we won't take up any more of your time," Liz says. "The boys did great. They will be so excited to see their dad in the morning."

"Thanks for being here. We really appreciate it," I say as Eric puts his arm around me.

"Our pleasure." Stephen says as they put their shoes on. We wave as they walk down the steps.

"They sure left in a hurry," Eric comments.

"I wonder why," I say teasingly.

I feel Eric's hand migrating down my back and I reach around and grab it.

"Not so fast. We need to talk first. Eric, I have been dying the last few weeks. I have felt so disjointed and alone. I know you can't talk with me about everything, but you need to give me something. I don't know what to think! I have been living in some weird sort of limbo, not knowing what was happening, not knowing if you were moving on...now this?"

My throat catches, and I quickly turn around and open the cupboard to get a glass of water. I know it didn't fool Eric, but I don't want to cry right now. But then his hands around my waist, and I can't hold it in. I turn and sob into his chest. He holds me, not saying a word.

When I can breathe normally again, I pick up my glass off the counter and fill it. The water soothes my throat, calming my nerves.

"We need to talk." Eric states, matter-of-factly.

"I think I just established that."

"But I said it now, so it's official," he grins. I've missed him so much. He turns on the faucet. "Seriously, Kate. We need to talk."

He tenses, and the worry and fear come rushing back.

"Eric, if you are messing with me with all of this physical energy, that is not cool. If you have something to say to me, just say it." I turn the faucet off and step back to look him in the eyes. He flicks the faucet back on and my eyebrows furrow.

"Leave it on. Just in case." He looks at me seriously, hesitating. "Berg has asked me to leave you," he says under his breath.

I stare at him bewildered. "What? Why would they do that?"

"Whisper," he mouths.

"Do they want you full time at headquarters?" I say more quietly and start frantically wiping the counters.

"No, Kate—"

"We could move there with you if that's the issue. I would happily change locations for my service—"

"No. Kate. It's more complicated than that." He puts his hands on my shoulders, and I stop.

"What do you mean?"

"You're a match." He puts his hands down, defeated.

"I'm a match? For what?"

"For..." he sighs. "For Nick."

"What?" I look at him confused. "Nick says he isn't looking for a pairing, and it makes no sense to run a pairing scan with someone who is *already paired*." I have no idea what he is trying to say.

"Kate. You're alleles match for TSG's. Berg initially told me there were eight matches in our region. There are actually nine. I haven't been at headquarters to train. I've been there to be away from you. To give you and Nick time to get to know each other. To hopefully create some distance between us."

I am dizzy. I shut off the faucet and walk into the living room. Eric comes and sits beside me. We sit and stare.

"I think we should go take a shower," he says after a few minutes, pulling me up after him.

We strip down and get into our cramped shower together. It's difficult to move, but at least the close quarters make it warm and steamy.

"Do you think we are being listened to?" I ask.

"I don't think so, but I have seen and heard some things over the last few weeks that just make me want to be careful." He grabs the soap and starts scrubbing my back.

"What kinds of things?" I ask. I haven't ever heard of the committee violating someone's privacy before.

"Nothing I can really put my finger on. I have just seen how seriously they are taking this research. They fully believe that this discovery supersedes all individual rights. I don't know if I believe that or not. Maybe I should? I watched them pull in those other pairs and completely turn their lives upside down. I experienced all of those same concerns that you brought up initially. It didn't feel right to dictate how people will be living their lives from now on. I know we do that in guided ways in Tier 1 every day, but this felt more, I don't know. Tangible. Real. More in your face, you know?"

"I do," I agree quietly.

"Kate I am completely dedicated to this project. If someone would have told me that they found a pair, but one of the individuals was a mother and paired already, I don't know that I would have hesitated to agree with the recommendations to pull her out of her pairing and start new. I am a hypocrite. I would have cringed a little, but I never would have stopped it. Then I find out that it's you. My pair. Instead of complying, I find a reason to come to you and then tell you confidential information..." He rubs his face with his hands.

"You weren't authorized to tell me?" I ask.

"No, of course not. This whole plan was in place to organically—at least on your side—separate us and then re-pair you with Nick."

I shudder. "Does Nick know? Do you honestly think that would have worked? What about the boys?" My mind is spinning.

"I do think it would have worked. You would have hated me, but I think you would have needed a partner with me out of the picture."

"I don't think I would have *jumped* into Nick's arms." I push away from him, hitting the cold, back wall of the shower. "Seriously Eric? And you didn't answer my question. Does he know?"

He pauses and pulls me closer. "Yes. He knows. And maybe it wouldn't have worked. The committee seemed to think that your profile would be compliant with this strategy."

"So all of this interaction with Nick has been planned? Is he actually Bentley's mentor?" Disgust wells up inside me. I feel used.

"I honestly don't know," he sighs. "But yes, I think a lot of your interactions with him have been planned. The timing of the mentor match is highly suspect in my opinion." He turns, and I scrub his back.

"Why? Why would they do this?" I hear myself ask. "Why wouldn't they just come to us and present the information?"

"Kate, you know the answer to that. You are so loyal. You never would have gotten on board."

"Maybe I am only loyal to society. My genetics may code me for that, but how does anyone know what I am loyal to?" I ask belligerently.

Eric turns and cups my face in his hands. "I know what you are loyal to."

I breathe deeply. It's true. And Berg knows it too.

"This doesn't make any sense, Eric. Everything we do is to make our conditioning ideal—family life is central to that. Why would they rip our family apart to create a new one? If it's just about genetic progeny, why can't they artificially inseminate and we can raise more children? I know it's not specifically ideal for us, but wouldn't it be better than this!?"

Eric runs his hands along my collarbone and doesn't respond immediately. "According to the Committee, that isn't better. They ran risk-benefit analyses for all of the potential pairs and cross-evaluated those results with personality markers. They did their research, Kate. You have to know by now how invested Berg is in individuals like Nick. They represent our future. Not only genetically, but also in terms of the contributions they can make."

"You can't tell me that Nick takes priority over you. Look at the contributions you have made—"

"Exactly, Kate," Eric cuts me off. "I made my big contribution. I am done, as far as Berg is concerned."

"Done? Being a father is as much a contribution as any research, as far as *I* am concerned. Did they factor that in?" I ask, my frustration palpable.

Eric laughs, but I don't find it funny. "I'm sorry!" he says. "You are just really cute when you're mad." He sobers up fairly quickly when he sees my face. "To answer your question," he continues, "yes, they did factor that in. Young kids, with the use of reversal therapy and a new, stable figure in their lives, can recover from the loss of a parent fairly quickly."

"Tal is not that young anymore," I quip.

"Tal is not who they are concerned about," Eric shoots back. This gives me pause. Of course Berg is mostly concerned about Bentley. And Nick. All my life I have accepted that priority should be given to genetically-superior individuals. But I didn't see it ever working like this. Not with my family.

"So, what now? What do we do? You have to go back in the morning, and I just...keep hanging out with Nick and pretend like I don't know anything?" I say.

"I don't know," Eric says softly, wrapping his arms around me. "I'm torn. On the one hand, I absolutely don't want to lose you and the boys. I don't know that I *can* lose you and be ok. These last few weeks have been torture. Hence the reason I am standing here. Naked. In the shower with you." He gives me a devilish grin and I smack his arm.

"But on the other hand, I am being completely selfish," he continues. "Have I become some Tier 2 individual who only looks out for himself? We have a responsibility to do what is best for society. Up until now, that has meant building a strong unit for our kids. Raising them, serving society through our research and mentoring, exploring new ideas and supporting people in their own self-discovery. Now there is this. We have an opportunity to be the pioneers in eliminating pain and suffering in future generations. So, as much as I can't lose you," he runs his hands through his wet hair, "can I live knowing that I chose myself over thousands of people?"

I look at the conflict in his face. A weight settles on my chest. Not knowing what else to say, I hold him. After a few minutes, my body begins to overheat, so I gently kiss his cheek and open the shower door. Steam billows around me into the cool air of the bathroom. Pulling my towel from the rack, I slowly begin to dry off.

CHAPTER 24

WE WAKE EARLY so that Eric can have some time with the boys before he has to fly out. Tal and Bentley are both surprised and elated to see their dad home. Eric wrestles with them while I make breakfast, and my heart is finally in a state of peace. I guess that's strange, considering all of the information I received last night, but it's just so comforting to know. Nothing in my life was making sense.. Now that all the pieces have clicked into place, I can at least start to deal with it. Thankfully, I have enough information to start processing the best options and outcomes.

If only I could believe that none of the responsibility for these future decisions rested on me. To believe that my brain would, over time, calculate the best option based on my previous experience and wiring, and that action would be inevitable. I could passively watch that process occur and not worry about whether my action was right or wrong, better or worse. It would be the only action my mind and body could come to—learning and progressing through a feedback loop. There wouldn't need to be any stress or regret. I continue whipping the eggs. It seems like a cop out.

We spend another hour together, then Eric has to leave. I hug him tightly, and I can tell he doesn't want to go. We all wave to him from the front porch, my newly validated self standing tall, watching his car drive away.

Almost immediately, upon reentering the house, my sensor dings. It's Nick, and I don't answer. How am I going to handle this? I can't say anything or let on that I know. I definitely don't want to give Eric any trouble. I have to act like nothing has changed, but I don't think I know what that would look like. Think. What space was I in before I saw Eric the other night? I probably would have answered Nick's call gratefully. I quickly call back after shooing the boys off to get dressed for the day. My assignments have been postponed this week. With all that was involved with preparing for the ceremony, the health center decided to lower my schedule. Initially, I was grateful, but now, I am desperately in need of a distraction.

"Hey Kate, how are you doing this morning?" Nick says, answering the call. I can practically hear the grin on his face.

"I'm good. Eric just left to go back to headquarters, and the boys are getting dressed. How are you?"

"I'm great." He pauses. "I didn't see you again after we went back into the ballroom, so I just wanted to make sure everything was ok."

"Yes, sorry. Eric and I left right after that. We wanted to spend some time together before he had to leave again."

"I totally understand," Nick says, a little too quickly. "Is Bentley available to go play some ball this afternoon? I am done with my shift at one o'clock and thought it would be a good time to hang out. We could play at the park across from your house, so it doesn't require any extra time for you."

"That would be great. Just message when you are on your way and we'll meet you there," I say.

"See you then!" He signs off and I lay my head in my hands. I have until one o'clock to figure out how ignorant Kate would act.

All morning, I go through scenarios in my head. If Eric came back and didn't say anything, what would that night have been like? Probably frustrating. It probably would have ended up like the last few conversations we tried to have weeks ago. I try to engage him in conversation, he responds noncommittally, I try to remain calm but can't help a little annoyance creeping into my tone, he gets frustrated, I get upset, and we each go to bed not talking anymore. Ok. If that had happened, how would I be feeling? Alone. Scared. Angry. If alone, scared, and angry Kate went to the park to meet Nick, what would she be doing? Noticing him. Enjoying his companionship. Seeking validation that she is, in fact, not crazy. It is disturbingly easy to drop back into that space, but I go with it. Good enough.

Nick should be here in about ten minutes, so I walk with the boys across to the park and push Bent on the swings while we wait. I suddenly realize I haven't talked with Shari since the cafe. I should probably call her so she knows I am not upset. I don't have time for a full conversation now, so I send her a message just as I see Nick's car pull up. He doesn't get out right away, so eventually I walk over to the window and find him sleeping on the pull-down cot. I can't help but smile. He looks so young, almost boyish. He opens his eyes and I look away, embarrassed that I was staring at him. I step back as he opens the car door.

"I'm so sorry, I didn't think I would fall so deeply asleep. I guess I haven't fully recovered from last night." Nick yawns as he reaches into the trunk. His hair is wild, and his movements are a little out of sorts. It's hard not to be amused, watching him try to act normally. He pulls out three gloves and a baseball. "I brought an extra for Tal. I didn't want him to feel left out."

"What about me? I feel left out now." I pretend to pout.

Nick laughs. "I did *not* think that you would be into baseball. We can rotate in?"

"I'm kidding. I'll throw a few, but then I actually have some files to catch up on from last week. I was planning to work on those while you guys play."

"Sounds good." He looks over to see the boys running our way. They have finally noticed he is here.

"We haven't checked out sports equipment in weeks. I think they are slightly excited," I laugh.

Nick jogs over to them, and they start sorting out who will use which glove. I leave them to it and head over to set up my tablet at one of the benches. Working through my notes, I find it difficult to stay focused. My eyes keep straying to where Nick is playing with the boys. I am doing a pretty bang up job of pretending to be ignorant Kate.

Allowing my thoughts to stray, I wonder if I could actually be happy with Nick. Could I give up Eric and make a new life with him? What would happen with the boys? I assume they would stay with me. Eric would definitely be sacrificing the most. He would be alone with his research while I still had our family. I would be able to have more kids, and I have to admit, this thought is tempting. Eric and I were maxed at three with our genetic matching. I glance around, irrationally nervous that someone would be able to sense my disloyalty for even entertaining the idea of this new life, but I remind myself that I need to explore all the options. I owe it to myself and to Eric. I play out the different possibilities:

Option one. Eric stays and gives up his involvement in the research. I don't even know what that means for our family. We obviously would not be keeping our commitment to put society above self. Would we be allowed to stay Tier 1? I have heard of people removing themselves and settling into Tier 2. Could that be a possibility for us—stay together, but sacrifice Tier 1? What would that mean for our kids? They wouldn't have the resources they need to fulfil their potential. So we stay together, but sacrifice our kids' future? That makes me feel sick. Maybe we stay together and move to Tier 2, but leave the kids with new parents in Tier 1? More sick.

Option two. Eric stays and somehow they allow us to remain Tier 1. They decide that our contributions to society are high enough that they won't require me to re-pair with Nick. Or maybe they find more pairs and it's not as necessary. Eric spends the rest of his life knowing that I am his selfish choice. Every day, he looks at me and feels worse about himself, becoming withdrawn and volatile over time. Maybe we stay together, but maybe we split up because we can't handle the pain we are causing each other.

Option three. Eric and I separate and I re-pair with Nick. We have children (quickly, because I'm getting old) and we do reversal therapy on Tal and Bentley, so they don't feel the loss of their dad so acutely. Or maybe Eric is still involved? No, that would be too hard for me. Eric is not involved at all. The boys lose their dad and I lose my other half. Literally. But, I am not alone, and Nick and I would likely grow close. The kids have the resources they need. We start the process of fulfilling Eric's life work. I miss him but am serving him every day by creating new potential for generations. Eric misses me, but he sees the good he has done. He re-pairs with someone else, most likely. He may even have more kids, too. We start over. We still love each other, just not together.

I know Eric. He is so dedicated to this program and how it could change the course of humanity. He believes in this research one hundred percent. He will not be able to just get over a choice that will make it more difficult for society to progress. My options are not to keep things the same or change; they have already changed. Eric and I won't ever be the same. This thought lands heavy on my heart.

My fingers pause on the display, and I am lost in thought, remembering a time early in our pairing when we didn't have children yet. I woke up one morning feeling lazy and tired. I needed time to recharge, and I wanted Eric to recharge with me. I laugh thinking about 'needing more time for myself' when I had multiple hours of discretionary time every day. That morning, though, I felt completely justified for wanting a break—I had been working hard and hadn't taken any time off all year. I rolled over to Eric and jokingly pouted, asking him to play hooky and stay home with me. I laid out a perfect day, with all of his favorite activities. He had research planned at the lab, and I remember being slightly offended that he wasn't even tempted to blow things off. I remember him, even then, saying that this research could change hundreds of lives. Our day of fun would only give us momentary pleasure and wouldn't even change anything for us, not really. Despite my protestations that this day *could* be life-changing, he didn't bend. I ended up going in for my shift that day, and it solidi-fied what I had already known about Eric: he was always going to put others first. The potential to help society was always going to outweigh selfish desires for him, and it always has.

The fact that he is struggling with this decision now shakes me. If Eric—the one person I have always counted on to be my compass— is tempted to choose us, I don't want to be the reason for his regret. I don't want him to go against his core beliefs. I know what I have to do, but I don't know if I have the strength to do it.

I type a quick message to Eric saying, 'I love you. Go save the world. I will do what I can to make sure your research moves forward.' I hope it is cryptic enough, but that he understands what I mean. My heart starts to beat fast. Is this right? Am I really going to do this? I close my tablet before I can bring myself to press send. I should at least sleep on it. Placing my things to the side, I walk over to play some baseball.

CHAPTER 25

THAT EVENING, Nick and I are sitting in the living room after I put the boys to bed. I don't know how to do this. I haven't flirted in fifteen years. I feel really, really old right now. Doubts come rushing into my head. He is so young. Why would he even want to be with me? Does he actually want this? Is he only doing this out of a sense of duty? I am doing it because I love another man, so I guess that's not much better. I speak, to break the silence.

"Nick, what you said last night— "

"I am sorry if that was weird," he cuts in. "I was so full of energy and warmth toward you. I realize I may have crossed a line. I didn't mean to overstep."

"No, I know. I have been thinking a lot about it. Eric and I talked some last night, but it ended like it always does," I lie. I never lie. My palms are sweating. "When he showed up at the ceremony, I hoped that he had returned to get our relationship back on track. I shouldn't have gotten my hopes up and am realizing that he needs to be invested in his research right now. This discovery is huge, with such far-reaching consequences. I don't know what that means for me, but I think it's obvious that Eric and I are drifting further apart every day. I worry about the boys, and I worry about being alone. I really appreciated knowing that you are here for us." I pause. "Here for me." My hands are shaky. This feels so wrong, but I can't see any option that keeps our family intact long-term.

"Of course I'm here for you. I'm sorry this is so hard." His face is sincere. I know he is probably very open to this change of direction, but he is also a genuine guy. I haven't seen anything in him that is self-serving. He only wants to do what is expected of him. He probably feels like he is making a huge sacrifice trying to settle in with me when he could have some beautiful, perfect 18-year-old bursting with energy and ideals. We are a sorry pair. At least he doesn't know that I know. Maybe that will count for something.

"I don't know where to go from here," I say. "I can't keep playing this game with Eric. It's killing me, and I think it's adding stress for the boys. They can see I am not myself." My emotions are so close to the surface that I stop talking, in fear of breaking down. Nick moves to the seat next to me and puts his hand on my knee and my body responds. Every time he touches me, my heart races a little bit—proof that we are genetically a good pair. I try to keep this realization in the forefront of my mind, so I won't chicken out.

"Kate, I would never...try to come between a pair. Ever. But these last few weeks have been slightly torturous for me. I am really attracted to you—"

"Nick—"

"No," he cuts me off. "Just let me finish, and then you can say what you need to say. I am really attracted to you. Like, really attracted. Every night, I go home and try to stop my brain from making up stories where we are together—where I met you before Eric did."

"You literally would have been a baby." I look at him seriously.

"I know, I know," he laughs. "In my daydreams, I'm the same age, though. Just roll with it. I have a hard time shutting it down. I think about you constantly. I love your kids, too, which doesn't help. All I've ever wanted is to find a pair, have a big family, and then follow whatever path will allow me to make this world a better place. Up until now, I haven't found anyone— "

"But— "

"I know!" He puts his hands up. "It sounds ridiculous, just stick with me. I need to explain. Of course I could have paired with a number of other women. I dated a lot, right when I turned eighteen, and everyone hit the minimum requirement. But nobody matched all of the most important markers. More concerning, nobody felt like my equal. It seemed like I would always be settling. I think I told you about the one girl I tried to make things work with. Honestly, she did me a favor. I wouldn't have been fulfilled; I was trying to do what was expected of me, but it didn't feel right."

I cut in, "And somehow, you think that you wouldn't be settling for me? I have so many flawed markers. I have been a mother and health assistant for my 'career.' My brain and body are used. I'm

28, Nick." I look at him, aghast. I wonder if he will come clean and tell me that Berg ordered him to pair with me.

He looks embarrassed. "Maybe your age and experience are what attract me so much. Maybe I was never meant to be with someone my own age. Maybe that's why I never felt like I could find someone who complimented me. I also—" he swallows hard, "I ran our numbers," he blurts out.

"What?"

"I ran our numbers. In a weak moment. I am so sorry. It was a total violation of privacy."

I am confused. And slightly upset that he isn't being totally honest with me about what he knows and how he knows it.

"How? The system doesn't allow you to run numbers on people who are already paired."

"I— " He looks down at his lap, his olive skin flushing. "Grace gave me clearance. She didn't know that's what I wanted. I told her that I needed access to run files for the ceremony. The following week, I was told that I would be Bentley's mentor. A part of me felt like I should decline, knowing my personal feelings, but I couldn't make myself do it."

Oh, I'm sure Grace knew exactly what she was doing. Is it possible that Nick wasn't in on this? That he was just gently guided in my direction? I try to keep my face straight as I analyze this possibility. Would that mean...that he *is* actually attracted to me? Heat rises to my face.

I clear my throat. "So, what did you find?"

"We are an incredible match, Kate. We far exceed the minimum match required for pairing. We wouldn't be limited to only one or two children. When I saw that, and I already knew that I was attracted to you, I...well, that's why I was so forward the other night. I feel terrible about how I acted. It was not okay for me to take advantage of that moment. Seeing Eric, so intent to be with you, made me a little bit desperate." He rubs his face with his hands. He looks exhausted.

"I had let myself hope that Eric might choose his research over family and that I could swoop in, but just saying that out loud makes me feel like a jerk." He starts speaking quickly. "Eric is obviously an amazing guy, and you have all of this history together. I am sorry, Kate. I don't know what I was thinking." He stands up, speaking more deliberately. "I feel sick just talking about this. I got carried away and I am fully aware of how selfish my actions have been. Rest assured, I will learn from this and move forward." He purses his lips and turns toward the door. As he walks past me, his hand brushes my chair and I reach out, grazing his fingers.

"Nick," I say softly. He stops, but doesn't turn around. "You aren't selfish." He is standing stock still. "Wanting to help others doesn't mean you have to be a complete martyr."

"It doesn't mean that I put my wants above those of another, Kate," he says, still facing the hall.

"Sometimes sacrifice isn't black and white. I have gotten to know you well these last few months. I don't think you would pursue anything you didn't feel was for the greatest good."

Nick turns around slowly and braces his arms on the chair, still not meeting my eyes. "How do I know that the greater good is worth short-term loss? Especially when it means *I* don't lose anything? I only gain," he asks quietly. "How do I know that I'm not justifying the 'greater good' for something I want?"

We sit in silence for a moment. "You don't," I finally answer. "I don't think we ever have enough information to know *for sure* that any one choice will end with the exact consequence we antici- pated. But, we can learn from past experience. In this case, looking at the results of past matches, we can be fairly certain that Eric's research is going to change our world. It will most likely change the lives of thousands—and then millions—of people. If he needs to dedicate his life there, how ridiculous would it be for me to stop him? I'm one person. *That* would be selfish." I try to avoid saying anything that would give Nick the wrong impression. That I know it's about more than Eric's dedication to his project.

He raises his eyes and looks at me, a pained expression on his face. "I know that I'm just a kid with very little relationship know-how. Like none," he laughs. "Unless you count dinner and small talk experience, which I have in spades." I laugh nervously. "I am in no way, shape, or form trying to take Eric's place. If you two work things out, I will do my very best to not—" He pauses and takes a deep breath, "To not look at you or want to be with you. I will help Bentley and do all I can to mentor him and aid him in reaching his potential."

He shakes his head in frustration and makes his way to the door to put his shoes on. I follow a few steps behind, stopping to lean against a wall. When the laces are tied, he stands and looks hard at me. I meet his gaze with a rather tentative smile.

"I will give you space to figure all of this out with Eric," he promises. "I won't bring it up again, and I will be strictly professional when I come to see Bentley." Sudden realization dawns on his face. "Oh wow, we need to set up a time in the next couple of days," he says, flustered. "I just realized we didn't make a plan for that. Do you know what will work?" he says, suddenly all business, tapping his sensor.

"Nick," I say slowly, "I'm not saying no." I stare at him intently, trying to look like I'm speaking with conviction.

He stops and lifts his eyes to meet mine. "No to getting together with Bentley?"

"No."

He thinks on this a moment. "You aren't?" he asks, with a quizzical brow.

"No."

A shy smile creeps onto his face and his cheeks flush. "I can deal with not a no."

Mustering my courage, I step over and pull him into a hug. He hesitantly puts his arms around my shoulders. He feels different from Eric, but still good. Solid. I breathe him in. I haven't had to be vulnerable with anyone new for a long time. It's scary and electrifying. I think of Eric, any excitement quickly fading to nausea, and pull back slowly, ending the hug awkwardly. I give him a half-wave goodbye, then he walks out the door. I rush to the bedroom and rummage through my bag to find my tablet, sending the message to Eric before I can find another excuse to wait. Tapping his contact, I block his number. It's done. I focus on what makes sense, rather than what my heart is screaming at me. Bile rises in my throat and run to the washroom.

CHAPTER 26

I CAN'T WAIT another second to call Shari, and am relieved when she is available to talk. Though I don't know how much she knows, or how much I should say, I need to bounce this off of someone.

"Hey friend." Shari says, smiling. "Long time, no talk."

"I know. I'm so sorry. We are due for a long chat and ideally, a lunch."

"What's been going on? You were fantastic at the ceremony. Did you see me? I was seated a few tables away from Eric in the back. I got to watch the whole show."

"You mean the whole ceremony?"

"No, I mean the whole show between you, Eric, and Nick."

"What are you talking about?"

Shari laughs. "Don't pretend to be that oblivious! Eric with his

222 / CINDY GUNDERSON

hands all over you, Nick watching you all night while you talked with Cassidy. You looking uncomfortable. It was amazing. I loved it."

I groan. "Was it that obvious?"

"Oh, chill out. I doubt anybody noticed besides me. And Grace. She was definitely looking your direction more than I would normally expect."

"Great," I mutter.

"Everyone else was so involved with their own agendas for the evening, I doubt they gave it a second thought. Except when Eric kissed you. A lot of people watched that."

I groan again.

"No, that was awesome. Who wouldn't want everyone to see how bonded they are with their pair? They were inspired." She laughs at the look on my face.

"Not so inspiring when you find out that was the first night Eric and I have spent together in weeks."

"It's that bad, huh?"

"It's that bad."

"Is he back down at headquarters?"

"Flew out the next morning. I don't know what the boys are thinking at this point. Eric and I have both talked with them about his research and the need for him to be involved, but I don't know that they really understand what this means."

"What *does* it mean?" Shari asks, suddenly serious.

"I just meant that it might go on like this. For awhile."

"What's going on, Kate?" When I don't answer immediately, she says, "Never mind, I am coming over," and signs off before I can object.

Fifteen minutes later I hear a light knock on the door and Shari walks in, giving me a brief hug before charging into the kitchen.

"I brought some herbal tea I really like. Let me make it up, and then we can talk."

She starts water boiling, finds mugs, and unwraps the tea bags while I search the pantry for our recently harvested honey. Once our tea is steeping, we sit down in the living room.

"Ok, fill me in," she says, curling up in the chair and blowing on her tea.

"I don't know what to say," I complain weakly. She raises her eyebrow, as if disappointed in me, and I sigh. "Things are kind of imploding, I guess?"

"You guess?" she says sarcastically. "C'mon, Kate."

Though I know she is goading me, it works, and I begin talking in a rush, the words pouring out of me. "I don't know, Shari! Eric and I want to be together, but there are demands on him that have changed things. He believes in this project. If he stays with us, he will always feel like he let society down. If he stays there, he will always feel like he let us down. I miss him. The boys miss him. I am sick of doing this by myself, but I *would* keep going if I knew that he would be back at some point. I don't have any guarantees, and you told me yourself that it might be best to un-pair—"

"I didn't say 'best'," Shari cuts in, "just possible."

"Well, whatever." I take a sip, almost burning my tongue. "I don't know whether Eric is going to be able to make this decision. He isn't telling me everything." I pause, inspecting Shari's face. It is a mask of calm, though she seems inordinately engaged with her tea. She knows.

"So what am I supposed to do? Just wait? Hope that it all works out? Or move on?" I ask.

"What would moving on entail?" Shari asks nonchalantly, as if simply inquiring about the weather. The question makes my nostrils flare, but I mirror her tone.

"Really, the question should be: 'Is it even possible?'. I love Eric and can't imagine myself without him," I exhale deeply, "but, the boys need someone besides just me. And, honestly, I'm lonely." I hesitate. *I* need someone besides just me.

"Are you thinking that you want Stephen to be around more?" she asks, her voice sweet and innocent.

"You know I'm not talking about Stephen," I mutter acerbically under my breath.

Shari smiles, taking another sip of her tea. "Just keeping you honest."

"Yes, Nick is incredibly attractive," I say, throwing my hands up.

"But he's 8 years younger than I am. What, we pair, have some kids, then I die and he has to raise them on his own? I'm old, Shari. Why would he want to do that?"

"I don't know why, but I know that he does want to."

"How do you know?"

"He ran your numbers."

"How do you know that?" I ask, exasperated.

"I get notified anytime anyone looks at your file, Kate. I saw him poking around. And I saw how he looked at you at the ceremony. Do you want proof?" Without waiting to hear my response, she pulls up a video on her sensor. "This," she taps forward on the video, "is Nick's face while you were introducing Cassidy."

I watch myself speaking at the podium, impressed with myself. I actually do look quite nice. Then, my eyes are drawn over my left shoulder to where Nick stands, watching me. His face is engaged, smiling, intense.

"That's just Nick," I say. "He's always dialed up."

"Not like that, Kate." She turns off the video.

"Ok, let's say I do pair with Nick. What happens to the boys? And what if I can't have as many kids as he wants? Do I need to repeat myself? I am *old*! I have stretch marks. I have literal brain scans showing my mental decline—"

"Slight."

"What?" I ask.

"Slight mental decline," Shari corrects.

"Fine, *slight* mental decline, but still. We would have only seven more years before we would be risking major mutations through procreation. I would have to be pregnant the entire time to even get four babies here."

"You could do fertility. Maybe have a couple sets of twins?"

I throw a pillow at her.

She laughs. "Seriously, Kate. It's an option. And you don't know how long you are going to live. Your body is doing great, and you haven't seen any DNA deterioration yet. You could live into your fifties, easy."

"That's wishful thinking, but let's say that does happen. Nick could still procreate much more effectively with another person. Someone who is young."

"What help would that be if it wasn't as good of a match? Who cares if they could have more kids? The point is that your kids would be genetically superior. Quality over quantity."

"How could they be so superior to put both of us through this?" I press. I want her to say it.

"I saw the numbers he ran. You two have incredible allele matches. I think it would be really difficult for him to find something better," she explains generally, without missing a beat.

"I just find it very convenient that all of a sudden my pair is taken from me and, out of the blue, this new, perfect match shows up.

What are the chances of that, Shari? Seriously. It was hard enough for me to find Eric."

We sit in silence, sipping our tea.

Shari finally speaks in a low whisper. "Kate, you're smart. I'm not going to pretend that there's not more at work here. But I need you to trust me on this. Eric is making the right choice. I love you, and I don't want you to be miserable." She looks at me intently. "Let him go. Let him move forward with this project. I can't say more than that."

I am grateful that she is at least trying. "What about the boys?" I ask gently.

"There are plenty of good options. They have a good relationship with their mentors. We can easily get them in for reversal therapy over the next few months."

This not-so-theoretical scenario starts to sink into me and I tear up. "I don't want them to forget their dad."

Shari sets her tea down and moves close to me. "They won't, Kate. They will just remember the good and...have manageable grief."

Tears start rolling down my cheeks. "I don't want to, Shari. I just want Eric."

She holds me while I cry. I am not strong enough to do this. More honestly, I just don't want to. I don't want to! I scream this over and over inside my head. The pressure around my eyes is almost unbearable. There is no way to escape this cognitive dissonance, because, after all, I am resigned to leave Eric. I know it's the right call, for his sake more than mine. Will this be how I feel for the rest of my life?

After a while, I pull away and grab a tissue to blow my nose.

"We can do reversal therapy on you too, you know," Shari says, gently. "You won't have to feel this pain forever."

My world seems frozen for a moment. It feels like such a betrayal to remove any of the hurt, because it would lessen the depth of the good. I shrug and tell her I'll think it over.

"I have no closure," I say. "I haven't said goodbye."

"I think it's probably better this way," Shari says, rubbing my back. "But I would be happy to arrange for Eric to come home for a day or two, if you think it would help. It might just make it harder."

"I'll consider it. I find it hard to believe that anything could make this harder."

She holds me again for a couple of minutes, then grabs our mugs and takes them into the kitchen. I follow her and thank her for coming over. She turns around, putting her hands on my shoulders.

"You are strong, Kate. Most people in Tier 1 only ever have to give up their time and energy. You are being asked to give up someone you love, a relationship that fulfills you. I can't pretend to know how that feels, but I do know how it feels to *want* someone to love and never find them. I can't help but think that having Eric for twelve years is better than never having him. And having another man ready and waiting to love you? I know it probably doesn't help right now, but maybe try to focus on shifting perspective from all that you are losing to all that you have." I give her a hug and thank her again. I watch her car as it glides away down the street. In that moment, I become deeply aware of how tired I am. My body seems to melt into itself, retreating from all of the unknown. I go through the motions of shutting down the house for the night, then walk down the hall, and bury myself in the bed covers.

CHAPTER 27

I WAKE up to Tal and Bentley running around. Loudly. My body aches from tension I held while I slept. Apparently, I can't will myself to truly relax with all of the unknowns rolling around like marbles in my head. Sleep is supposed to help with clarity of thought, but this morning, I still don't have any good answers. Stepping into my morning routine allows me to shove those concerns down deep.

Today, I had planned to take the boys to the Tech Museum. Leaving the house is quite possibly the very last thing I want to do right now, but I press forward nonetheless. Tal and Bent always spend hours at that museum trying to figure out how to use the old technological devices that rotate through the hands-on exhibits. Our society needs more people to go into tech, so I am hoping the more they see it, the more likely it will light a spark of interest in them.

"Hi Mom!" Bentley shouts as he catches my figure walking past their door.

"Good morning, Bent. Hey Tal," I say, walking into the kitchen.

The boys run after me. "I don't want to go to the museum today, Mom," Tal says quickly. "I think I've seen everything there. It will be a boring repeat."

"It might be," I agree, "but it's been a while since we've been. You never know." I reach into the fridge for the sausage I saved for this morning.

"I want to go," says Bentley. "I hope they have those square phones with the old games. I love those."

"Their graphics are so bad," Tal criticizes.

"Graphics don't matter. They're good games," Bentley counters.

"I am sure they will have something with games," I interject. "Can you guys go wash your hands for breakfast? After we eat, we can change and get going. Tal, we don't have to stay there for a long time, if you aren't enjoying it." He shoots me an appreciative smile.

The boys obediently follow my instructions, and we eat as soon as the sausage is done cooking. After inhaling their breakfast, they run off to get changed. So much for not wanting to go.

"I'm going to take a shower!" I call after them. "We're leaving in 30 minutes!"

They don't respond, but I pretend they heard me as I simply do not have the energy to say it again. I hear more playing than changing coming from their room, but at least that buys me a few minutes.

Being in the shower is like a swift kick to my gut. It tangibly reminds me of my last conversation with Eric. Every single day, I am tempted to unblock my sensor. To find a way to be with him. I still don't know what I am going to say when the boys start asking when he will be home again. I wash my hair and body as quickly as possible, wanting to escape this tragic space. Maybe closure would be good. The warm water wash over me and, though I know we are probably approaching our water limit for the month, I can't bring myself to care.

I pull on my favorite jeans and a t-shirt, needing to be comfy today. Walking out of my room, the boys' voices reach me. They are chattering to each other. I slowly sneak up to the door, wanting to hear what they are saying without disturbing the moment.

"This is your final warning," Tal says, mimicking a loudspeaker. "We are taking this city and you can either surrender or die."

"Tal, don't kill my guys! I just want to have a battle." Bentley whines.

"I'm not actually going to kill them, this is how the battle starts," Tal says, annoyed. "Besides, your guys are all Tier 3 so it doesn't matter if they die."

My eyes widen. Where did he learn the idea that Tier 3 lives don't matter?

"My guys are not all Tier 3! It's a mix of everyone." Bentley is getting increasingly frustrated. This isn't going to end well.

"Ok, well, then I kill all the Tier 2 and Tier 3 people." Tal starts dropping pretend bombs. Bentley squeals and I walk into the room, hoping to mitigate the damage.

"Guys! What's going on? Why are we fighting?" I ask as I pick Bentley up, avoiding his kicking legs.

"Tal is killing all my guys and saying they are Tier 3!" Bentley accuses, crying now.

"I was just trying to do the battle he wanted," Tal responds defensively.

"Ok, let's take a few minutes to calm down, and then we can talk about this. Tal, please get dressed so we can go. Bent, what do you want to wear today?"

While the boys get dressed, I grab some snacks out of the fridge and fill up the water bottles. We hop in the car and buckle in.

"Can we talk about what just happened?" I ask gently. They both nod. "How do you two think we can avoid getting into a fight next time?"

"Bentley could stop throwing a fit," Tal says. I see Bentley's eyes flash.

"Let's only talk about what we individually could do differently, not what others could do. So, what could you do to avoid a fight, Tal?"

"I don't know. Maybe talk about the rules ahead of time?"

"I think that's a great idea. What about you, Bentley?"

"I didn't do anything. I just tried to play, and then Tal was making stuff up," Bentley complains. Tal scoffs.

"Well...what if you let Tal have a say in how the game goes?

Maybe you both get to make half the decisions? If Tal wants to kill everyone, maybe you get to kill his guys, too. Or maybe only some of them die. Do you think you could discuss rules like Tal suggested?"

"Maybe," Bentley says, as he looks down at his shoes.

"My other question is for you, Tal. Why were you talking that way about Tier 3?"

"What way?" he asks, confused.

"I heard you say that it didn't matter if they died, because they were Tier 3."

"They weren't Tier 3! They were a mix!" shouts Bentley.

"I know, buddy. I am not talking about the game anymore, just asking Tal about his thoughts and feelings," I explain, rubbing his back.

"I thought Tier 3 is full of people who have bad markers. Why would it matter if they die?" Tal says, honestly wondering.

"That's a good question," I say, trying to hide how disturbed I am by this line of reasoning. "Do you know the history of Tier 3, Tal?"

"Kind of. I know that when Berg took over, there were a lot of people who didn't want to get on board with the new system. They didn't think it was fair that certain people had access to more resources. But Mom, why would anyone be okay with not getting food or water? How could Berg expect people to just say 'OK, you're right, I should starve while other people get what they need'."

"They didn't expect that, because you make a good point. Nobody would accept that. Our drive for survival is strong, regardless of whether we have a good chance of surviving or not. Our brain doesn't take that into account naturally. It wasn't a situation that anyone would have chosen to be in. To have to decide who lives and who dies is pretty terrible, but it had to be done. We had only so much food, so much water, so many safe locations; and they had to determine how to distribute those in a way that would ensure the survival of our species. Outright war among an already-damaged population was the other option, and everyone knew that we wouldn't survive that." Tal and Bentley sit thinking, their brows furrowed.

"What would you have done?" I ask Tal.

"I don't know. I don't think I could tell people that we were choosing for them to die. I would probably just surprise bomb them, so I didn't have to make them suffer."

"That option was considered, actually. They didn't go through with it, but the discussion resulted in a group of people who caused a lot of problems—terrorizing the Berg camps and starting small uprisings."

"Yeah, if you were going to die anyway from a lack of resources, why not fight?" Tal says.

"Exactly. Those people, as terrible as it sounds, were eliminated out of necessity. There was no other option. There were, however, other individuals who didn't meet the requirements to be considered for higher resources, but they weren't actively causing problems. These are the people who became Tier 3 as we know them today. Berg decided to distribute resources in a way that gave everyone who met the marker and health requirements what they needed. Not wanted, but needed. Then, they gave whatever was left to those people who weren't qualified, but who were still living peacefully outside of the safety zones."

"Why would they give any resources to those people? If they weren't in a safety zone, their chances of survival were low. And they shouldn't have been allowed to reproduce," Tal says, puzzled.

"They weren't allowed to reproduce. In order to gain their resources, they were required to undergo sterilization."

"What does sterilization mean?" Bentley asks.

"It means that you can't have kids anymore." Tal says. "If they were sterilized, how come we still have Tier 3 today?" he asks.

"Great question. We don't have nearly as many in Tier 3 as we did then. Also, because of terrahealing projects, new farming technology, and less population, we have plenty of resources to go around. Tier 3 isn't stuck with leftovers; they get what they need now, along with the rest of us. But back to your question. Genetic pairings still aren't 100% predictable. Especially when matching is at the low end. It is very common for couples in Tier 1 to end up with Tier 2 or even Tier 3 children. Sometimes their pairings are just unlucky, resulting in mutations that we can't control. And sometimes people end up having children when they haven't been approved for it. All of this combines to introduce kinks in the system. We do our best to select for the variations that will serve society in the future, but when things don't go as planned, we have a place for those people to fit."

"So, what do Tier 3 people do?" Bentley asks as he ties and unties his shoes, happily entertaining himself.

"They do lots of things. Often manual labor, since they don't have the genetics to justify spending time on higher learning. They learn skills and trades, and they contribute to society, just like we do. They are responsible for many of the raw materials that we receive in order to build, do research, and create new technologies. In exchange, they receive resources."

"Are they still sterilized?" Tal asks.

"Yes. It really does have to be that way. As a society, we can't afford to build populations that aren't sustainable or that could compromise more promising groups. Tier 3 populations are extremely low, and Tier 2 is getting lower every year. Eventually, I think the goal is to move back into an integrated society, but for now—"

"Like, there would only be Tier 1? But how is it fair not to give others a chance?" Bentley demands, incredulous.

"But, we do! We give people chances. That's my whole job! I teach people how to heal their bodies from the inside out. Some of them repair their DNA to a point where they can actually move to Tier 1. When people are close to the cut-off, Berg doesn't require sterilization—they only require semi-permanent birth control. That allows them to work toward advancement and eventually, if accepted, they may be able to have children. Those who are far from making the cut are still given information that helps them lead happier lives, but sterilization happens at 16-years old. It's less risky to undergo that procedure at a younger age, before body systems are set. At that point, it's already quite clear they won't be able to qualify for Tier 1."

I sigh. "I guess that was a really long answer to your question, but the short version is: We don't want Tier 3 people to die because they contribute without endangering society. We have plenty of resources now and aren't in a crisis situation, so there's no reason to eliminate them. These people can live full—albeit short—lives. Their existence also gives us an opportunity for service and learning. It's good for society to have diversity."

"Seems like Tier 3 is the place to be. No responsibilities, just food and some physical work. Can I transfer?" Tal jokes.

"Ha. Ha. You would not be happy there—your brain is coded for more. It sounds nice to be lazy, but it isn't actually fun long term."

We pull to a stop, arriving at the Tech Museum. The angular facade is juxtaposed against the trees, making the leaves look even more vibrant. I am not ready to be done talking, but the boys are. They unbuckle and jump out, running through the natural grass toward the entrance.

CHAPTER 28

NICK IS TAKING the boys for the afternoon, so I can meet with Cassidy. I have been writing down all of the questions that have been weighing on my mind. It is slightly ridiculous that I know so little about life in Tier 2, considering that I work with these individuals weekly. Clipping my bike into the stand, I see Cassidy already sitting on a bench. We decided to go on a walk together today to meet her physical fitness goals.

"Hey Cassidy," I say as I sit down next to her.

She closes her display. "Hey! How are you?"

"Great. I have been looking forward to this. We didn't get to chat the other night, with all the Ceremony excitement."

"I know, this will be great." She motions toward the path. "Should we do a loop and see how far we get?"

"Absolutely."

We start walking, and I allow the fresh air to seep into me. I haven't been in nature much the last few days and I suddenly feel desperate for it.

"Now that we aren't at a table of strangers, you can tell me what you really think about Tier 1. No need to hold back," I say.

Cassidy laughs. "I wasn't holding back the other night! I really do love it. I love feeling useful and holding myself to a higher standard."

"Do they have you assigned for service yet?"

"Yep, I am a distribution specialist for Tier 2."

"Oh, no way! My family and I just went and helped out at one of the Tier 2 centers. Which one are you working at?"

"I'm actually at the central location most of the time. I order and organize resources, and every once in a while, I'm able to actually go into the field. There was a sharp learning curve at first, but once I became competent at the ordering process, I have felt really comfortable."

"That's great, Cassidy. Good for you," I say, looking out over the lake. The pristine, glassy surface of the water is calming for my soul. An occasional ripple erupts and slowly dissipates as it moves toward the shore.

"Do you miss Tier 2? Your family and friends?" I ask.

"Yes, of course, but it's manageable. I still see my mom regularly. I didn't really have many close friends in Tier 2. I was so focused on qualifying that it became a full-time job for me. A lot of other people didn't understand that, so it was hard to connect."

This is foreign to me. Everyone in Tier 1 has the same goals, the same ideals in common. As an adult, I've never had a conversation with someone where I felt like an outsider. I do remember a few conversations I had with one particular girl at conditioning when I was younger. Her world-view was confusing for me, but even then, I felt like *she* was the outsider. And we were seven.

"Tell me more about that—actually, I would love to hear about Tier 2 life in general. Technically, I know that Tier 2 has service assignments, but I have never asked anyone about it. What were your days like there?"

"It's funny, because for me, they weren't all that different. My service assignment was to look after some of the elderly people in our immediate neighborhood. That included my mom. Every day I would check in and make sure they had what they needed and that they were completing their health requirements. Many of their children were—and still are—serving in the south gardens. I loved hearing their stories of picking fruits and vegetables, then cleaning and bundling them for distribution. I actually wished many times that I could serve there," she says longingly. "As a consolation, I applied for extra service hours in our gardens. Time in the dirt makes me more functional. More able to problem solve, better perspective. If that makes any sense," she finishes, slightly out of breath.

"Oh, I think it absolutely does. It's great that you made that connection. Being with my kids does that for me, too. I guess those are my 'extra' service hours," I laugh. "After being with them, I see things differently when meeting with patients. I also feel more grateful for the quiet moments in my life that I tend to miss otherwise. It's so important to find a balance, otherwise it's difficult to give our best."

"That's exactly what I love so much about being here. In Tier 2, I just didn't have the flexibility to explore—anything, really. My days looked very similar, but I lacked the control and opportunity to shift and grow. I feel freer here. Like I can blossom and follow whatever path I need to. That is really powerful."

This idea of limited freedom has also never occurred to me before, having always been encouraged to explore and discover.

"Have you completed your initial testing yet?"

"I go in next week. I have been working hard and reaching all of my goals. I don't feel nervous. I am sure it will come back positively. I feel better than I ever have, so if the results don't reflect that, I would be shocked."

"I'm sure the fact that you aren't nervous about it will only improve those scores. And then you will be fully integrated." I nudge her. "You can start dating, hey?"

She laughs. "It's funny, I was so excited for that initially. Now my mind has been opened to all of these new possibilities. I know I definitely want to pair and have kids at some point, but I feel more stable. Like it doesn't have to happen immediately."

I am amazed at how much more confident she is. She seems grounded, whereas before in our meetings, she came off as desperate and unsure.

"This might be a strange question, but now that you have seen inside both Tiers...do you think the Tier system is right?"

She stops walking. "You mean, do I think it's a good system?"

"Yes. I guess I just wonder if we really need to be separated? Now that resources aren't as scarce as they were back then? Could we all live together and be happy? I don't know. Maybe that's crazy. It would probably turn out the way it always has."

"Yeah," Cassidy agrees, "I think it sounds idyllic, but I am not convinced that people in Tier 2 would willingly take on the responsibilities needed to properly integrate. They are conditioned for giving less, and being satisfied with less. I don't know how that would work," she admits, hesitating. "Right now everyone receives resources equal to their societal contribution. In the past, conflict was caused by people trying to receive more, whether by working harder, or smarter, or simply breaking the rules. I think the fact that 'getting more' isn't an option makes it easier for all of us, don't you? When we are all equal, that stress doesn't exist. We don't have to try to get ahead."

"But, many people in Tier 2 *are* trying to get ahead, to move into Tier 1. But, like you mentioned, that marked you as different from the rest of your peers. So maybe it isn't a majority mentality."

We walk in silence for a moment. "I hadn't really thought of it that way," Cassidy muses. "But, it didn't ever feel like I was trying to *get* more. Only that I wanted opportunities for growth and to be able to contribute. Maybe, for those of us who are borderline, Tier 1 feels more like an eventual home. Even for others who have qualified, it didn't ever seem like they thought they were 'moving up'. Just trying to be the best they could be."

I nod, slowing as Cassidy stops on the trail. She pauses, balancing and lifting her foot to pull a rock from her shoe. "I mean, I have definitely heard rumors that some people in Tier 3 feel like the Tier system is bad for society, that they have been left with less purely because Berg wants order so they can retain control. I did hear some members of Tier 2 discussing things like that, but I guess I have always viewed it as a natural thing. Of course people with lower genetic and social capabilities would come to false conclusions," she says, replacing her shoe and continuing on.

"It's true. That's exactly why the Crisis happened. It did turn into a power struggle. Those who understood the best options couldn't make headway with so many people holding them back. I guess there has to be some element of organization to keep that from happening again. I think a part of me just wants to believe that we can help everyone, that we have enough resources to give everyone the best. I don't know if it's actually true or not, but I want it to be."

"It probably isn't realistic, but definitely a nice thought."

We pass through a canopy of low-hanging trees into a small clearing. Taking in the surroundings, I realize we have returned to our meeting place. We sit on the bench we started from, taking respite from the growing heat under the shade of a massive honeylocust tree.

After taking a small break, we decide to walk one more loop. The sun feels good on my skin, and I am not ready to head home yet. We talk of frivolous things for the most part, but my mind is still focused on our initial conversation. I have always viewed Tier 2 as being less desirable, but her responses have shifted my understanding. It's just a different place. People there are comfortable because their way of life suits them. What would it be like not to worry about growing, stretching, pushing? Are my desires inherent to my coding or societally grown? Would I have those ideals if I had grown up in Tier 2? I can't wait to see how E—I stop myself. Nick, how Nick feels about this. I am sure he has an opinion worth hearing.

CHAPTER 29

THE NEXT FEW days pass by slowly. My day with Cassidy felt fine, normal even, but now, a fog has somehow slowly descended on my entire life. I go through the motions of each day with my heart not fully in it. Every once in awhile, a piece of me surfaces and anticipation of a potential day of normalcy surges within me, only to be squashed again when the moment is short lived.

This morning, I sit in a chair, reading training materials. Movement beyond the front window catches my eye and I recognize Nick walking up the steps. Before I have time to react, the bell rings, and I answer it.

"Hey Kate, how are you doing this week?"

I respond honestly. "I am ok. I have kept busy with the boys, so I haven't had a lot of down time to think about things."

"Have you talked with Eric? Do you know what you plan to do moving forward?"

"No. I think I'm going to talk to Shari about having a day of closure, though. I think that would help me and the boys move on." I motion for him to come in and distract myself by putting the dishes away.

"Do the boys suspect anything?"

"They have noticed their Dad isn't around, but I think they are definitely expecting him to come back at some point. We need to sit down and discuss it. I don't think I can do that without Eric—"

A plate slips from my grasp and hits the floor, shattering. Nick and I both jump out of the way, then survey the damage. I apologize, reaching into the closet for a broom.

"Here, let me help," he says, offering to take it.

"It's ok," I say, beginning to sweep up the shards. This is one thing I can actually fix, and I need to do it. As I sweep, I continue.

"I have been feeling like they need to see Eric and know that he loves them, that it's not their fault. I still don't know how they are going to take it." Saying these words, as I sweep up pieces of shattered glass, triggers something in me and I am overwhelmed with emotion. Nick notices and navigates the hazardous conditions to kneel next to me on the floor. He wraps me in his arms and I sink into him, noticing the strength of his chest, his soft shirt, and a slight scent of ginger. I close my eyes and breathe.

"I'm sorry, Kate," he says softly. Pulling back, I see the genuine concern on his face. Being next to him makes my body ache for Eric. For closeness. Not for the first time today, I feel anger and frustration well up inside of me.

Bentley walks in and sees Nick. He begins running toward us.

"Stop!" I shout, hand outstretched. Thankfully Bentley freezes and I am able to clear the floor before he insists on greeting us both with a hug.

"Hey bud! You ready to go? Is Tal coming with us?" Nick says, ruffling his hair. Ah. That's why Nick is here. I had completely forgotten.

"Tal doesn't want to swim. He is going to play frisbee with Stephen and Liz," Bent replies.

"They should be here in a few minutes to pick him up," I say, grinning at Bent, pretending I have everything under control.

"Kate, do you have plans? Want to come with?" Nick asks with a hopeful grin.

My stomach drops. This was not in my plan for the day, nor do I want to show any more skin around Nick than is absolutely necessary. Arms. Arms are good.

"Mom?" Bentley's voice brings me back to reality.

"Ummm...not sure, bud," I hedge, trying to compose a response, but it is not happening fast enough to avoid awkwardness. Bent's pleading eyes soften my heart.

"I would love to come with you, but I do need to prepare some files for tomorrow," I say, recognizing that it is an extremely weak excuse as the words leave my lips.

"I could help you with that when we get back," Nick offers, grinning.

Bentley's face lights up at the prospect. "Can you come now, Mom?" he asks pulling on my hands.

"Okay, okay, I'll come," I laugh, wondering how hard it would be to quickly 'lose' my swimsuit.

We arrive at the lake to find perfect weather. Just hot enough to make the water feel relaxing, but not chilly. Already dressed in our suits and having preemptively applied skincare, Bentley darts toward the water. Nick pulls off his shirt and races after him, while I set our snacks and water bottles on the picnic table. I can't help but notice the perfect curves of his muscles. I am shameless as I stare in Nick's direction.

I don't know what has gotten into me. Am I *that* desperate to see a man with his shirt off? I guess it has been over a month. And, I remind myself, I should actually be fostering this attraction. It will hopefully help me move forward with this new normal, I guess? I cringe, still feeling dirty all over, despite my rationalizations.

Then, Bentley is waving for me to join them in the water. I sigh, pull off my wrap, and bravely walk toward them, knowing there is no perfect musculature here.

"Mom, will you throw this ball for me to go get and bring back? Throw it far, otherwise it will be boring," Bentley shouts as I get within earshot.

I laugh and take the ball from his outstretched hand, throwing it far to the right. Bentley immediately starts toward it. He is a great swimmer, due to the physical conditioning he did last year. Last year, his skill focuses were swimming and climbing, and it has obviously payed off. It's impressive to see such a small body move through the water so effortlessly.

"Thanks for letting me come along," I say, looking Nick's direction. "It's been a while since I have come here. I forgot how nice it is to feel the water and sun on my skin. And to watch Bentley swim. I needed this today."

"So, you're not mad that I wouldn't let you get out of it?" He grins, splashing a little water my way.

"Not mad," I admit, smiling. "Was it that obvious?"

"Yes," he says, and I splash him back.

Bentley returns with the ball, and this time Nick throws it even farther in the opposite direction. I wriggle my toes into the soft mud and notice a few minnows swimming around my ankles. When Bentley gets bored of his game, I am sure he will try to catch them.

Something grazes my hand and I look down to see Nick's fingers interlacing with my own. My heart speeds up, but I don't pull away. I look up at him, but he is completely engaged in watching Bentley attempting to catch the ball. I stand there, the water lapping coolly against my thighs, my hand in his. As soon as Bentley finds his prize and begins to turn back, Nick gives my hand a squeeze and pulls away. He silently makes a show of cheering in support of his win, and then starts toward Bent, who takes off as fast as he can. I smile as I watch them play tag for awhile, my hand still tingling.

CHAPTER 30

LATER THAT NIGHT, after Nick has gone home, I call Shari.

"You don't need me to come deal with another crisis, do you?" she says dryly.

I laugh. "No, but thanks for the vote of confidence."

"What's up?" she grins.

"I have been thinking a lot about moving forward. I just don't see the boys getting through this well without having some closure with Eric. I think we need to set something up. I think I will talk with them tomorrow, and then maybe we could all meet together at the end of next week? Or do you think we should do it sooner?"

"I think it will depend on when Eric is available. I will send a message over there right now. What are you going to tell the boys?"

"Just the facts. That Dad made an amazing discovery and that we all have to sacrifice to allow him to follow that path. He loves them, but he can't be with us. We are all sacrificing so that humankind can benefit. I know it's cliche, but does that sound appropriate?"

"I think so. Are you going to tell them about Nick? And what did you decide about reversal therapy?"

"I don't think I am going to say anything about Nick yet. They will need to process this awhile before we get to that point."

"You don't have awhile."

"I thought about that, too," I say, without thinking. "Wait, what do you mean?"

"You know what I mean, Kate."

I guess we aren't pulling punches anymore. She must know that I am aware of the details of the situation. Does that mean that Eric talked with her?

"Would it be possible for us to pair and not...live in the same house right away? Do people do that?" I ask, hesitantly.

"Not usually. I'm sure you can imagine the strain that puts on a relationship."

I nod. "Maybe I will have to talk to them sooner rather than later." I pick up an apple and take a bite. "I will definitely have the kids do their first reversal session after we meet with Eric. Who would help me set that up?"

"I can take care of it," Shari says. "What about for you?"

"Not yet. I don't feel good about it. I might grieve longer or harder, but Nick is a compassionate guy. I think he will understand, and I can't—I can't bear the thought of forgetting any part of Eric," I say, not willing to openly admit that I'm doing this for him. I can't give that knowledge up.

"Up to you. And if it gets too hard, you can always reconsider," she says.

I am sure I won't. "I'm really tired, so I think I will head to bed. Thanks for helping me with this."

"My pleasure," she says, giving a fake curtsy.

My smile is purely out of social obligation. It feels like I just put the nail in the coffin for me and Eric, and the finality of it is hitting me.

"Will you let me know what day works? I want to make sure the boys are prepared," I choke out.

"Sure, hon. Sleep well." Shari signs off with a wave and an image with a heart appears on my display. She might not say it, but she knows how hard this is for me. I really am exhausted. I wash my face, change out of my clothes, and drop into bed.

The next morning, I continue to push through our regular routine, and we all prepare for physical conditioning. Historically, this is something that Eric would take charge of, but today it's up to me. I get our water bottles and make sure we have a protein-rich breakfast, then initiate our ride to the park near the community center. Today we will be working on balance and ligament strength. Not my strongest area.

When we arrive, we see slacklines strung between trees at varying heights. While I am slightly nervous, Tal is practically bouncing off of his seat. He parks his bike and runs toward the nearest line that isn't already occupied. I move to check in with the site director. It's Shandra, a friend I haven't seen in months.

"How are you doing?" I ask warmly, embracing her. "It's been a while since we had an assignment together."

"I know. I have mostly been running physical conditioning these days, so I don't see anyone anymore!" She scans my sensor. This initial scan will give a baseline for the session.

"It's our loss. Do you enjoy it?" I ask.

"I love it. I also get to work with new Tier 1 initiates. I actually worked with someone you know last week. Cassidy?"

"Yes! We got together just the other day."

"It seems like she is transitioning really well. She is working hard and appears happy."

"She is one of my favorites."

"She is quickly becoming one of mine, as well," she agrees. "It's so good to see you, Kate."

"You too." I smile as I walk over to the boys. My service assignments have allowed me to draw close to such high quality individuals, and I love reminded of that, randomly like this.

Bentley is attempting to get on the line without falling, while Tal can already take a few steps. I stand next to them and offer a hand.

After a few passes, Tal can do it almost all the way across without my help.

"Is Dad ever coming home?" Bent asks, taking me by surprise.

"We are actually going to meet with him soon," I say, trying not to give away the seriousness of the situation.

"Why do we need to meet? Can't he just come home?" I should have used a different phrase.

"We need to make some decisions as a family. You guys remember seeing Dad's work at the lab, right? He is working so much and it isn't going to slow down anytime soon."

"Why do they need him? Why is it so important?" Tal asks.

"It's important because if they get this right—if they can use the pairs they have found to successfully create the allele matches that Dad discovered—it could start us on the path to eliminating really deadly types of cancer."

"The kind that Grandma died of?" Bentley says.

"Yes, the kinds that all of your grandparents died of. We don't have many disease markers in Tier 1 anymore, but this is a huge one. If we can start cleaning this genetically, in a couple hundred years, it won't be an issue anymore."

"But what about for all of us right now? It doesn't really help us," Tal says haughtily. "We just have to give up time with Dad. And probably still die of cancer."

I respond, pretending I didn't notice the attitude. "True. But we don't make decisions simply based on what is good for us. You know how that turned out over and over again for our predecessors. It never worked. Society was repeatedly driven to destruction with that mentality. We have to be better than that. We have to be willing to sacrifice for the greater good. And, as far as we are concerned, our lives are pretty great, don't you think?" I help Bentley step on to the line.

Tal sighs. "I guess. Sorry, Mom. I just really miss Dad."

"I know. I do, too. I don't want to sacrifice this either, but I know it's right. When we meet with Dad, we can explain more."

"Are we ever going to be a family again?" Bentley asks, causing my throat to constrict. I let his question hang in the air and just keep holding his hand.

CHAPTER 31

Shari contacts me to confirm details the next day. Eric is helping with training in Centennial, about two hours south of us. Erie, our community, is located in one of the original safe zones. Once the initial Crisis was over, there was no longer a need for the people living here to be quarantined. Though some of them potentially could have applied to return to their homes, it would have been costly and difficult to do so. They had built lives here. Our population was still so small that it didn't make sense to try to rebuild outlying neighborhoods; it would only have made it less efficient to deliver supplies.

Once our population began to grow and people were less hesitant about stepping outside of the safe zone boundaries, the Berg committee began to organize supply chains reaching beyond our limits. They utilized old buildings and structures, developed ancient farm and ranch lands, treated water supplies, and began to make new communities not only habitable, but desirable. Centennial is one I have never been to.

I suddenly feel desperately jealous that they get Eric's attention when I don't. Shari confirms that he will be available for a meeting with us next Thursday, which means I will see Eric in less than a week. My stomach flips.

I jump full force into my tasks at home, trying to keep my mind off that meeting. Being around Nick is a great distraction, too, especially in the evenings. He eats dinner with us almost every night, and I see the boys clamoring for his attention. They miss their father desperately, though they don't complain. Not consciously, anyway. Tal has definitely been more moody than usual.

Watching him change makes me wonder if I'm ready to handle the new stages that are coming for him. Every time my children progress into a developmental phase, I realize how important our mentors are. It is invaluable to have insights from other males, so much closer to my boys' ages. I spoke with Stephen the other day and had my eyes opened to a few teenage boy thought processes. Slightly disturbing, to say the least, but it helped.

The boys are at conditioning this afternoon, so I am preparing files and cleaning up around the house. I hear a knock at the door and wonder if I've forgotten something else. I already know it's Nick; who else would randomly stop by? I haven't really been putting forth much effort to build friendships lately—new or existing. Even our usual friends don't really reach out now that Eric isn't around. I guess it would be kind of strange for them to invite me, alone, over for dinner or a walk.

I open the door and see Nick standing there with his hands in his pockets. He isn't smiling as widely as usual and I can tell something is off.

"Hey Nick, come on in." I open the door wide.

"Actually, I was hoping I could take you...out."

"Out?"

"Like for lunch. On a date."

He is nervous. His hands still haven't made an appearance and he is shuffling his feet. Suddenly, his energy rubs off on me. So far, I have been able to remain in the companion zone with Nick. I knew it couldn't last forever, though a part of me really hoped it would.

"Sure. That would be fun. I have until four o'clock, when the boys are done for the day. What were you thinking?"

"I know you and Shari love that cafe downtown. I have never been. Could we go there, or would it be overkill for you?"

"Not overkill. That sounds great." I pause. "Like, now?"

He laughs. "Yes, like, now. We can take my car."

I put my work away, slip on my shoes, and follow him to the car. Once inside, I type in the destination. The Old Mine. They got the name from a sign, a relic from society before Berg took over. I am sure some people would have liked a different name, but since the sign was there and still working, it didn't make sense to switch it. The management, cook staff, and servers all rotate every few months. That type of work isn't ideal for Tier 1. But, the community as a whole values being able to go out to eat every once in a while, so we have quite a few restaurants on our side of the city. People take breaks from other service appointments to work there.

I had a stint back before Eric and I paired. It was a nice respite from training, honestly.

"How was your morning?" I ask, leaning back into my seat.

"I actually did some health training today."

"Just regular training, or was it something special?"

"My mentor and I were tweaking some things based on my most recent scan. I need more magnesium in my diet, and I need to focus more on balancing the muscle strength in my upper body."

"It doesn't look like your body needs any more balancing," I tease.

"Well, it's not about looks!" he jokes back. "It's about making sure that my spine is balanced—that nothing is pulling or straining. It was a good reminder for me. I like certain exercises better than others, so I need to be more self-disciplined."

I sigh. "I need to adjust some things, too. As my body ages, I can see how much building muscle will help my bones and joints. I am *old* remember?"

"Kate, you are older than I am, true. But it doesn't mean you are old. We might be the first generation to far exceed our parents in life expectancy. Think about it: when your Mom was your age, was she as healthy as you?"

I think for a moment. "No, definitely not. She already had cancer at that point. She lived until she was 45, but she fought it the rest of her life, which meant a lot of suffering."

"Right. Did you know that you have an allele that is linked with a strong tumor- suppressing gene response?"

I pause, taken aback. "I know that," I say guardedly. "How do you know that?" I ask, fully knowing the answer to that question.

"I ran our numbers, remember? I noticed it because I have the same allele variation. That means it is highly unlikely that you or I will die of cancer. Even if we see tumor growth, our body will have the tools to shut it down with minimal treatment. Kate. We could live well into our seventies."

I stare at him. I don't know why I hadn't thought about that before. I guess I didn't ever expect to have a better or longer life than my parents. And honestly, until Eric's research, I hadn't ever thought twice about that gene or allele variation.

"What will society even do with us at that point?" I joke. "Don't you think we will be bored?"

"I looked into it, and there are people in Tier 2 already starting to live past their fifties," he says, ignoring my question.

"I know," I say. "I met with one of them that same day I ran into you."

"Right," he goes on. "With adherence to health and nutrition standards, even those with poor genetics can extend their lifespan—their healthy and functioning lifespan. People in Tier 1 have been living into their fifties regularly. I even know of a few in their sixties. Cancer and a few mutated virus strains are the only things between us and living who knows how long. What if we can suddenly live to see our grandkids and great-grandkids? What if we can create close-knit communities of families like they did in the past? We wouldn't need such a structured society because older family members could teach and mentor the young. Don't get me wrong, mentoring is great, but this would take advantage of that biological link—the drive to keep your offspring alive. Families and individuals would be even stronger. We could see a population boom like before the Crisis, but this time it would be set up in a healthy, sustainable way."

I can see that Nick is extremely passionate about this, so I hold back my reservations. I'm not sure it *is* sustainable for a population to boom so quickly. We have things under control right now, but it seems like Berg thinks that they can predict and control the trajectory of life on Earth. It isn't that simple.

Eric was always talking about the need to factor in random variations, incidental mutations, unpredicted change. Our research has obviously been so necessary in helping us repopulate and live in harmony with ourselves and nature, but history shows that many groups of people have achieved this in history. Some variable always changes, resulting in collapse. Whether from disease, new settlers, or environmental shifts, the population wasn't ready to adjust. How do we know we will be ready to accommodate when something else happens?

"Do you really anticipate it being sustainable?" I ask, trying not to burst his bubble. "One of the major factors that contributed to the Crisis was disease…" I trail off, not sure if I should say more. The population during that time was so large, and deadly illnesses could spread like wildfire. So much of it was preventable, but people didn't know which warnings to trust. They had access to massive amounts of information, but it was arduous to sift through, none of it very reliable. New material was being created constantly, making it virtually impossible to discern what data was real and what had been massaged to meet an agenda. Large groups of people became convinced that scientific research was doing more harm than good, and they refused to follow any recommendations.

People simply stopped listening. Perhaps most significantly, many stopped using scientific and medical research to build immunity against disease. Old diseases came back and absolutely decimated the population. That, along with all of the other factors Grace talked about in her speech, was a major catalyst for decreased lifespan. Add in a lack of family stability and trust in society, and you can imagine why the situation was able to reach a boiling point.

"I think it could be," Nick says. "Our general attitude is different now, as is our dissemination of information."

"Do you think our overall immunity is strong enough that a population boom wouldn't be begging for disease levels to increase?" I ask skeptically. I don't see how Berg can keep close enough tabs on hygiene and compliance to prevent a similar problem in the future. Maybe with some better protocols in place. I don't know. Beyond that, who is to say that we wouldn't respond similarly if fear somehow crept back into our society? If an infectious illness mutated, can I really say that I would act in society's best interest? None of us in our generation have been faced with a test like that.

"It's a good point," he says slowly, and I realize I have unintentionally killed his excitement.

"It's not that I don't think it's possible," I backtrack. "I do really hope that we can create a world like that. And I love that you are so sure we can. I guess I am having trouble imagining what that will look like." I pause. "Would we spend those elderly years with our families? Continue to serve in the community? Would we still be allotted full resources if we are past the years of being able to reproduce?" I ask, growing more concerned at the thought.

"I don't know, but I think Berg is discussing and researching all of this now. They know it will happen. Especially with Eric's discovery. It seems completely within reach."

Eric. I will be seeing him tomorrow. My stomach fills with butterflies and I remind myself that I have to be strong. Unselfish. Thinking of society improving to the point where there isn't suffering makes it easier.

The car slows down in front of the cafe. Nick opens my door for me and we walk in. We are seated at a table in the corner, along the exposed brick wall. Sunlight is streaming in, bathing us in warmth as we take our seats. It's cozy and quiet at this time of day, with the hustle and bustle of the morning already past. I order a fonio bowl, Nick orders an omelet. As our server walks away, I feel exposed and vulnerable. I hide in the motion of drinking my water.

"What are we doing, Kate?" Nick asks softly.

My heart starts to race. "What do you mean?" I say, stalling.

"You know what I mean. What are we doing? Where is this heading?"

I want to tell him everything. I want to say that I love Eric, but I also know that I have a responsibility to society. I want to tell him that I know we are one of five matches in our region, that if we don't pair, we will exponentially affect the growth of a resistant generation. That I am so worried about what this will do to my boys, but I know there's no going back to how life was before, either. I want him to know that I care about him, that I am attracted to him, but that Eric is an extension of me, and I don't think that will ever change. That I feel like I can't be fair to him. But I want to be.

I want to be the type of person who can move forward and do something important. I blocked Eric so I could try. I want Nick to know how grateful I am for his companionship. That I love how strong he feels when we embrace. I love his dedication to the greater good and how he is such a good example for Bentley and Tal. I want to kiss him. I want to never see him again.

I look into his gentle eyes. And I do it. I say it all. When I'm done, Nick is still staring at me. He doesn't say anything for a minute, and he is about to speak, when our server returns with our plates. I clear my throat and look down, waiting for him to leave, then look up and all I see is Nick. Nick with tears welling in his eyes, and I am worried that I have wounded him.

"Kate," he starts and then pauses. "I know that you and Eric are bonded strongly, and I never thought or hoped that I could replace him." His eyebrows furrow. "Did Eric tell you about the match?"

"Yes," I admit, and it feels so good to be free of the information. "I have known for a couple of weeks. Since the night of the ceremony. I am sorry I didn't tell you then. I didn't know what to do."

"No, this is exactly what needed to happen. Your brain needed time to process. Just allow yourself to move through this without judgment. I am not convinced that any of our conditioning really prepared us to deal with something like this."

"Yours obviously did," I laugh.

"I told you, Kate. I have nothing to lose here. I just feel really lucky."

"So you are okay pairing with someone who might not do this gracefully? Who might have constant second thoughts? I likely will have a tougher time reproducing at this point. Who knows how my body will respond. And how the boys will respond? I am planning to do reversal therapy with them, but it will likely be a process. You are fine with *all* of that?" I motion with my hands and realize too late that my voice has gotten loud. Other people are looking in our direction. I place my hands on my lap as my cheeks flush.

"I am," he says, amused. "Like I said before, I'm one hundred percent in. I know that it might take time for us to bond the way you and Eric have, and maybe we never will. I know that. I accept that. But I think we will have a lot of fun, and I will be a full partner in raising a family with you. At the end of it, we will be able to say we did our part. That's enough for me. And," he clears his throat, "are you remembering that I do actually want you? I think about you all the time, Kate. Just put me out of my misery, please." He laughs nervously. "I need to know one way or the other."

"Okay, yes. You say that," I counter, "but would you have wanted me if you hadn't been forced into it? You were told that we needed to pair. Would you have ever thought about me had that not happened? When did you get that information?"

When he speaks, it is hurried and intense. "I don't think I ever would have had a reason to hope, without the match. My mind wouldn't have gone down that path, since I knew you were paired. But, don't think that I didn't want to. I didn't know until Eric knew. When he left on that first trip, we met together at headquarters. When I ran into you at Washington Park and had that first meeting to start forming introductions, I didn't know anything. I was attracted to you then and shut it down, because I knew those thoughts weren't helpful. Then, when I knew...well, I didn't shut it down as easily anymore." His blue eyes sear into me.

We haven't even taken a bite of our food. I pick up my fork and start to eat, sitting in in his revelation for a few moments. Nick is the first to speak.

"So," he says leaning back. "Am I understanding correctly that you have hesitations and concerns, but you *do* want to pair with me?" He puffs up his chest and has a mock arrogant look on his face.

I laugh with food still in my mouth. "Now I am rethinking my decision..." I say, taking a drink.

"I use humor as a distraction. I'm sorry." He looks at me seriously, all of his defenses down. "Have you actually made a decision? Are we doing this?"

"Yes." I say definitively. "I have decided. It's the right thing to do. I'm terrified, though."

"Okay, then. I can deal with terrified." He smiles and reaches out for my hand. We finish our food and let our server know that he can log our meals as he takes our plates.

"What do we do now?" I ask. "Will they let me dissolve my pairing with Eric and submit this?"

"I think you know the answer to that. Berg is highly invested in us."

"True."

"Should we head down there and take care of it now?" He sees the hesitation in my eyes. "Too soon?"

"I think we should wait until after I meet with Eric, so I can tell him in person. Who knows, maybe he has already dissolved things," I say, choking up a little bit.

Nick stands up and pulls me from my chair, into his arms. "You don't have to do this alone," he says, stroking my hair. Not worrying about the people around us, I softly cry into his shoulder. Then he walks me to the car, and we ride home.

CHAPTER 32

NICK STAYS the rest of the evening with us, even offering to pick up the boys from conditioning so I can finish my work. Tal and Bentley walk in the door laughing, and the sounds makes me cringe. I am going to have to crush that silliness by prepping them for our meeting tomorrow. Tomorrow, I think, and my lungs refuse to breath. Their worlds are going to be rocked. Tomorrow.

I consider asking Nick to leave, but realize it might be helpful for him to see and hear the boys' reactions. After dinner, I ask them all to join me in the living room. Tal immediately stretches out on the couch, tempting Bentley to jump on him, which predictably causes a commotion. Once they are settled—on opposite sides of the couch—they are still, the busyness of the day finally seeming to sink into their small bodies.

"Bent, Tal, do you remember what we are doing tomorrow?" I ask.

"Yep!" says Bentley excitedly. "We get to meet with Dad!"

"I still don't know why we have to have an official meeting," Tal mumbles.

"I think you will understand more tomorrow," I say. "I am sure Dad is so excited to see you two." I pause. "We are also going to meet with the doctor at some point after the meeting."

"Why?" asks Tal. "We already had our annual checkup and scans."

"I know, but there is a new therapy that we have been selected to try. I think it will be great. Really similar to what you experienced at the center, Tal."

I called Shari earlier, and she walked me through the reversal therapy process. The first treatment should be fairly quick and simple, but also very helpful after our meeting. It will soften the blow for the boys. I made their appointments, still refusing to do so for myself.

"Do you have any questions?" I ask.

"No," Bentley says, flipping himself upside down.

"I am just really tired, Mom," Tal says. "Can we go to bed?"

"Absolutely. We have a long, exciting day ahead of us. Run, brush your teeth and I will come tuck you in."

"Can Nick tuck us in?" Bentley asks.

I look at Nick and see him smile, obviously honored. "Sure," I say. Bentley races to the washroom and Tal follows.

I reach over and squeeze Nick's hand. "Thanks for being here."

"I wouldn't want to be anywhere else." He cups his hand around my face and gently kisses my lips. Every nerve response in my body is heightened, and my lips tingle. My head spins at the unexpectedness of it.

"Nick! We are ready to be tucked in!" Bentley yells. They must not have brushed for the requisite two minutes, but I decide to let it slide. Nick stands, quite enjoying the stunned look on my face, and walks down the hall.

I hear his voice waft down the hall, the words a familiar bedtime story, and smile. We will be ok. This will all be ok, I think. I force myself to get up and clean the rest of our dinner mess, but all I want to do is sit there, feeling.

About half an hour later, Nick returns to the kitchen, as I am just finishing up.

"The boys are fast asleep," he says, quite proud of himself.

I grin, giving him a thumbs up. He leans on the counter.

"I don't want to go home, Kate," he says softly.

I rinse out the cloth and hang it up to dry.

"Then don't," I say, turning to meet his eyes.

He moves with purpose around the counter and pulls me close. I am guilty and desperate and ecstatic all at once, but I turn those thoughts off and just enjoy being held. Being touched. My body lights up as his hands move across my neck and through my hair. He doesn't kiss me softly, and I am more than okay with that.

CHAPTER 33

NICK LEAVES EARLY the next morning, so we don't have to explain anything to the boys. We plan to meet the next day at the Town Hall to officially submit for pairing. Cerebrally, I am second guessing our decision to spend the night together before making things official, but my body is humming, and at peace. We made the decision to pair, and that's all society requires. Filing our status is secondary. I am sure Berg is probably already aware, since our sensors were in the same location all night and they are likely monitoring us closely. They are likely thrilled. As if on cue, a notification on my sensor alerts me to a call from Shari.

"Good morning," I say, smiling.

"Good morning? That's all you have to say to me? Why didn't you tell me you were officially pairing with Nick?"

"Shhh! The boys are still sleeping! Let me turn your volume down."

"Sorry. But seriously, why didn't you tell me?" Shari says, almost in a whisper. She looks genuinely hurt.

I laugh. "I'm sorry! We just talked about it yesterday. I think I made the decision a while ago, but I needed time to process."

"Well, a message would have been nice. Instead I wake up to an alert."

"What kind of alert?"

"The kind that says 'warning, a new sensor was detected during off-times'. Before I saw it was Nick's, I was worried you had been murdered."

I laugh again. "I am really sorry, Shari. That is pretty funny, though."

"So funny," she says sarcastically. "Seriously, though. I am really happy for you. Are you still going to meet Eric today? Won't that be hard, considering?"

"Yes. It will be hard. But honestly, being with Nick has made me less nervous about it. I know I will miss Eric forever, but Nick is wonderful. It makes my decision easier, knowing that I can do what is best and still have something to look forward to. I know I should be willing to do what is best regardless, but...I guess I am not there yet."

"You are willing, and that's all that matters. I have to go, but I hope all goes well today. I know it will. You and Eric are strong."

"Thanks, Shari. I will call you later." She waves and signs off.

CHAPTER 34

THE BOYS and I are waiting in our meeting room. Tal, whether consciously or subconsciously, is aware that this is more than just a meeting. His shoulders slump and he hasn't said two words since we arrived. Bent, on the other hand, sits in his chair, legs swinging, humming a tune that only he knows. Oblivious as far as I can tell.

It's a few minutes after our appointment time, and I find myself getting antsy. Finally, the door opens and Eric walks in. I catch my breath. He looks awful. He is thin with dark shadows under his eyes, his face almost ashen. My heart wells up in concern. How hard are they working him?

Bentley runs and hugs him tightly around the thighs. Tal walks forward with his hands in his pockets, slightly hesitant, but Eric reaches out and grabs his shoulders, pulling him in, squishing Bentley in the process. They all laugh and fall against the wall. Eric has tears in his eyes and, I realize, so do I. He looks up at me and time seems to stand still for a minute. His eyes are desperate and almost animalistic in their intensity. The air feels thick, and

I have trouble breathing. My body begins to shake uncontrollably.

"Hold it together, Kate," I mentally chastise myself. He whispers something to the boys and they let go, allowing him to stand. Walking forward, he nearly crushes me with his embrace. His stubbled face seems to become a part of me, pressed so tightly between my neck and shoulder. I squeeze him back, knowing that we won't be able to say everything we want to say today. I let loose all of the thoughts of fear, frustration, love, longing, desire, and gratitude, allowing them to flow into the air around us. I visualize them seeping into him and hope that he knows how much I love him. That I will never stop loving him.

When he pulls away, he traces his hand down my arm, and places something in the palm of my hand, so subtly that I barely notice it. I take my cues from him and place the small slip of paper in my back pocket as he retreats to give his attention to the boys. Should I have written him something? Why is he being so secretive? The questions swirl in my mind, making it impossible for me to focus.

"So, how have you been?" I ask, attempting to create normal conversation.

When I speak, it's as if I have broken down any last defenses Eric may have had. A sob escapes his lips and he has a difficult time composing himself. My body is frozen, watching him break. I have never seen him like this.

"I have missed you all so much," he says, pulling the boys to either side of him. "Tell me everything I've missed."

The boys immediately launch into all of the fun things we have done, all of the new conditioning they have experienced. Bentley mentions Nick a few times, and I see Eric biting his lip, doing his best to hold it together.

"What about you, Dad?" Tal asks. "How is your research going?"

"It's great. We have quite a few pairs moving forward already." He pauses, not meeting my eyes, and I want to throw up. "We were able to find more pairs than expected in some of the other territories, so we are working around the clock training teams to support them. I am tired and fulfilled and...really sad that it's taking me away from you," he finishes softley. Bentley reaches up and wipes a tear from his neck.

"Mom said—" Tal starts. "Mom said that you might have to do this full time. That we might not see you much anymore."

Eric sighs, and the tears roll in an unending torrent down his cheeks. "I have tried to find any way possible to be home and be with you, Tal. I want you to know that if there is any way, I will find it. Right now...that just doesn't seem to be possible. It's not fair for your Mom to be alone all the time."

Bentley pipes up, "She's not alone, she has Nick! He can help her until you come back."

Eric laughs, concealing another sob, and strokes Bentley's head. "I think that's a great idea, bud. Look at you, looking out for your Mom."

He is completely wrecked. I feel flayed open on the inside, and I don't know what to say, or if I can say anything at all. The guilt of being with Nick last night is unbearable. I knew how hard this would be, so why did I ask for this meeting? I guess I thought that Eric would walk in uncaring and distant, the way it has been for weeks, and it would solidify my decision? Why did he choose now to be vulnerable!?

This Eric makes me shrink. Who would do this to the person they love? The horribly tragic piece of it all is that I really thought I was *helping*. Doing the right thing. But, obviously not. And what about Nick? How can I continue on now, knowing that I have absolutely destroyed a person I love, the father of my children? I am dizzy and lean on a chair for support. Eric wipes the tears off his face and gives the kids another hug.

"Dad, can you come home for a while?" Tal asks.

Eric laughs. "I wish I could, bud. I wish I could." To me he says, "Kate, I will call you tomorrow to talk logistics. Other than that, I won't really be available after this weekend."

I nod. I don't trust myself to do anything else. After he leaves, I rush out with the boys, completely forgetting about their appointments, and head home.

Later that night as I am taking off my clothes to get ready for bed, I remember the slip of paper I put in my jeans pocket. I frantically search for it, opening it up to see that it is, indeed, a long note from Eric. The paper is thin and folded into a small square. The print is nearly microscopic, and I force myself to read slowly.

"Kate. I can't do this. I know you might be decided, but I have to

*try. If you have moved on with Nick, I respect that. If you are unde-cided...I plead with the intensity of a broken man: please come with me. I don't know where we'll go, or what we'll do, but I want it to be together. I have had plenty of time to think about my options. There is a part of me that wants to embrace this path, but a much larger part of me wants you and the boys. I don't know if that means there is something wrong with me, but I have done all that has been asked. If my brain is pushing for this, there must be a reason. I am choosing to trust my instincts, and hoping Berg will understand. I want to discuss our options and find a different solution. I am allowed to call to finalize things after our meeting. I don't have a plan, but I thought we could meet at the Peace Celebration next weekend. I know you will be there with the boys, and I have asked to attend. If you are in, just mention the celebration at any point in our call. If I don't hear it...know that **I will be ok**, and I love you. Forever. --Eric"*

The celebration. I had completely forgotten about it. Our lives have been so distracting and out of routine that it was completely off my radar. My mind goes into planning overdrive. I need to prepare our traditional meal with the boys and see which activities they want to attend. They usually love the shows and live music. Though I haven't participated in the Ceremony regularly, we always fully participate in this one opportunity for family frivolity. The organizers always include something completely silly and impractical that we get to enjoy for the evening. Last year, it was fireworks. I am sure this years' event has been announced and I just missed it.

"Wait," I stop myself. "This is what I'm thinking about? That's what I got from this? That I need to plan our traditional celebration activities?" I throw myself onto the bed in disgust. This note changes everything and I am thinking about the celebration!?

I read Eric's note again and feel my body shutting down, the full weight of it hitting me. Deep, wracking sobs of relief and horror burst from my body, and I throw the note out of the way so it won't get hit with my tears. What a mess. I am with Nick. We are supposed to go *tomorrow* to submit for pairing. The boys will be doing their first session of reversal, since I failed to show up today.

I'm doing all of this for Eric! How do I know if he is making the right choice now? I previously weighed the options and decided I couldn't be the person who made him regret his life forever. Can I be that person now? Can I trust that he won't regret this in five years? My body aches to be with him, but I still don't see how it can end well. On the other hand, can I continue on this path *knowing* it isn't what Eric wants? I imagine explaining this to Nick and my head begins to throb, pulsing so hard that I wonder if my skull is up for containing the pressure.

I reach for the note, folding it up and placing it in my drawer, then move to the washroom to splash water on my face. I have to sleep. I have to process.

CHAPTER 35

WHAT DO I TELL NICK? This is the only question on my mind when I wake up, feeling slightly more sane, but still missing the answers I so desperately need. I am supposed to meet with Nick this afternoon. Would it be appropriate to ask him to wait until after the celebration? That would give me time to think, time for the boys to do therapy...if we go forward with that. Every part of me feels stiff, and my neck aches. I have to decompress before I get another headache.

The door to my bedroom opens.

"Hey Mom!" Bentley says, jumping up on the bed with me. I grab him and hug him close.

"I can't breathe," he says laughing.

"Sorry. I needed a hug this morning," I say, plastering on a smiling facade.

"I'm hungry."

"I knew you would be," I laugh. "Go on out and I'll come make breakfast." He runs out with his pants falling down, as usual. I sit up and tap my sensor, sending a message to Nick.

Hey, yesterday was rough. I think we are going to need a bit more time before officially moving forward with this. Can we plan on waiting until after the Peace Celebration? I completely forgot about it, and the boys look forward to it every year. I am hoping to do some preparation with them this week. Want to join in on celebration planning tomorrow?

P.S. I am so sorry to put this off. I am doing my best, Nick. I know this isn't easy for you.

I know this sounds like a total cop-out, but it's the best I can do. The repercussions of these decisions determine everything and it's too much for my brain to take in. I breathe. I will take Eric's lead and trust my instincts, as well.

Entering the kitchen, I assemble oats, salt, and apples to make oatmeal. Tal is going to complain, but it's all I have the energy for right now. I squeeze half a lemon into a glass of water and take a drink while I wait for the pot to boil.

"Bent woke me up," Tal complains, pointing to Bentley as they enter the room.

"It's time for breakfast!" Bentley announces excitedly.

"Let's let people wake up naturally, okay?" I say. "If he sleeps in reeeallly long, I'll let you know when to wake him up."

"K," says Bentley, somewhat disappointed.

"Hey guys, guess what is happening next week."

They stare at me blankly.

"It's the Peace Celebration!" I say with exaggerated enthusiasm.

"What? That's next week?" says Tal, as Bentley looks at me wide-eyed.

"Yes! I have been so busy, I completely forgot about it."

"I remember they said something in conditioning last week, but I forgot to remind you!" Bentley says, throwing his arms up in the air. His energy is contagious.

"You guys have been busy, too. It's totally fine, we still have plenty of time to plan," I say, giving the oatmeal a final stir, then reach into the fridge to pull out the blueberries and walnuts. Tal pulls two bowls out of the cupboard, and Bentley picks the spoons out of the drawer. I am impressed that Tal hasn't said anything yet about the oatmeal. Maybe all this excitement is a good enough distraction.

"What are they doing this year?" Tal asks.

"I'm not actually sure. I was thinking I would look it up after breakfast."

"Can you look now? We could read about it while we eat!"

"Let me take a few bites and then I will," I say, hurriedly adding my blueberries and slurping some of it down. I pull out my tablet and turn on the display, directing it to the community website. The first image we see is of a gigantic balloon.

"That's a hot air balloon! We learned about those at school!" Bentley says.

"I'm guessing...that this is the main event at the celebration," I say as I manipulate the image to see the information below it. "Yep, check it out. It says here that they will be doing a balloon launch on Saturday morning, early. Hey Bent, maybe you could wake Tal up *that* day," I say teasing. Tal rolls his eyes but smiles. "Do you guys want to do it? I've never been on one. It looks like we can take a ride if we want, or we can just watch."

"Aren't they really dangerous? Like they fly with a ball of fire in them or something?" Tal asks.

"I think there's definitely a reason we don't use them anymore, but I don't think they are dangerous for small rides. Who knows—I haven't actually ever seen one in person!"

The boys both get a kick out of me not knowing something. I remember when the air of mystery surrounding my parents expertise began to burst for me, and I felt the same way. The best was when I knew something they didn't. One time, my dad was having trouble figuring out how to use his new health sensor. I was eight at the time and had just seen my instructor showing someone else how to use one at conditioning. I immediately jumped in and taught Dad how it worked. The look on his face was priceless. After that, I wanted to earn that look from him every single day.

I take another bite of oatmeal and see a call coming through on my sensor. It's Eric and I panic, almost choking on my food. I haven't had enough time to figure out a plan of action. Tal reaches over and answers before I can stop him.

"Dad! Are you coming home today?"

I hear Eric take in a deep breath. "I wish! I'm actually a territory away. How are you guys doing?"

"Mom is showing us the hot air balloons for the Peace Celebration!" says Bentley excitedly.

"She is? That's so cool. Hey, can I actually talk to Mom privately for a minute?"

"Yes," I say, laughing at the boys' pouty faces. "I promise you can talk for a few more minutes after, okay?"

That seems to appease them. I turn my sensor to private and walk out onto the patio. "Hey," I say quietly.

"Hey, Kate." There is a long pause. I don't know what to say. I mean, I do know what I want to say, but...it's complicated. How do I tell Eric that Nick and I...How do I tell Nick...I can't even form a complete sentence in my brain, let alone out loud. Eric breaks the silence, clearing his throat.

"So, like I mentioned, I am just calling to figure out logistics. I need to pick up my things from the house, and I thought that might be best to do when the kids aren't home." He stammers, struggling to get through this.

His face from yesterday haunts me. I have never seen him in such terrible condition before. And it isn't like we haven't been through hard times together. We have both lost our parents and—my mind transports me to four years ago.

We had been cleared to have a third child. We conceived easily, as always, but lost the baby at around ten weeks gestation. It was terrifying for me. I had felt some cramping and called my doctor, but he told me that there really wasn't much to do besides wait and see. At that young age, the baby wouldn't be viable. All tests up to that point had seemed normal, and I think that's why it was so hard. We had already made plans.

We hadn't told the boys yet, since I was still in the first trimester, so at least they were spared. Eric took it extremely hard, mostly because analysis showed that his DNA contribution caused the miscarriage. It was doubly hard because we found out shortly thereafter that we were not cleared to try again. He felt like a failure, despite my constant insistence that it wasn't the case, and took a few months to come out of it. Even then, he never looked as bad as he did yesterday. The pain in his voice strikes me deeply, and I can't handle it.

"Maybe you could do that the morning of the Peace Celebration," I blurt out. In that moment, I don't know if I'm right, but I do know what I am going to do. I care about Nick, but this is Eric. I have tried embracing the societal ideal, but I can't live in a world where I know I didn't try every possible option to stay with the man I love and have committed to. If we crash and burn, if Berg moves us to Tier 2, if Eric becomes bitter and depressed...I guess I will have to live with that.

I repeat to myself that this plan of action represents where I am at, nothing more. There is no blame, just observation of my brain coming to conclusions. It's easier to accept that than feel responsible for the potential breakdown of my family. And another incredible human being. And generations of people who will suffer for my decision. I force myself to stop thinking about it.

Eric's voice is throaty when he speaks. "As it turns out, I asked for leave to attend, so that works great. I will be there."

"We were planning to attend the balloon launch in the morning," I say. "I'm not sure what else we will be attending, but we will definitely be there at 7am."

"I will plan on that timing then," he says. "Thanks for everything..." he says and trails off.

My eyes fill with tears, and for the first time in months, my heart feels full. I will meet Eric in a week, and we will be together. I focus on that and not all of the unknowns that come along with it.

"Have a great week, Eric."

"Thanks. Enjoy the balloons."

It's like we are dating again. Neither one of us wants to be the first to end the call. I remember I promised the boys they could talk, so I tell Eric to hold on. They can be the ones to sign off.

After they talk for a few minutes and end the call, we get on our bikes and ride to conditioning. The boys chatter nonstop about the celebration and how they can't wait to discuss everything with their friends. We have missed quite a few classes lately, and I didn't realize how much they look forward to sharing and talking with kids their age. It's been a while since they have played with anyone besides each other, I realize. I should set something up.

Before I start the ride home, I check my sensor and see that Nick has responded. My stomach drops. I select the message and begin reading.

Hey Kate, I am so sorry it was tough. I expected it would be hard for all of you, and honestly, it's hard for me knowing you are in pain. I feel somewhat responsible even though...even though. I just want you to know that I love you. Take all the time you need. If you want someone to talk to, I am here. Would love to help with celebration planning.

I'm smiling and I immediately want to slap myself in the face. How can I be smiling at a message from the man I am about to leave? After we have paired? I think back to all of the things he shared, about feeling rejected, alone, unable to find someone to move forward with. Tears start rolling down my cheeks. He is young, and I know he will find someone else, but I might be a terrible person. The most terrible person. I want to curl up and sob. I see someone walking up the street and don't want to attract attention or have to explain my emotional distress, so I start riding. I zone out as I pedal. When I pull up in front of my house, I wish I would have continued on. Grace is sitting on my front porch.

CHAPTER 36

I QUICKLY TAKE off my helmet and try to pull myself together. It proves to be impossible. With my eyes red and puffy, I step off the bike and move slowly up the walkway. Grace stands as I approach, looking stiff and out of place on my whimsical porch in her crisp, white shirt and black slacks.

"Hi Kate, I am sorry to come over unannounced. I wanted to check in on you and see how you are handling everything," she says flatly.

I look at her with my wrecked face, daring her to comment. "It's been hard," is all I can get out. I really just want to go inside and curl up in bed. Instead, I say, "Can I get you some water or herbal tea?"

"That would be great."

I open the door and walk into the kitchen to get the mugs.

"When you didn't show up for the boys' first reversal treatment, I was so concerned. I wanted to personally come by and make sure everything was alright."

I sigh. I completely forgot to call today. Of course that raised red flags. I place the teapot on the stove.

"Our final appointment with Eric was yesterday," I don't know why I even bother to say that, of course she already knows, "and that was difficult for all of us. Then we discussed him collecting his things this morning. The boys seem to be doing ok, but I'm not. I completely forgot to cancel that. I think I want to wait until after the Peace Celebration to move forward. They are so excited about it, and it's providing a great distraction. After that, I think they will need it more."

I hear the pot whistle, take it off the burner, and pour it over the tea bags in our mugs.

"I am sure the last few days have been a blur," Grace says empathetically. "Have you talked with Nick about it?"

"I really haven't had a chance. I've been trying to keep everyone together here."

"Talking to someone you trust can be really helpful in this situation."

I'm not an idiot. Of course I know talking with someone would be helpful. Why does she only bring up Nick and not Shari? I really hate feeling like I am a pawn. Like I am being manipulated.

I take a deep breath, and a thought occurs to me. Why haven't Nick and I been asked to do training? Eric talked about how they are doing training and conditioning with the other pairs that have matched. Why haven't they said one thing to me? I assume they are meeting with Nick at this point, but who knows.

It can only be one of two things. Either they don't trust me to react the way they think I should...or they already know that Eric has told me. Is there something in my behavior that is tipping them off? Or in Eric's behavior? Is there anything I have done in my life to make them think that I would have a propensity to rebel against something? But that's exactly what I am doing. I am rebelling. Eric and I have already set up a time to meet. Do they know about that? I don't see how they could, but my heart starts to beat faster.

"That's a great suggestion. Thank you," I say calmly. I remove the bags from the mugs and pass one to Grace. She blows along the surface and takes a small sip.

"Do you need anything from the Committee? We so rarely deal with un-pairing that I don't think we have the best resources. Have you considered doing reversal therapy as well?"

She says it like our un-pairing is an unfortunate occurrence, not something that she orchestrated. Anger again rises up in my chest. I take a drink. It's too hot, but somehow that helps.

"I've considered it. I just need more time to really see how my brain is going to deal with this. I haven't had many experiences in my life when I have been pushed to the max emotionally like this. I don't know what to expect."

"Don't you?" Grace says quietly.

I pause. "What do you mean by that?"

She looks at me with what I can only assume is her version of a kind smile. It feels forced. "I have just been thinking about when your mother died. I remember it being very hard for you."

It's as if she threw cold water over me. Of course losing my mother was difficult. Am I really being judged for my emotional response then? I had a 3-year-old and a 6-year-old, and both of my parents died within a year of each other. I wasn't responding just to my mother's death, I was responding to all of it.

"There were so many things creating chaos for me during that time. I don't feel like I can expect that level of reaction to this event."

"But this is someone you have built a life with for eleven years. Do you honestly think your level of emotional response will be less?"

She makes a good point.

"I don't know that I can directly compare my level of emotional bonding and investment with my parents versus with Eric. I was also emotionally and physically stressed with child-rearing when my parents died. I think I am in a better place now."

"Well that's good to hear." She takes another sip.

I think about what I was like when my mother died. It wasn't pretty. Back then, I assumed life would continue the way it always had. That every day would get better and happiness was an unlimited resource. I was very optimistic then. I guess I still am, but it's more steeped in reality now. When my mom died, my brain literally couldn't process it, despite the fact that I had been given plenty of warning.

Looking back at that period now, I recognize that I was only paying attention to the good. I only ever allowed myself to hear that the treatment was working. I heard about the increase in her platelet and red blood cell counts. I saw that she wasn't weak and throwing up when we went out for her birthday.

I didn't see the days when she couldn't lift her arms, or when she slept on the washroom floor so she wouldn't throw up in her bed. I didn't see the scans showing her body lit up in every place imaginable. I wrote those things off as part of the process, just something that we had to pass through on the way to recovery. Because of course she was going to recover. Never once did I think otherwise.

The day that she died, I was right there holding her hand. She was lying in her bed, and I remember the privacy curtain lightly blowing in the breeze. Her window must have been open, but I don't remember checking it. That image will stay with me forever. Her face, creased with pain, suddenly at peace. The curtain kept gently blowing, the sun still shining. Nothing changed. I sat there for a long time, waiting for her to take another breath, frozen until Eric put his hand on my shoulder.

The next few weeks were an incomprehensible blur. People have told me that I seemed normal, that they were impressed with my ability to 'handle' everything so easily. I wasn't handling anything, I just checked out.

We had a simple gathering with those who knew her, to share stories and give closure. The next day, it was like a switch was flipped in me. I lost all motivation to do anything, and I couldn't explain myself. I spent weeks like this. Eric took care of everything for our family and later discussion have helped me understand that he, too, was terrified and felt helpless. I eventually pulled out of it, but only because of his love and support.

Of course, Grace doesn't know that I am in no danger of that happening again. She doesn't know that I don't intend to lose Eric. Because I don't know what else to say, I sip my tea and wait, hoping that this meeting will pass quickly.

"Well, I guess my fears were unfounded," she says simply. "Is there anything we can do to support you through this?"

"I don't mean to sound naive, Grace. I know it will be a long road. I think I know what warning signs to look for, though. I will let you know if I get desperate."

She stands and sets her mug by the sink.

"Thank you for the tea. I had better get going."

I breathe a silent sigh of relief and walk her to the door, politely sending her off. Now to curl up and cry.

CHAPTER 37

I WAKE the boys early for the celebration. Actually, I wake Bentley and allow him to wake up Tal. With supervision, of course, so it doesn't get out of hand. My heart is fluttering, and I am having difficulty thinking clearly. I couldn't sleep last night, so I used the time to pack our lunch and jackets. The boys get dressed quickly, and we head to the public transport station. We don't have the car this month, so we have to plan in a little extra time to walk down there.

Tal and Bentley are a little slow this morning, but that's to be expected. I think anything would feel slow to me, considering I have had to wait an interminably long week for this moment. Every nerve ending in my body is tingling. I am both excited and terrified. I can't wait to see Eric, but my body screams for answers regarding the aftermath. What will we do? Where will we go? I hope Eric has thought this through. He has more information than I do, so I don't see the benefit of me getting my heart set on a plan that most likely won't work.

The train arrives at the open space, and we step out into the cool morning air. The morning light is barely creeping up along the horizon, hinting a new day, and the air is fresh and clean. The crisp sensation against my cheeks centers me. I hold onto Bentley's hand, and we follow the map to the balloon launch.

At first, I worry that we are in the wrong location. I see only vehicles with trailers, spaced out across the field. Checking the map again, I conclude that this is indeed correct. There is a playground nearby, so I invite the boys to go run around for a bit, assuming that the organizers haven't quite set everything up yet. I sit on a bench and pull out my thermos. Even though it is insulated, the exterior exudes enough heat to warm my hands. I watch Tal and Bent run around, chasing each other as the sun slowly gets brighter, shooting rays of light through the eastern sky.

I notice what look like large, wrinkled blankets being pulled out along the grass behind us and call the boys over to look. I assume these are the balloons. Sure enough, we see an operator tinkering with a mechanism that shoots out flames, with another person beside him, pointing a fan into a large circular opening in the bag. As it begins to inflate, my eyes widen. This thing is going to be huge. The whole process is very physical. Men and women are hanging on to the basket attached to the balloon, keeping it steady. Others are holding the fans and testing the blowers. We see partially-filled balloons popping up everywhere now, our eyes taking in all of the colors and patterns. It's magical, and the boys are entranced.

A hand slides around my waist, and my heart leaps. I turn to face

Eric and pull back. It's Nick. His face suddenly turns from a smile to a look of concern, probably mirroring my own.

"I'm so sorry," he says hurriedly. "I didn't mean to frighten you."

"No, I'm so sorry, I just wasn't expecting— "

"I know. I thought I would surprise you. When we got together the other day, the boys mentioned that you were hoping to watch the launch. I was planning to be here already, so I thought I would find you guys. I probably should have said something."

My heart is racing. Where is Eric? Is he watching this? I specifically didn't mention anything to Nick, to avoid a situation like this. Leave it to the boys to complicate things. I mentally scold myself for blaming them. *I* should have said something. But how would I have explained to them that I didn't want Nick to know? I figured by *not* saying anything, my chances were higher that they would forget to mention it! I figured wrong.

I force a smile to my face. "No, it's fine. I was just surprised, which you just said was your goal right? That was nice of you to look for us."

He drops his arms. "I can go watch on my own if you were planning on spending time with the boys," he offers, looking slightly dejected and confused.

"No, watch with us for a bit. Then maybe I will spend some alone time with the boys before we take our ride." Tal and Bentley notice Nick and give him quick hugs before continuing their game of tag. I am desperately hoping that Eric will wait to find us until after Nick leaves. I want so badly to tell Nick what is going on, but I can't do it. He is so happy to be there. My mind flickers to what I imagine him to be thinking and feeling when he hears the news from someone else. I am selfish and a coward, yes, and I am going to accept that for now. He will be better off without me. Besides, I rationalize, I don't even know how all of this will end up. I don't know if Eric has a plan. I would rather wait until I have something more solid to tell.

We watch the balloons fill and rise to their full height. Standing by the heaters, we feel the warm, dry air on our faces as we watch them begin to leave the earth, growing smaller and smaller in the sky.

I notice five balloons at the edge of the field that are filled, but still tethered. I assume those are the ones that will be open for rides. I begin to make a plan for our exit. My hands are still in my pockets, even though it's plenty warm out. I know Nick is probably confused by my standoffish behavior, but if Eric is watching...well, I don't want to send mixed signals.

I am about to open my mouth to tell Nick where we are heading, when I see him. Eric. He is walking through the crowd toward us. My heart leaps and then almost immediately sinks when I realize that he is focused on Nick. Though it's only been a week, Eric almost looks like himself again, the dark shadows only a hint of their previous shade. The boys follow my gaze and see their dad, immediately running toward him.

"Kate, what's going on?" Nick questions.

"Nick..." I start, but Eric and the boys approach before I can finish.

"Hey Nick," Eric says gently. He doesn't embrace me, in what I can only assume is respect. Eric points out another balloon to distract the boys.

"Eric, what's going on?" Nick asks quietly. "I don't think you are supposed to be here."

"I'm not," Eric says. "Kate, why don't I watch the boys for a minute and you can have a moment with Nick to explain." He looks at me and in that moment, I know that he knows. He understands what I have done and what Nick and I have been through. A weight seems to physically rise off my body, as if floating into the air like the balloons. He isn't walking away, even though I tried to.

Nick looks hurt. "Explain what?" he says. My eyes are already filled with tears. I nod and hold on to Nick's arm, leading him away from the boys.

"I'll meet you at the balloon rides, Kate." Eric says.

Nick and I walk arm in arm for a few minutes without saying anything. We come to the gardens, and I lead him to a bench, still covered with morning dew. I sit down anyway, and Nick joins me.

"What's going on, Kate?" he asks quietly.

"Nick, I don't know what to say." The tears roll down my cheeks. "I wanted to move forward, and you are such an amazing guy, I thought I could. But Eric doesn't want to, and I can't do this knowing that he isn't on board. I just...I can't. It would eat at me from the inside out. Forever. Knowing that Eric was somewhere miserable, I just..."

Nick reaches out and pulls me to him. His shoulder quickly becomes damp with my tears. I feel his chest shaking and realize that he is crying, too. I have never seen Nick cry. I hold him close in the best apology embrace I can muster. Eventually, I slip out of his arms and look at him.

"Is this why you wanted to wait to file for pairing?" he asks.

"Yes. I'm so sorry I didn't say something sooner. I wasn't sure, and I didn't know if Eric would change his mind."

"So you were stringing me along as your second option?" he asks, the hurt evident in his eyes.

"Nick, I've been with Eric for eleven years. Eleven years! We have had children together, worked together, grown older together. Every part of me is connected to him. I wasn't trying to string you along, I was trying to do what was right. And I didn't want to hurt you unless I knew...I had to be sure that Eric was sure."

Nick's tone is more intense when he speaks again. "Sure about what? Sure that he wants to do what's best for him as an individual? He, of all people, should understand the consequences of this action." He pauses and takes a deep breath. "I'm sorry. I don't mean to preach to you, I am just shocked that he is so...weak."

My cheeks burn. Eric is anything but weak. I breathe, acknowledging the position I have put him in, and take a moment before responding. The last thing I want to do is offend Nick when I am the one turning his world upside down.

"Maybe we both are. I don't know, Nick. I am unsure about a lot of things right now."

"What is your plan?" he asks crisply.

"I don't know. I haven't had a chance to talk with Eric about the next step. I know we will have to talk to the Committee. I am not looking forward to that," I chuckle. Nick doesn't.

"I am obviously extremely upset about all of this, Kate. I don't understand it. I think I need to go." He stands to leave but looks lost. He eventually goes right, and I watch him begin to walk away.

"Nick!" I call. "If we had met under different circumstances—"

"Don't." He cuts me off. "Goodbye, Kate." He turns and walks further into the garden.

I stand, shaking, my pants wet from the bench. I walk quickly back the way we came, then toward the balloon rides.

CHAPTER 38

THE LINES for rides come into view, and I start scanning for Eric and the boys. I look up and down each line but don't see them. I am already feeling extremely on edge, and my hands begin shaking even more intensely. When I scan the first line again, my stomach drops. I see two faces looking directly at me. Shari and Grace. They start moving my direction. Why would they be here right now? Why are they even together? I know Shari doesn't particularly care for Grace, but they have worked together multiple times. Maybe they came together for the celebration?

Despite my interpretations of the situation, my gut tells me that something is terribly wrong. *Where is my family?* Cognitive processes end, and I turn and run. I don't know why I am running or where I am going, but my legs continue pumping. I bolt directly away from Grace and Shari and have only gone a few steps when I feel something hit me in the shoulder blade. It stings. Before I can see what it is, my vision recedes slightly, and I fall to my hands and knees in the grass. The soft earth shifts under my fingertips and I wonder why I haven't looked at grass up close before. Its color is variable, not just pure green like I thought. I allow my face to sink into it and close my eyes. Just for a minute...

CHAPTER 39

I HEAR HUMMING. A low, consistent humming. Is it the car? Did I
fall asleep in the car again? I open my eyes and stretch my jaw,
feeling mucous crusted to my lips and the edges of my mouth. I
move to wipe it away, but can't. My arms won't move. Looking
down, I see that they are restrained. The chair I am propped up in
is slightly reclined. Everything is soft and comfortable, considering. My eyelids feel like lead, and I still can't keep them open long
enough to figure out where I am or why I am here.

I hear a door open and a woman walks in. It's Shari. She walks to
the chair, sitting close to me, and uses a damp cloth to wipe my lips
before brushing the hair from my eyes.

"Shari, where am I?" I ask. My voice is thick and slow. I clear my
throat.

"Hey, it's okay. Just breathe. I will explain everything in a few
minutes. Just let yourself fully wake up." She smirks. "I don't want
to have to repeat myself."

I do what she says. I breathe. Suddenly, I remember, and my body jolts.

"There it is," Shari says wryly.

"Shari! Eric and the boys, I don't know where they are! I was talking with Nick and then...then I saw you and Grace. What is going on?" My heart is racing and I am pulling furiously on the restraints. My legs won't move, and I see that they are fastened as well.

"I know, Kate. I know. It's okay. I promise we are going to talk about all of that, but you need to calm down. Eric and the boys are safe."

She should have led with that. "You're sure? Why weren't they in line?"

"I'm sure. Just calm down and we can talk about everything."

I try to calm my heart rate. I take deep breaths, hold, and then release, focusing on calming images in my mind. It's extremely difficult, but I trust Shari. If she says they are safe, I believe her.

"Good job, Kate. Your vitals are normalizing. Just a minute more and we can start."

I continue to breathe, forcing my questions to the back of my mind. Shari pulls up a chair close to me, my body feeling cold on that side as she shifts into it, taking her warmth with her.

"Ok. Ready?"

I nod.

"Do you want me to start?" Shari asks.

I nod again. I don't even know what questions to ask.

"I obviously know how hard the last few months have been for you, Eric, and the boys. I was really impressed with how willing you were to adjust and move forward with Nick, once you understood the situation. I surmised that Eric had told you everything after he came back after the ceremony. It didn't make sense that he would suddenly want to come home for a night, just to support someone he knew he couldn't be with. You acted strong that next week. I assured Grace and the rest of the Committee that you were well on your way. They are completely committed to these pairings and were very concerned about yours in particular. There were only a few pairs that were taken from existing pairings. A majority of the matches they found were between young or single individuals."

"There are other pairs like mine?"

"Only a few, but yes. Not in this territory."

I motion for her to continue.

"I was sure that everything would go perfectly, as long—" she sighs and looks down at the blanket over my legs. "As long as Eric was committed, too. I knew that you would fiercely defend whatever you thought was best for him. As soon as you asked for that meeting with him, I was worried."

"Worried about what?" I ask, my voice still hoarse.

"Worried that seeing each other would make him—or you —reconsider."

"Why is that such a terrible thing? I mean, I know it's definitely not what the Committee would deem best for society, but how do they know for sure? What if Eric and I have some other purpose we need to fulfil? What if our kids need us and *they* have another path to walk? How can they be sure that gene propagation is the *only* best interest?"

"I hear you, Kate, but you already know the answer to that. This system works. It has created peace, safety, health, all of it. We are so much better off now. You can't expect everyone to throw that away because one pairing isn't as cut and dry," she replies, her voice biting.

Yes, this system works, but it's been so long since we tried selection like this. It seems like moving forward with caution would be recommended in this situation. It is completely different from past initiatives. I don't understand how the Committee isn't seeing this.

"Kate?" Shari asks.

I realize I have been staring past her.

"Are you ok?" she puts her hand on my shoulder.

"Yes, sorry. Just thinking."

"Should we take a break?"

"No, I really want to continue."

"Ok. So, rewind. As soon as you set that meeting with Eric, I was extremely nervous that something would derail. I recommended that we record the meeting."

I open my mouth, but Shari cuts me off.

"I know. I know that probably makes you upset with me, and I wish I could say that I'm sorry, but Kate. Look what happened! Eric passed you a note, yes?"

I stare at her. "Yes."

"We couldn't see what it said, but after hearing your conversation—"

"You have been listening to us?"

"We had no choice!" she nearly shouts, exasperated. "You haven't been completely upfront with me. Or Grace. Or Nick. What were we supposed to do?"

I am absolutely shocked. This is not the world I know. People who have done their conditioning and are compliant with continued training have complete flexibility in Tier 1. We fulfill our societal responsibilities and are then expected to take care of ourselves, work on projects we are interested in, raise our children, and find new ways to contribute. Never would I have guessed that someone was spying on me—or anyone, for that matter. I thought Eric was being paranoid. Apparently not.

"You were supposed to trust me!" I blurt out. "You, of all people, should know how I felt, the kind of stress I was under. You should have been my advocate, not recommending that the Committee invade my privacy!"

"Kate. I am your advocate. I advocated for you up until I felt like you were distancing yourself. I stepped in to help. And if you felt like someone's actions were endangering society, I know that you would have stepped in as well."

"How am I endangering society, Shari? By wanting to stay with my pair and raise my children, I am a danger?" I try hard to keep the emotion out of my voice, but I am not entirely successful.

"Yes. Exactly. You and Eric both know what's at stake here, and you are moving toward an easier path. A more comfortable option. *That attitude* is a danger."

"Just the other day, you were telling me that our differences are a strength. Our actions are determined by our genetics and social inputs, right? So Eric and I are acting in the only way we can act. When Eric couldn't move forward, I couldn't continue either, knowing that he was suffering. It is what it is. We aren't strong enough, we haven't had enough societal preparation. Or our bonding is strong enough that it overpowers the conditioning we do have. Or we are faulty! I don't know!? You tell me!" Now it is my turn to shout, and I immediately regret it. I know Shari is trying to help.

"Exactly, Kate. Exactly," she nods, her voice calm. "Eric's actions and your response made it very apparent that you did not have the conditioning and subsequent mental and physical strength to be able to handle this." Shari's voice becomes strained and, for the first time, I notice that she also has dark purple circles underneath her eyes.

"What does that mean, then? Eric and I are open to possibilities. We knew—or at least I knew—that there wasn't much chance of us staying in Tier 1 once we were back together. It would be blatantly disregarding our societal responsibility. So, what do we need to do?"

Shari looks at me unblinking.

"Can we take off the restraints and discuss this?" I ask.

"No, Kate. I feel horrible that you have to be in this condition, but I do think it's for the best."

"What do you mean?" I ask, my voice a mere whisper. "Where is Eric? Can we discuss this together?"

"The Committee has decided that in order to proceed, we will need to do reversal therapy on you and Eric. We can take you both back to a point where you remember each other, but not as deeply. It will help with the transition."

My body tenses. "What transition? Shari, are they seriously going to try and force us to move forward with this? I already told Nick. There's no way he will want to proceed now. He knows how I feel. Not to mention that this is completely violating my freedom to act."

"It is not a violation. You are not willing to fulfill your societal obligations, and that alone is enough to justify action by the Committee."

"What if our 'obligations' are not agreeable? In every other aspect of my life in Tier 1, I was given flexibility to find the path that suited me. Flexibility to learn from my own actions and results that come because of them. How is it justified that I would be forced into a pairing? Forced to procreate? All of that should be determined by my brain and my body."

"I hear you." Shari smiles wanly. "I know that it doesn't sound right. But, in situations like these where there is so much riding on a specific action, Berg is not willing to leave that solely up to you and Eric. They see this push-back as a failure on their part. How did two Tier 1 individuals act in their own self-interest over the whole?”

It's a valid question. We have been taught and trained since the day we were born to protect the whole over self. What went wrong? Did our family become 'the whole' in my mind? I feel more strongly about doing for them instead of doing for society? Maybe it feels too disconnected? I have let everybody down, including Eric. Yet, I am still fiercely against this plan of action.

“Shari, you can't believe that this is the best option. I don't know much about reversal therapy, but I do know that it isn't as effective when someone is unwilling.”

Shari sighs. “Kate, honestly. Can you not see that we are trying to help? Something has gone wrong and I, along with the Committee, am trying to fix it. To put you in a situation where you can be successful.”

“But it's success on their terms!” I plead.

“No, it's success on everyone's terms. We have all agreed that this is the life we want to protect.” She stares me down. “You have to accept that your logic is flawed. Let me help.”

My eyes fill with tears. This is unimaginable. These last few months have been unimaginable. Where did I go wrong? What did I miss?

“Please,” I say. “If this is going to happen, can I please see Eric and the boys one last time?” Before she protests, I continue. “It shouldn't change anything. You are going to reverse it anyway. If I can see them, I will do it. Willingly. I won't fight. It will be more effective that way, and Berg should be happy."

I can see that she is considering. She taps her sensor and sends a message.

"I will ask, Kate. I can't promise anything."

CHAPTER 40

I WAKE up to continue staring at a blank wall. My room is comfortable, but bland. It is basically a glorified holding cell. I still have no idea where I am. Shari said we are within Tier 1 boundaries, but I am at a loss as to where this facility could be located. There are a lot of things that I have no idea about, apparently, but I didn't ever think to question.

I have never encountered someone who was in this position before. But then, I guess I wouldn't ever know if I had. My friends at work won't ever know it happened to me. Will they? Will I forget about conversations I've had or things we've done? Would anyone even notice if I did? Shari will notice, but obviously that doesn't make a difference, she will also know why I have forgotten. Eric. Eric would notice.

My eyes start to sting. Nobody outside of those core people really knows me well enough to have the chance to recognize that I have changed. Maybe people who don't have children have stronger relationships with other adults? If connection is one of our goals, then how is it possible for me to feel this lonely in a moment like this? I make a mental note to ask Shari. Of course, I may not remember her answer.

I lie there and think about the boys. I remember the first time I gave birth. The incredible pressure that suddenly gave way for me to grasp a new little human. A slippery, squishy bundle of flesh. I was in shock and awe holding Tal. Theoretically, I knew that he was alive inside me, but until I saw him. Touched him. It didn't seem real.

I remember our ride home. Eric and his goofy grin, his tired eyes. Pure, terrified bliss. My mind is definitely skipping over all of the hard parts. The lack of sleep, the problem solving that never seemed to end, the feelings of inadequacy and failure, the constant worry. I think only about the smiles, the milestones, the joy I felt the first time his tiny arms closed around my neck. Then Bentley with his contagious energy. I laugh to myself about all of the times he has taken me by surprise or made me smile with his sweet innocence.

When I was willing to go forward with Nick, I still had the boys. I wasn't losing them. I now understand what it must have been like for Eric. I couldn't have lasted even close to as long as he did. I know that he had his research as a distraction, but still. That man. I honestly do not understand how anyone could be strong enough to deal with what Berg has asked of us. Shari said there are other pairs. I wish I could talk to them. Understand how they have been better prepared. Berg knows those answers, but I haven't been given any helpful information, nor do I understand what our family will look like after these procedures. Will I have the boys? Will Eric? The uncertainty eats at me from the inside out.

A knock sounds at the door, and a few seconds later, a woman enters. She greets me with a smile and motions for me to follow her. Her hair is in a tight bun, and she is walking quickly, making it difficult for me to keep up on my stiff legs. Making it to the end of the hall, we turn the corner. Shari is there, and she smiles at me. I want to smile and embrace her, but everything feels different now. She is the corrective parent, and I am the petulant child. She is not on my level anymore.

"Hey," she puts her arm out and brushes my shoulder. "You can see Eric and the boys."

My heart leaps. "Thank you," I say, my voice barely audible.

"It's only for a little while," she reiterates. "Then we will go down the hall for therapy. This is it, Kate."

I start to ask one of the million questions I have, but she holds up her hand to stop me, her eyes warning me to take what I can get. Right now, I can only focus on these minutes. I nod, and she points me toward a room on her left. I walk hesitantly to the door, turn the knob, and step in.

CHAPTER 41

Eric, Tal, and Bentley are sitting on soft chairs along the wall. The room is small and simple, but not overly cramped. When I enter, three heads jerk up in unison and the boys run to greet me. I hold them tightly. I feel Bent's disheveled hair and Tal's strong shoulders. It's been only a day, but I swear they look older. They are both sobbing. I am sure they are terrified. Eventually I release my grip, noticing Eric as he stands.

He holds me. His steady arms completely envelope me, and I want to stay there forever. I feel his chest rising and falling, so comforting. So familiar. I laugh through my tears when Bentley worms his way in between us, so he can be in the hug as well. I look at Eric, taking him in as he smiles at Bent. I hate this. All of it.

We sit down and the boys move close. Even Tal, who is usually too big to want to snuggle.

"What happened yesterday?" I ask.

"I shouldn't have told you to go," Eric says in a rush. "I was trying to be considerate of Nick, which I still think was the right thing to do, but I had no idea the Committee was aware of what we had in mind. I thought we would have more time to figure something out. That we could go to them with a plan." He looks down. "I was completely naive."

"What is happening?" Bentley asks.

I breathe. "I don't really know," I say. "Dad's research has made it so we need to make some adjustments, but Dad and I don't want to be apart. Somehow we haven't been able to make the choice that is best for the most people." I don't really know how to explain this. "We are stuck. Berg is trying to help us. I know it's really hard, guys."

"I don't want to be split up!" Tal shouts. "This is crazy!"

He obviously understands more than I gave him credit for.

"I don't want that either. But do you remember when we used that machine on the tour? How good it felt? They are going to use that to help us all get through it," I assure him.

What else can I say? I am at a loss. They don't want this. Yet, here we are. I know their brains are malleable enough that they will likely be fine after just a couple of sessions.

"But why? I don't understand *why* this is happening," Tal says. I look at Eric. It won't hurt to tell them the whole story. It will be gone from their brains after today, anyway.

Eric starts. He explains everything. How his research was used to create pairs and how I was paired with Nick. He lays everything out factually, but stops when he gets to the part where he came back for the ceremony. Bentley and Tal are both looking at him expectantly. I jump in.

"Dad came home because he was having a really hard time being away from us. He thought he would never get to be with us again. We talked, and he told me what was going on. It was so helpful for me to have more information." I pause. "Have either of you had a situation where you assumed one thing and then found out more information that helped?"

"Like right now!" Bentley says excitedly. "I thought you and Dad didn't love each other anymore. But really, you were trying to do a good thing."

His comments pierce my heart. Did it really seem to him that Eric and I didn't love each other? I thought I had been able to play off his absences without disrupting their opinions. I guess not.

"That's a great example, Bent. I'm sorry we didn't say anything sooner."

"It would have been helpful," says Tal.

"Do you understand why we couldn't, though?" Eric says. "I wasn't even supposed to tell your Mom. I was supposed to let her move forward with Nick. I just...couldn't. I am not strong enough to lose you all. That's why we are here." He clears his throat in an effort to hold back tears. "We are here because I wasn't able to go through with a course of action that would have been best for society. I couldn't give you guys up. And now... I'm going to lose you anyway. I just won't know it."

"It's okay, Dad," Tal says. We all sit there. It's not often that life with two boys is quiet, but in this moment, they are unconscionably still.

Tal speaks first. "What is going to happen? Are we still going to be with you?"

"I don't know," Eric answers. "They haven't given us much information, and I'm sure it's because they don't feel like it matters anymore. We really don't have a say in anything at this point. We just have to trust that they will use the evidence to determine the best option for all of us."

I do believe that Berg has everyone's best interest at heart. I do. But it is a terrifying feeling to have someone else in control of your family. Taking charge of your life. My mind desperately craves some control over the situation.

"So what do we do now?" Bentley asks, always the rational problem solver.

I don't know how to answer that. What do I say to the people I love most when I am not sure if I will see them again? How do I express the strong emotions I hold for them?

Eric says, "We just enjoy these last few moments together. Enjoy being who we are now. We had a pretty great run, didn't we?"

My throat constricts. Eric looks at me and smiles. He rises and moves toward me, his motions so familiar that they comfort me. The boys stand up, too. Eric reaches down and pulls up Bentley's pants and I laugh. I guess we didn't ever get that one solved. He looks both boys in the eyes and tells them he loves them. I drop to my knees and hug each of them, intently. Individually. Then Eric asks them if he can talk with me privately for a moment. They sit down obediently, pretending as if they aren't waiting to absorb every word.

"Hi," he murmurs, looping his arms around my waist. He pulls me close.

"Hi," I say. "Not quite the day I had planned for us."

"What did you have planned?" he asks.

"Lots of entertainment for the boys," I whisper conspiratorially.

"Seems like that would leave us on our own," he says, softly kissing my cheek.

"Huh," I say, heat rising to my face. "Pretty sure they are watching us in here."

"Does it look like I care?" Eric says, moving his hands under the back of my shirt. It's so familiar. I am losing all of this. All of this knowing. A wave of emotion swells up from my gut and I suppress a sob. His fingertips press into my back as he crushes me to his chest. His breathing becomes shallow, and I bury my face in his neck, tears streaming down my cheeks, soaking his shirt collar. We stay frozen like this for what seems like hours—yet not nearly long enough.

"I love you, Kate," he whispers. His voice is coarse and shaky. "I don't care if that makes me weak or hinders me from doing my societal duty. I believe in my research. I know it will make the world a better place, and even then, I can't force myself to leave you. I made myself physically ill trying."

I push back and look up at him, trying to gain some semblance of clarity.

"You do look terrible," I choke out, and he laughs heartily, coughing at the unexpectedness of it.

"Thanks for validating my self-diagnosis," he says when he can breathe again.

"Sorry, I think I am a bit hysterical," I say, patting his face. The contact with his stubbled chin immediately sobers me. "I don't want to do this, Eric. And I am so sorry that I moved forward with everything...with Nick. I was trying to do what I thought— "

Eric puts his fingers on my lips. "No, it's ok. You are amazing. I am so grateful that you were willing to be strong. Sorry I couldn't be."

The door opens and our heads whip around. It's Shari. Our time is up. I look back at Eric. He leans down and kisses me deeply. Bentley clings to our legs, and Tal hugs me around my waist. I give them all one last, desperate hug, and then we follow Shari out into the hallway.

CHAPTER 42

THE STIFF BACK of the chair supports me while the electrodes are placed on the sides of my head, the metal cool against my skin. I can't stop shaking; my hands and feet feel freezing, almost numb. My jaw is chattering so violently that Shari notices.

"Kate, are you ok? Are you cold?"

I don't answer. Anything that I say right now will be put through my current emotional filter, and I don't want to hurt Shari any more than I already have. She opens a cupboard, removing a blanket from the top shelf. She gently wraps it around my shoulders and tucks it between my back and the chair to prevent it from slipping. I look at her, and she meets my gaze, looking almost apologetic.

A voice breaks the silence, coming from the speakers overhead. "Kate, we are going to go ahead and start the session. There won't be any pain. There will likely be a warm and tingly sensation along your skin where the electrodes are located. We anticipate it being a mostly pleasant experience. As discussed, this first session will be the longest. Are you comfortable?"

Though comfort is not remotely possible at this point, I nod nonetheless.

The machine begins to hum and warmth diffuses into the skin near my temples. It isn't uncomfortable, just...strange...

"Hi Kate." It's Eric. I have been so excited for this date. Something about this guy feels different and I tell myself not to blow it.

"Hey, it's good to see you."

"Are you ready to go?"

"Yep."

He stands there and smiles for a minute, just looking at me. I shift my weight, my heart pounding, waiting for him to say something. He motions to my pants. Looking down, I realize that I am still wearing my pajama bottoms.

"Oh! Wow. That...is embarrassing. I'm sorry. I will go change really quick." I rush back to my room. How did I forget to change my pants? I had been looking forward to this all day, but I was also working on a lot of cleaning and preparation for conditioning on Monday. And these bottoms *are* extremely comfortable. I guess it slipped my mind. I quickly put on some actual pants and throw my pajamas on the bed. Eric is still waiting patiently when I emerge properly dressed.

"I personally would have been fine with you wearing those pants, but I didn't want you to feel uncomfortable," he grins. "I would wear pajamas all day, if I could."

"Well, apparently I was living the dream today," I laugh nervously. He reaches for my hand and we walk down the steps.

I poke Eric. I don't know what time it is, but I am exhausted and I can hear Tal crying again. His turn. He groans and shifts positions. I poke harder. He begins to stir and I immediately shut my eyes, adopting my typical sleeping breathing pattern. I know it is a cowardly move, but I don't want to explain why I am not getting up. I have already woken twice, and I physically can't do it right now.

Eric registers the cries and rolls out of bed. A few moments later, I hear him talking to Tal, who quiets down. Now that he is up, I feel a pang of regret. With my mind buzzing, it's unlikely that I will actually be able to go back to sleep. I sit up and figure I could go apologize and take over.

Glancing at the clock, I see that it has only been an hour since I was last with Tal. He can't possibly be hungry already, so why is he awake? I yawn and stumble down the hall, stopping short when I hear Eric humming. Slowly walking the last few steps, I peek through the door. There isn't a light on in the room, but moonlight streams through the window, giving off a heavenly glow, and it's just enough light to make out Eric sitting in our rocking chair. Tal is bundled up against his chest, and Eric is gently patting him, rocking back and forth, humming a lullaby. Warmth swells in my chest, and I prop myself against the door frame for balance. I remain a silent voyeur, not wanting to disturb the sacredness of this moment.

I am yelling. Screaming. Slamming cupboards in the kitchen.

"It's too much! I can't take it, Eric! I don't want to do anything right now, and they won't leave me alone. The boys need things from me at every moment. They are hungry, sad, fighting, or touching me. Constantly touching me! I just want to be by myself. For even an hour! I want to curl up in the closet and never come back out, okay? If you want to know how I feel, that's it. I love them so much and...and I really hate them. I know it sounds ridiculous and weak and horrifying, but it's true. I am just so sad..." the sobs escape from my throat involuntarily.

Eric rushes to me and holds my head against his chest. He doesn't say anything. He just holds me. I lean into him, breathing in the fresh scent of his recently laundered shirt, and let him carry most of my weight for a moment. Not having to hold myself up is salvation. I have barely been sustaining myself for days. When my limbs stops shaking, Eric turns my face up to his.

"Kate, it doesn't sound weak or horrifying. It sounds like you need some help. Maybe more than I can give."

I start to object, but he cuts me off. "I don't mean you need help like you aren't good enough. I mean that after a woman has a baby, hormones are crazy and can sometimes be out of proportion in your brain. There could physically be a problem, and I think we need to get it checked out. Just like we would get it checked out if you broke your arm. I know you haven't been wearing your sensor lately— "

"It's so tight— " I whimper.

"I know. I totally understand. I just wonder if maybe there is some physical data we are missing. Would you be willing to go in with me tomorrow? I can take care of the boys and call Shari to help. I know you aren't totally sure that I can handle them by myself— "

"It's not that, I— "

"It *is* that, and I get it. If I had come home to you trying to fix the door while Bentley was crying in the chair, I probably would have questioned it, too. But just for the record, it had literally only been two minutes and I was so close to finishing."

I laugh, giddy.

"What do you say?"

I nod. "I don't want to find out that I'm...broken." I choke back a sob.

"I know you aren't broken. I simply want you to feel like yourself again. Deal?"

"Deal."

"This is it!" Eric says, raising his hands over his head.

I scan the exterior of our new home. It's breathtakingly perfect. Sloped roof, forsythia blooming around the steps, original brick. I don't know how it's in such great condition, but I am over the moon that it's ours. The houses on both sides of us have obviously been renovated. They must have been in much worse condition than this one. We got lucky. Eric lifts me up and cradles me in his arms. He walks up the steps, trying to make it seem easy, but I can feel his chest heaving a little. I am not tiny, and this is completely ridiculous. I laugh out loud.

"Don't laugh! I'm doing so well!" Eric grunts.

We get to the door and he fiddles with the knob, realizing it's locked. I start to push off to get down, but he stops me.

"Nope! I am doing this. Just...let me get the key out my pocket."

I burst into more laughter, feeling his contorting arms.

"Why is it locked in the first place? Nobody locks their doors," I say, attempting to commiserate.

"I think it's just been empty for awhile. Maybe making sure nobody accidentally comes in?"

He finds the key and it turns easily. The door swings into the entry and we bumble into the house.

"Now, I will give you the tour!" Eric announces, breathing heavy, beads of sweat forming on his forehead.

Our laughter makes it difficult to remain upright. He struggles into the kitchen and living room, but can't quite reach our bedroom without my legs slipping. I quickly hop down and move behind him, jumping on his back.

"Try this, less arm work," I suggest between giggles.

He laughs, his breath coming in short bursts. "Perfect!" Walking the last few steps into the bedroom, he throws me on the bed in a victorious maneuver. We both laugh until our stomach muscles ache. I take a deep breath and look over at him. He is mine. This is our house. It all seems surreal.

Rolling over, he places his hand on my cheek and traces my jawline. Heat explodes underneath his fingertips. I stare into his eyes as his nose grazes mine and then he slowly kisses my lips. I close my eyes, and everything fades to black.

EPILOGUE

"NICK!" I call. "Nick! Come here! You have to see this!" His footsteps echo down the hall as he comes running.

"What is it?" he asks nervously.

"Come here," I laugh. "Sit down and just watch for a second." I point at my protruding belly as it rises and falls with my breath.

"I don't see anything," he says, obviously disappointed.

"Just be patient! Watch closely." Of course, as soon as we are paying attention, the babies have gone still. After another minute, though, I feel movement.

"There! Did you see that?" My eyebrows shoot up and I whip my face toward his, watching for his reaction.

"I think so..." Nick says, his eyebrows furrowed in concentration. "Oh wow, I definitely saw that one. And that one! Whoa, that is insane! I can't believe those are little people in there." He places his hand tenderly on my bare skin and feels the tiny kicks.

It's been so long since I felt this. Bentley is already eight years old. After Eric passed, I was so nervous about pairing again. At the time, I said it was because I didn't think that Bent could handle it, but I recognize now that it was me I was trying to protect. No part of me wanted to be vulnerable again. I honestly wasn't convinced that it was even possible.

Nick and I had known each other through work. I was always attracted to him, but he was young enough that I didn't consider him a viable option. Plus, I was so busy and focused on my service and Bent that I hadn't made dating a priority. I probably should have. When my parents died, I retreated into myself for a few years. I don't know that I would have paired organically had Nick and I not been given the opportunity to pair through Berg's new research program. When we found out about our pairing numbers from the Committee, it shocked both of us. There was some new research that came out a couple of years ago, specifically focused on matching for disease eradication and...we matched. Nick was—amazingly—completely willing to pair, despite the fact that we didn't know each other very well. I was more hesitant. It felt like such an intense life shift, and I had Bent to think about. Eventually, Bentley and I made the decision together.

"I'm almost finished putting those shelves up in the bedroom," Nick says, still running his fingertips along my taut skin, sending tingles up my arms.

"That's great, thanks so much for doing that," I sigh, relieved. He gives my belly a final rub and heads back to his task. I watch him go, admiring his strong physique. Turning my head to the kitchen, I notice the time. Bentley should be home from conditioning soon.

We live close enough that he can walk back to the neighborhood with his afternoon group.

My heart swells within me, myriad emotions wrestling for control. I loved Eric. I wish we had been given more time. One year wasn't enough, and I don't even remember details well enough at this point to give Bent more information about his dad. I was such a mess during that time, I didn't even keep anything of his to pass on. Another kick to my bladder brings me back to the present. I stand up and head into the kitchen to prepare an afternoon snack for all of us. No more regrets. I have Nick and soon-to-be three beautiful children. Life may not have turned out how I expected, but I love and am loved. I can't ask for more than that.

ABOUT THE AUTHOR

Cindy is first and foremost mother to her four beautiful children and wife to her charming and handsome husband, Scott. She is a musician, a homeschooler, a gardener, an athlete, a lover of Canadian chocolate, and most recently, a writer.

Cindy grew up in Airdrie, AB, Canada, but has lived most of her adult life between California and Colorado. She currently resides in the Denver metro area. Cindy graduated from Brigham Young University with a B.S. in Psychology, minoring in Business. She serves actively within her church and community and is always up for a new adventure.

Made in the USA
Columbia, SC
05 September 2019